I0457853

When A Warrior Comes Home

Pete Barber

Published by: PJ Publishing
106 West Hill Avenue North
Hillsborough, NC 27278.

First Edition.
ISBN 978-0-9855230-4-6

Fiction is the lie through which we tell the truth

—*Albert Camus.*

Pete Barber

ONE

January 2008 - Fayetteville, North Carolina

The front door opened, and Sarah poked her head out of the kitchen. Daniel, her fourteen-year-old, stepped into the hall with a finger to his lips. Mike followed, carrying Christopher—fast asleep—his flushed cheek pressed into his father's shoulder, legs dangling halfway down Mike's thighs. He was going to be tall, like his daddy. Mike gifted Sarah a proud-dad grin and carried their son upstairs.

When she returned to the kitchen, Daniel had the fridge open, browsing. "There's pizza from last night on the middle shelf. But only one slice—we're eating dinner in an hour," she said.

He folded a wedge, crammed the point in his mouth, and popped open a can of soda with his free hand.

Mike snuck up behind her, wrapped a powerful arm around her waist, and pecked her cheek. "Smells good in here."

"Me or the sauce?"

A low laugh rumbled his chest and vibrated against her back. "Both."

Still encircled, Sarah turned to face him. With a lip-smacking sound, Mike stole a kiss. She wriggled free. "Why don't you *men* play a video game while I finish in here?"

Daniel sprinted from the room. "I'll set up *World of Warcraft*."

"Ten-four, soldier." Mike, still smiling, looked deep into Sarah's eyes.

"What?"

"Snapping a mental picture. You with a flour-smudged nose in a kitchen filled with the aroma of spaghetti sauce—a memory to treasure."

When Mike deployed, she'd miss these moments—simple things but hard to define—a look like this one, deep and tingly, or

1

a casual comment keenly felt. Mike wasn't a touchy-feely kind of guy. She didn't want that from her man. But to think he'd remember this ordinary domestic moment with fondness meant the world because it showed how much he valued the life they'd built. To hide the mist in her eyes, she spun away and stirred the sauce. "How long has Chris been asleep?" she asked.

"He passed out before the end of the movie and snored all the way home. That boy can sure sleep."

"He's had a big day. Let him rest until dinnertime."

They'd gone to the Waffle House for breakfast, then to the local park to feed the ducks. After Mike had dropped her at home, he, Daniel, and Christopher had headed off. A boys' outing. Seeing a movie the day before deployment was a ritual. And it had been a lucky one. Mike had always come home healthy and safe.

Superstitions were only stupid if they didn't work.

The spaghetti dinner was part of it. Tomorrow morning, they'd say good-bye at the front door. Butch, Mike's battle-buddy, would drive him away. Later, she and Butch's wife, Rosa, would collect their vehicle from the base. A convoluted system designed to ensure Mike's last memory would be of his wife standing at their front door, waving and smiling. That was the memory he wanted, the memory he needed, so that was the memory he'd have.

Most army wives had a routine. Tonight, across Fayetteville, NC, two hundred families would try to soften the sense of losing someone dear, try to dull the edge of an aching heart, to blunt the fear that they might be parting forever.

After dinner, Daniel hugged his dad, said good-bye, and went to stay with his friend. Last year, when Mike left for his second tour, Daniel had gotten upset. He didn't want his dad to see him cry again. Also, their son was maturing fast, and Sarah suspected he knew Mom and Dad needed alone time.

Later, Sarah came downstairs from checking on Christopher. "He's asleep."

Mike pulled the cork from a bottle of Chardonnay. He poured, and she joined him at the kitchen table. They chinked glasses. "To being home by Christmas," Mike said.

Sarah sipped and then smiled.

"What's funny?"

"Remember your first trip to the Sandbox?"

"Christopher was only, what?"

"Two," she said.

"Daniel was just old enough to grasp what it meant."

She nodded and the emotion, still raw four years later, dried her mouth and roughened her voice. "Rosa and I went to all the deployment briefings. I sat at the back of the room in a daze—in denial. I had a drawer full of brochures and checklists, but I didn't do a damn thing with them." She focused on her wineglass, avoided his eyes. Anxiety warmed her cheeks; she shouldn't have brought the memories back.

He laughed. "You *were* a little unprepared."

But it still wasn't funny to Sarah. The night before he left, three feet from where they now sat, she had leaned against him and grasped his shirt in both fists. Tears streaming down her face, snot bubbling from her nose, she'd begged him not to go. Of course, he told her he had to. She knew that. But fear overwhelmed logic, and she had pummeled his ribs and screamed at him before stomping up the stairs and slamming their bedroom door. "I gave you a horrible send-off."

He reached across and stroked her hand. "But this is nice. We've learned."

For the ten months he was in Iraq, a ball of guilt camped in her chest, ever-present, choking, immovable. How could she have behaved so selfishly? How could she put that pressure on him when he was already handling so much?

Sarah wet her finger in the wine and circled the lip of her glass. "The week after you left, we had a power outage, and the electric company wouldn't take my call because I wasn't on the account. I'm glad my mom didn't hear the names I called that poor woman on the switchboard."

Mike squeezed her fingers. "We're old hands now. I don't need to worry. I know you've got my six."

Yes. She had his back, and it meant a lot to hear him say it. Even when he was away, they were a team.

"From what I hear, not many wives are as organized as you, Mrs. Braeman."

When she raised her head, the intensity of his stare sent tingles tripping across her belly. She touched her glass to his. "When you're not here, that's my job."

The run-in with the power company had delivered the kick up the butt Sarah needed. She had spread the brochures on the table and cried her way through the information. Her family was unprepared. This was her responsibility, and she'd flunked out. If something happened to Mike in Iraq, she had no power of attorney, no last will and testament.

Not anymore. His will and their marriage certificate and his military id and Social Security card and emergency contacts and phone numbers were in a safe deposit box at the bank. Sarah kept copies at home in an indexed three-ring binder. Their credit cards, bank accounts, and utilities were all in joint names.

He topped up their glasses, and she took another slurp and let the liquor ease her throat. When he had returned home from that first deployment, she had tiptoed around the idea of writing a will. However you spun it, she was preparing for his death. But Mike didn't see it that way. Knowing his family was taken care of *reduced* the pressure on him. Every time Mike shipped out, he prepared for the possibility of death.

"Anyway, you're worth it. I guess." She grinned.

"Hmm. Well, to make sure you remember that—here." He stuck a hand in his side pocket and produced a small black box, which he placed on the table. "I got you a going-away present."

She opened the lid and lifted out a gold necklace with a heart-shaped locket engraved with her name. "Mike, it's beautiful."

He grinned. "You like? It matches the earrings I bought you."

"I love it. Thank you." Emotion swamped her chest and stung her eyes. Sarah cleared her throat and stood. "Finish the wine. Give me twenty minutes to shower, then come upstairs and I'll wear it for you. I may not wear anything else!"

At six a.m., Christopher—in Spiderman PJs, his blond hair poking up in tufts—stood beside Sarah on the front doorstep. They waved until Butch's car turned the corner at the end of the street.

"When will Daddy be home?"

"As soon as he finishes his job."

Christopher frowned. Only this morning had he learned that Mike was going away. But their son was six years old. They couldn't gloss over a deployment again. Next time, if there was one, he'd need to know, need to prepare for the worst, need to feel the fear that his father might never return. Damn. Army life was tough on kids. The longer she could postpone that conversation with her son, the better.

"Come on," she said, "I'm hungry. How about a Pop Tart?"

His frown melted. "Strawberry?"

"Of course."

He took her hand and pulled her into the kitchen, but when she pressed down the toaster handle, the sound echoed in the empty house. With forced lightness, she said, "Shall we visit with Aunt Rosa after breakfast?"

"Yay!"

Rosa and Butch had a four-week-old baby boy. Her kitchen would also be echoing and empty.

Pete Barber

TWO

Ten Months Later – December 2008, Southern Iraq

The Humvee swerved at high speed through a series of orange cones. A plume of dust and stone clattered against the vehicle and sprayed the air behind. At the end of the half-mile course, the driver executed a skid turn, stopping fifty feet from a five-stack of aluminum bleachers. Engine racing, the Humvee rocked on its suspension—a thoroughbred pawing the ground, ready to race.

"Very impressive, Master Sergeant."

"Thank you, sir." Standing next to Brigadier General Swain on the bleachers' bottom tier, US Army Master Sergeant Mike Braeman suppressed the urge to punch the air. A screw-up today would have been typical Murphy's Law. To continue with the project, Mike needed Swain's approval, and the general had earned his reputation as a stickler for details—*all* boxes must be checked before making a recommendation—everything would be done by the book.

"Tell me again, what's the operator's name?"

"Brian Matthews, sir—civilian contractor, software specialist."

"And he is located where?"

"At Camp Liberation, sir."

"Very well. Please proceed."

Mike spoke into his headset. "Cleared for second phase."

The driver's door of the Humvee opened. Instead of a soldier, a machine rolled out on three-foot-long twin tracks that tilted and bridged the gap between cab and ground. Once clear of the vehicle, the front of the machine hinged, Transformer-like, until a metal stick figure, five feet tall with two multi-jointed arms, stood erect on top of its miniaturized tank base. Late afternoon sun glinted off two camera lenses set as eyes in its flat, rectangular face.

An electric motor whined as the robot sped from the vehicle.

Twenty feet from the viewing gallery, it stopped and rotated its body away from the observers.

The general and the five civilians standing behind him on the bleachers raised binoculars and focused on a distant row of targets.

A three-foot-long rifle barrel hinged out from the robot's torso and six rapid-fire shots cracked downrange. After the firing arm had retracted, the robot returned to the Humvee. The body folded, the tracks tilted up, and the machine rolled into the driver's compartment. A metal claw slammed the door shut. Engine screaming, the Humvee sped back through the obstacle course. It cleared the final cone on two wheels before spinning, as before, and skidding to a halt.

Sergeant Braeman waited while a second Humvee approached from the range. The driver climbed out, carrying a gray folder. Mike brought the papers to General Swain.

"Shot distance?" Swain asked.

"A half mile, sir."

"And the weapon?"

"A modified XM110 sniper's rifle."

The general flipped through the targets. "Six bulls, impressive."

"Thank you, sir."

As they passed among the spectators, the paper targets received nods of approval.

"Master Sergeant, have the robot repeat the maneuver. No, wait." Swain stepped off the bleachers and spoke to the Humvee's driver. The soldier saluted and climbed into his vehicle. He drove toward the course, picked up the second obstacle, and moved it fifty yards to the right. He altered the positions of five of the twenty cones.

The general returned to his place next to Mike. "The only certainty in combat, Sergeant Braeman, is change."

"Yes, sir."

"Now. Have him drive back."

Mike spoke into his headset. The Humvee started toward them. As it reached the space created by a moved cone, the vehicle swerved and rounded the obstacle in its new position. After zigzagging through the course, the Humvee pulled up in front of the observers.

The robot, code named VCOM for virtual combatant, opened the driver's door and rolled toward the bleachers. It covered the ground at speed, stopping three feet from the general. The VCOM looked up at the six-foot-tall military man who held its future in his hands.

"Does the controller have audio and visual reception?"

"Yes, sir."

The general stared into the lenses, centered on what passed as the machine's face. "Mr. Matthews, congratulations on an excellent demonstration."

The stick-man lifted its right arm and performed a crude salute.

A mile away, in a trailer at Camp Liberation near the Kuwait-Iraq border, Brian Matthews sat at a metal desk. His thin, pale hands were bathed in a blue cube of light projecting two feet above a flat panel, similar to an iPad. The VCOM's cameras delivered video to his heads-up display, worn as a pair of oversized sunglasses. Brian saw, heard, and controlled everything the robot did.

He *was* the robot.

Uncertainty flickered across the general's face. He hesitated, then saluted the VCOM, and said, "When I return to the US, I will recommend we begin field trials. Dismissed."

Brian grinned, and with a flick of his wrist, he returned the robot to the Humvee.

Humvees collected the general and the observers from Militec—the company responsible for the VCOM hardware. Once everyone had left, Mike climbed into the passenger seat next to the robot. "Home, Brian," he said. "I think drinks are in order."

They drove a mile cross-country, in silence. Although he knew Brian could hear his voice, it weirded Mike out to talk to the VCOM. After clearing security and parking in the main lot, Mike and the machine climbed out.

Camp Liberation served as temporary quarters to three thousand troops, many fresh from boot camp and awaiting deployment north to Iraq. Mike and the tin-man marched across the camp's sandy outer perimeter. They passed through a narrow opening between two fifteen-foot-high concrete blast walls. An upside-down tee in profile, dozens of similar barriers surrounded and protected the housing compound. Within the T-walls, air conditioners hummed in hundreds of trailers. The drone of generators delivered a constant background noise.

As they approached Brian's trailer, the robot moved ahead and used its three-pronged hand to open the door. Mike followed the machine inside and sucked in a lungful of cool, dust-free air. "That robot has better manners than my kids," he said to Brian's back.

With a couple finger flicks from its operator, the VCOM parked against the wall and folded itself in two. Brian removed the virtual display headgear, laid it on the desk, and powered off the LightCube. He spun his chair and sprang from his seat. Grinning, he offered Mike a high-five.

Mike pushed the hand aside and delivered a man-hug and a hearty backslap that shuddered through Brian's bone-thin frame. "You kicked butt out there today, my nerdy friend."

"Thanks."

"Can you believe that sneaky bastard moved the cones?"

"Not a problem." Brian pointed to the goggles. "I have a wider field of vision through those puppies than any human soldier."

"Don't go telling everyone. You'll put us grunts out of a job."

"I thought that was the plan." Brian retrieved a pair of wire-rimmed glasses from the desk and slid them on. "That's it then. At least you can ship out feeling good about the project. How's the family?"

"Excited. Especially Christopher. He can't wait for Santa to climb down the chimney."

"Well, after today, VCOM has a bright future. Looks like we'll be working together in 2009."

Mike shook his head. "Not sure. I'm slated to re-up mid-year, but Sarah and I are considering taking the hit and starting over in the civilian world. It's a big risk, but there are more important things in life than a guaranteed pension and healthcare—right?"

"Wouldn't know. Don't have either."

Mike smiled and punched Brian playfully on the arm. "That's what Sarah says. The first ten years we were a family—together most nights, and I got to see Daniel grow up. But this is my third deployment in four years. I'm missing out on Chris, and he's missing out on having a dad."

"It's not such a big bad world out there."

Mike grinned. "So you say."

"When will you decide?"

"We're going to talk it over at Christmas when I'm home."

"Do the guys know?"

"Butch is thinking the same; he just missed Noe's first birthday. Skype's no substitute for holding your baby boy." Mike's face grew warm. This was the first time he'd revealed his plans to anyone outside the military. Talk of leaving made the possibility more concrete. Sarah could go back to work. They had equity in their home if things got tight. It'd be a struggle. But life wasn't a rehearsal.

Brian tapped Mike's arm. "Drink? You promised?"

"Give me time to wrap up the paperwork and shower, then come to Butch's trailer."

"Need For Speed, again?"

"Yeah, but *you're* playing left-handed."

When Brian mimicked a shocked face, a lock of black hair shook loose from his fringe. The civilian had the worst haircut on base, but Mike liked the man. Lanky, and so thin he disappeared when turned sideways, Brian was a deep thinker. All brains and no balls, Butch said. But for six months, this VCOM project had kept Mike away from the front line and left no time for boredom— better fare than most.

He slapped Brian on the back and triggered a coughing bout. "See you at six thirty. Beers are on me."

At six fifteen, Brian strode between two rows of box-trailers. Staff Sergeant Paul (Butch) Cassidy's accommodations sat five trailers over. The night air chilled him enough to generate a shiver. This wasn't the humid, clinging cold of a North Carolina winter, but the twenty-degree temperature drop that happened minutes after sunset left him wishing he'd worn a jacket.

Identical to hundreds of others, Butch's thirty-foot-by-twelve box had a bunk at each end and a TV in the center. When Brian opened the door, his nose wrinkled at the heady aroma of body odor and stale pizza. "Stinks like a locker room in here."

Mike, lounging on Butch's bed with a headset on, glanced up

from the laptop resting on his knee. He held up one finger and waved Brian in.

Butch, and Yaz—his roommate, Staff Sergeant Mark Yazinski—sat on canvas chairs at a small table, each nursing a beer. Yaz sprang to his feet. "Finally! Ready to get *served*, Nerdman?"

Butch's soft rumbling laugh filled the room. Six foot six or seven, he was a bear of a man with a blond buzz-cut. His melon-sized right biceps sported a blue scroll with "Rosa" tattooed inside. On his right wrist, a heart enclosed the name of his only son, Noe. Butch stood, and the room grew smaller. In a deep bass southern drawl he said, "Now, Yaz, don't go callin' Brian names or he might take off the blindfold while he whoops your ass."

Brian laughed. "You guys go ahead. I'll play the winner. I need a beer."

Butch slapped Brian's shoulder hard enough to jostle him a step backward. "Good idea, maybe the liquor'll slow you down. C'mon, Yaz, prepare to be humbled."

The men dragged their chairs in front of the TV and a virtual racetrack filled the screen. In seconds, their heads were bobbing and weaving.

Brian peeked at Mike's laptop—he was on Skype with his wife, Sarah, and their two boys back home in North Carolina.

"I miss you too, Christopher," Mike said to the monitor, in a voice far gentler than the one he used in camp. "I'll be there in a couple weeks." As he listened to his son's response, Mike's face lit with a soft smile. He nodded. "Yes before Santa arrives." Mike laughed aloud at whatever was said next. Brian, feeling like an intruder, made for the fridge and snagged a Budweiser. Without the camaraderie of these men, his six-month project in this desert in the middle of nowhere would have seemed longer and been lonelier.

But their Iraq was worlds apart from his.

Four weeks into this deployment, these warriors had seen action together when series of IEDs had demolished the second vehicle in Mike's convoy. Butch and Yaz and Mike had spent two hours combing the wreckage and collecting the remains of five soldiers. They brought the body parts back to base. They knew the men from Fort Black. They knew their wives. They knew their families. Families who were waiting for those men to come home.

He had heard of the incident, but not from Mike or the guys.

When he'd asked, Butch simply said, "We ain't never going to talk about that." Then a screaming silence filled the trailer and made Brian squirm.

He popped the cap, took a long pull on the beer, and wandered to the door. A family portrait hung on the wall to the right of the door jamb. Butch touched a finger-kiss to it each time he passed. In the photo, the big man, dressed in a green hospital gown, towered over his wife. Leaning against her husband, Rosa's dark hair draped her shoulders and spilled over the front of a pale-blue nightgown. Her even, white teeth sparkled amidst tanned Hispanic features. Head tilted, her chocolate eyes, brimming with a mother's love, gazed at baby Noe.

A perfect family.

Someday, he hoped to find his own Rosa. The infant snuggled in her arms was hours old. Butch had deployed four weeks later. In two days, Butch would head home, hoping to see his boy take his first steps and say his first words before the next deployment. Brian hoped so too. No wonder the man was thinking of quitting. Who'd willingly be separated from Rosa and Noe?

Outside, the missile warning Klaxon started to screamed, drowning the soft sounds of Mike whispering to his family. Counterintuitively, Brian opened the door. Mike waved at him and shouted, "Shut the door, Nerdman. I can't hear… No, honey, it's okay, just the siren. I told you; it goes off all the time."

Brian stepped out and closed the door behind him. The Klaxon had sounded at two a.m. the day after he had arrived at Camp Liberation. Brian had lain in bed, covers pulled over his head, sweating and trembling like a petrified puppy. Amazing how he'd adapted to this strange life. He stood on the small wooden deck and let the deafening sound course through him. A shiver spilled down his spine and his heart rate spiked—evolutionary flight responses triggered by the ear-piercing noise, but no deep fear remained. As Mike said, this was a regular occurrence.

The siren was just a warning. If an attack happened, the Phalanx antimissile system protected the camp by spraying thousands of 20 mm rounds into the sky to destroy incoming mortar, artillery, or rockets. The troops called the weapon R2-D2 because its radar detection dome resembled the Star Wars robot. But the Iraqis aim was poor. Phalanx probably wouldn't even fire.

The wailing stopped and Brian listened to the ringing in his ears until the echoes faded and the camp's night sounds resumed. TVs blared from the half-dozen trailers backing onto Butch's—windowless, gray, and identical on the outside. Inside, though, many of the young men and women had arrived that week fresh from boot camp. At their age, Brian was a newly minted freshman in college. These kids were going to war, moving toward danger. If that had been their first warning siren, they'd be terrified too.

The Klaxon wound into a scream again. This time, the missile defenses triggered. Hundreds of white tracers lit the sky. Phalanx roared like a ten-ton lawnmower—loud enough to rattle Brian's teeth. A lead weight dropped into the pit of his stomach. The din wiped out his bravado, and his hand trembled as he spun around and grabbed the doorknob, desperate to escape the tumult.

A percussive sound wave staggered him backward, scrambled his head, and sucked all air from his lungs. He covered his ears. A fraction of a second later, the trailer door slammed into his arm, flipped him like a plastic toy, and smashed his chest against the deck's guardrail. He crashed through the wooden pickets, and the world exploded in sound and light and pain.

In Fayetteville, Sarah stared at her husband's image, frozen on the laptop's monitor. Mike was wincing, right hand lifted halfway to his head as though fending off a blow. *Michael Braeman is offline* pulsed in a small dialogue box at the bottom of the screen.

"Mommy, what's happening?" Christopher sat beside her on the sofa. Pale-blue eyes, his father's eyes, stared into hers. Worry creased her son's brow. "Why did Daddy stop talking?"

Sarah opened her mouth, forced air into her constricted chest and gripped the sides of the keyboard so her hands wouldn't shake. Nervous nausea knotted her stomach.

Daniel, standing behind her, stretched an arm over her shoulder. "What's that?" He pointed to Mike's headboard where a white crack had appeared. The dark wood, bowed at the center, appeared ready to snap.

Sarah managed a breath. "We lost signal, is all. Daniel, why don't you take Christopher to the kitchen and put a couple Pop Tarts in the toaster while I call your dad back?"

Christopher bounced to the floor and ran around the couch. He grabbed his brother's sleeve and pulled. "I want strawberry. Come on!" He dragged Daniel across the room. Sarah glanced at her older boy, following his kid brother but still facing her. Face drained of color, his eyes locked with hers, full of worry. She shooed him and looked away, tried to conceal her concern, tried to suppress the fear-monster that gripped her chest and shortened her breath.

Unable to reconnect with Mike, Sarah called Butch's wife, who lived four blocks away in the same subdivision. Keeping her voice calm, Sarah asked, "Have you heard from Butch?"

"Not since yesterday." Rosa's pitch changed, became nervous. "Why?"

Army wives existed with a compartment of terror locked inside and primed to be sprung open by an unexpected phone call or a knock on the door. During deployment, she and Rosa inhabited a false reality, forcing themselves never to dwell on where their men were, pretending to be unaware of the dangers they faced.

"Probably nothing," Sarah said. "We were on Skype and I lost the connection."

"Phew, you had me worried for a minute. Their Internet goes down on a daily basis, sweetie. I think the army scrambles the signals just to make us crap our panties."

Sarah laughed. "Yeah, I expect you're right."

"What else?" Rosa asked. "There's something else."

She glanced at the open kitchen door, lowered her voice to a whisper, and cupped her hand over the mouthpiece. She shouldn't worry her friend over this. But sometimes sharing was all they had. "The Phalanx sirens were blaring."

The line stayed quiet.

"You there, Rosa?"

"Uh huh. Butch told me those things go off all the time."

"Mike says the same. I'm sure he'll call back soon."

"Let me know when he does, okay… and, Sarah."

"Yeah."

"Tell Mike to say hi to Butch from me."

"Will do."

Sarah hung up. Before rebooting the laptop, she squinted and leaned closer to the frozen screen image, and tried to convince herself that the look she saw in her husband's eyes wasn't fear.

Pete Barber

THREE

Flat on his face in the dirt, spitting blood and grit, Brian lifted onto all fours. Pain streaked up his spine, whipped up his neck, and speared his temple. He took a breath but cut it short when hot sparks stabbed his ribcage.

A medic standing next to him screamed into a handheld radio, "Get a fire truck over here!"

Brian flipped over and followed the man's gaze.

Flames and acrid smoke spewed from a gaping hole where the door of Butch's trailer used to be. A wind gust fanned the fire and blasted searing heat into Brian's face. He sprang up, slapping sparks from his head. The action radiated pain around his chest and back as though a steel band was being twisted and tightened, crushing him. He bent double and grunted, gagging from the stink of his burned hair.

He and the medic backed away from the heat, shielding their eyes.

"You'd better let me check you out," the medic said.

Brian yanked at the man's sleeve, and shouted, "Did they get out?" His voice sounded odd, distorted, as though he were calling from the end of a long tunnel. "Butch, Yaz, and Mike, did they get out?"

The man stared back, blank eyed, clearly baffled by the question. Yellow flames reflected from his sweat-slickened face. "Who?"

The Phalanx roared. The Klaxon squealed. Soldiers spilled from their trailers, shouting, swearing, screaming. An officer barked orders at a crew of medics as they checked on dozens of men kneeling or curled fetus-like on the ground. Flashing blue lights signaled more help arriving. Soldiers with gurneys spilled through the T-walls from the access road beyond.

Four or five trailers had sustained a hit, but Butch's was on fire.

The heat forced everyone back. The stench of burning plastic stung Brian's throat and stole his breath, forcing him to double over, coughing and choking and clutching his chest.

He stepped forward, toward his friends, and stubbed his toe on the front door, lying on the ground between him and the trailer. It had saved him, protected him from the full force of the blast. Gritting his teeth against anticipated agony, he bent, grabbed, and lifted. "Gnah!" Brian screamed with the effort but raised the door. Using it as a shield, he stumbled toward the trailer. When he could no longer bear the heat, he pushed the door away from him. With one foot jammed against the bottom, it pivoted, and the top lodged against the trailer's deck, forming a ramp.

Flames scorched his face and forced his eyes shut. Bent at the waist, arms clamped across his chest to hold in the pain, he spun away. In an old-man hunch, Brian ran. He bypassed befuddled soldiers sitting, legs splayed, on the sand. He veered around a teenager with blood snaking from both ears who staggered around like a drunk in Jockeys and T-shirt. He swerved and swayed through obstacles, until he turned sharp right and climbed the ramp into his trailer.

Inside, he fired up the LightCube. Feet and knees vibrating under the desk, he screamed at the machine, "Come on. Come on!" The thirty-second-long boot routine seemed to stretch to minutes before the tablet initiated and hundreds of pinpoint light beams projected from the device's surface to form the control cube. He slipped on the heads-up display goggles, plunged his hands into the blue glow, and woke the VCOM.

Brian rolled the machine out the door, and retraced his route. He navigated the wounded and the frantic first responders until he reached Butch's trailer. The burning roof tiles belched smoke and dripped flaming tar balls that exploded like fireworks when then dropped. He drove the robot up the door ramp and into the burning box.

The VCOM's cameras projected the scene inside. Jagged holes, basketball-sized, peppered the walls. The center rear panels had blown in; shredded, they littered the floor. To his right, a three-foot-long spear of blue flame roared from a propane gas heater like a huge blowtorch. Flames swamped the carpet and wrapped the walls. Clothes spilled from an upturned dresser burned and glowed tinder red.

The smoke was densest ahead and right, so he turned left. Mike was at the far end trapped beneath the bed he'd been lying on when Brian last saw him. Mike's arm was straight out, pointing toward the middle of the trailer, near the busted paneling. He was shouting. Brian couldn't understand, but he rotated the robot and followed Mike's finger. Rolling forward, he spotted Butch's head poking out from under a tangle of chairs. A series of black tar balls peppered his scalp—remnants of the big man's blond buzz cut. A splintered two-by-four burned against his bare, outstretched arm, singeing the Rosa tattoo.

No time to consider the soldier's injuries. Left here, Butch would die, and Brian didn't know how long the prototype's hardware could survive the heat. He bent the torso, grabbed Butch's wrist, and reversed, dragging the sergeant down the makeshift ramp and twenty feet across the sand before dropping him and rushing back to the fire.

As he reentered the trailer, to Brian's right, a ten-foot section of roof caved in, showering sparks and debris. Greedy for oxygen, flames licked the wall, straining toward the new hole. Smoke blinded him, or maybe the lenses were failing. The prototype VCOM wasn't constructed to withstand combat conditions. He rolled away from the fire, toward Mike's bed. Three feet from the upturned mattress, the master sergeant came into focus. Both hands clamped his left leg. A jagged metal spike protruding from his calf pinned him to the floor. The digital readout on Brian's heads-up display ticked off the seconds.

Hurry!

Mike, face blackened and contorted, pointed toward the far wall where the propane gas blazed, and screamed, "Get Yaz out!" Brian rotated the cameras one-eighty. Butch's fifty-inch flat-screen TV had blown full across the room and lay at an angle against the upturned heater. Next to it, Yaz's red-checkered bandanna peeked out from under the toppled television. Brian rolled toward it.

He clamped the VCOM's crude grasping hand on the corner of the TV screen, and pulled. The heat-softened frame stretched like chewing gum. Flaming, molten plastic splashed the floor, splattering Yaz's chest. Brian moved in again, hooked the TV's metal mounting bracket, and dragged the set off the soldier's back.

Yaz's legs, enveloped in a roaring cone of propane flame, resembled two blackened Sunday roasts. Fat bubbled and oozed from cratered skin. Brian recoiled and sent the VCOM into a spin. "Get a grip. Get a grip!" Jaw clamped, he ground his teeth, forced air into his lungs, and regained control of the machine. When he grasped Yaz's left arm, the image swam, distorted, and then the feed from the right camera failed. He turned the robot toward the doorway and dragged the soldier outside.

A brace of medics were attending to Butch. They sprang back from the robot as Brian dropped Yaz, circled them, and returned to the trailer. He moved to the bed and grasped Mike's arm, yanking it away from his injured leg. A piercing scream sounded in his headset. Mike's agony swamped Brian's ears and sent shudders through his stomach. Body rigid, face twisted, tense and tight, knees shaking, he focused on maintaining steady hands. The LightCube was sensitive to the slightest movement. And this was no demonstration, no dry run. When he swiveled the cameras toward the door, his video feed flickered.

Then went blank.

Blinded, fingers poised, Brian froze—an orchestra conductor who'd lost his place in the music. Sweat dripped from his chin, but he dared not move a muscle. If he lost orientation, he might drive the robot into a wall.

Focus.

He closed his eyes, forced a slow breath, in, then out. Visualizing the floor plan, he pictured the last image he'd received. His fingers edged through the blue light. Drawing on years of experience with the controller, he judged an eight-foot straight-ahead maneuver, stopped, and then executed a standing turn. *Please be right.* After rolling thirty feet, he gave the command to open the claw. If he'd missed the door, the robot and Mike would still be inside the inferno. With no way out.

Brian put the robot in standby, jumped from his chair, and flew out the door.

He rounded an ambulance, and Butch's trailer came into view. The VCOM stood in the dirt thirty feet from the blazing trailer.

Medics were loading Yazinski onto a gurney. Butch had already been moved. Brian scanned right. Two soldiers jogged with a laden stretcher toward the gap in the T-wall. He raced to them, ran alongside, and stared at the face of the injured soldier.

Mike.

Brian dropped to his knees. Sobs wracked his body, each one

laden with pain so severe it lit sparks against his closed eyelids. He dug nails into his trembling palms and reverted to short gasping breaths. When he opened his eyes and glanced back at the trailer, fire crews had arrived, arcing water onto Butch's home and dousing the sides of the adjoining buildings. He grabbed his ribs, bent forward, and the ground came up to meet his face.

Pete Barber

FOUR

December 24th, 2008, Fayetteville, NC

Daniel stepped from the attic-access ladder and handed Sarah a large package wrapped in snowman-motif paper. "That's the last one, Mom."

"Good job."

He closed the hatch. Sarah shook her head at the mound of presents covering the landing. Most were for Christopher. She'd gone overboard. "Compensating, I guess."

"Huh?" Daniel raised his eyebrows.

She put a finger to her lips. "Shh. Come on. Let's take these downstairs. Don't want to wake your brother and spoil his Santa obsession. I thought we'd never get him to bed tonight."

He picked up a half-dozen packages, steadying them with his chin. Smiling, Sarah tracked his blond head down the stairs until it disappeared into the living room. With Mike recovering in Landstuhl hospital in Germany, Daniel had taken on the mantle of man of the house. War was a greedy mistress. Not satisfied with robbing her of a family Christmas, it was stealing Daniel's childhood, forcing him to grow up too soon.

They stayed up until eleven watching *Miracle on 34th Street*—the original, 1947 version.

At midnight, with both kids in bed, she stood alone in the living room. Wrapped gifts overflowed the base of their artificial Christmas tree. Strings of flashing colored lights blurred in her tear-filled eyes. Sarah lifted her wineglass toward the angel on the topmost branch and drained the dregs. "Well, we managed without you again, Mike." Four years earlier, on his first Iraq deployment, they had been apart for Christmas, but this year was tougher. Duty wasn't the obstacle. According to the doctors, severed tendons in Mike's left leg would keep him in the hospital until mid-January.

Why had this happened? The world was set against them. All year they'd discussed Mike's future with the army. Now they were close to a decision, close to choosing family over army—at least that was her choice—and this happened. She placed her empty glass on the coffee table and checked her inbox.

No new messages.

Sarah snapped a picture of the tree, uploaded it to the computer, and attached it to a message. She wrote, "Merry Christmas, honey. The kids helped with the ornaments. Daniel handled the higher stuff I normally leave to you. He's growing up so fast. As you can see, the presents are piled high. I'll keep yours under the tree. I drank our traditional toast, but it's not the same without you here to clink glasses. I miss you."

Sarah grabbed a Kleenex and dabbed her eyes. After a few deep breaths, she continued, "It's midnight here, and I'm going to bed. I'll Skype you at five fifty a.m. our time. Christopher is wound like a spring. Daniel will try to keep him occupied with a stocking we've hung at the bottom of his bed. As soon as you're online, I'll let him loose. That way we can at least have a virtual family Christmas. Good night, my love. I'll see you in the morning. I love you. XXX."

Once she'd pressed *send*, Sarah positioned the computer on the coffee table, aligning the webcam with the tree. Cold and distant, but the best they could manage. She'd wanted to take the kids to Germany. Cheer him up. Give him a family hug. The army offered to arrange the flight, but Mike persuaded her to stay home. The hospital ward was too depressing, he said. He didn't want the boys to see him until he could walk again.

After the rocket attack, it had taken four days before the Casualty Assistance Calls Officer contacted her. And then just to say Mike was in Germany and not seriously injured. Triage and transportation and chain of command—Sarah understood the reasons, but her gut had been coiled like rope until she received the first email from Mike: "I'm a bit banged up, but okay. I'm trying to get hooked up with Skype. Will let you know, Mike."

Flooded with relief, she printed the words, kissed the paper, and read them again, and again. She showed the note to the kids, and to her folks, but every time she saw his name written there, she wondered why he hadn't signed it *Love, Mike*.

During their first Skype call from the hospital, Daniel asked if

Mike's black eye and swollen face hurt. "Naw. You should see the other guy." Mike grinned, and they shared the first family laugh for a long time. But the call only lasted a few minutes. Mike was tired. Sarah told him she loved him. The kids told him they loved him, even Daniel. "Me too," Mike said, but his face didn't reflect any love. Probably she was making too much of it. After all, he was hurting, and far away. She should be grateful Mike's injury wasn't serious. Apparently, Yaz was worse off. Mike hadn't been allowed to visit him yet because he was in the Landstuhl ICU.

Sarah collected her wineglass, put it in the dishwasher, stabbed the *on* button, and sighed. After unplugging the tree, she climbed the stairs with leaden legs and a heavy heart. She wanted her husband back.

The next morning, Christmas morning, she tried for twenty minutes to Skype with Mike, but he wasn't online. Unable to contain Christopher any longer, she let the kids come downstairs, and they opened presents watched by the blank laptop screen. After gathering the discarded wrapping paper into a trash bag, she headed into the kitchen to make breakfast. As she was buttering toast, Daniel touched her shoulder from behind. She jumped and dropped the knife.

Sarah pressed a hand to her heart. The knife clattered on the tiled floor. Then a momentary silence filled the kitchen.

"Sorry, Mom."

"Not your fault. I was miles away. Breakfast's nearly ready. We'll eat in the living room, and you can show me your new video game."

Daniel held out a wrapped box. He'd reused the paper from one of his gifts. "This is for you."

"Oh!" Sarah wrapped him in her arms and squeezed, clinging to him until he tapped her shoulder for release.

"You shouldn't have."

"It's not much," he said.

She tore the paper off a box of candies and smiled at him, her eyes filled with tears, her heart filled with pride. "My favorites. Thank you. Now go and enjoy your game."

At ten thirty, Mike finally connected on Skype. Christopher held each present in front of the webcam for his father's approval. Her husband made appreciative noises, but his voice sounded flat, and his eyes kept drifting from the screen. Once Christopher began repeating toys, Sarah told him to go and play.

"You missed the excitement this morning," she said.

"I know."

Daniel, sitting beside her on the sofa, said, "Where were you? Mom was upset you didn't call."

Sarah turned to her son. "Daniel!"

"Well?" Daniel, chin jutting, face set, glared at the screen.

Mike's eyes darkened. His mouth flattened into a tight line. He barked, "Don't speak to me in that tone, young man!"

Body rigid, Daniel held his ground. Sarah placed a hand on his arm. "It's okay."

"No it's not." He pointed a finger at the camera. "Dad made you cry on Christmas morning." He sprang up and marched from the room.

"What was that about?" Mike asked.

"He misses you. We all miss you. It's hard when you're not here, Mike, especially today."

"Daniel shouldn't disrespect me."

This wasn't like Mike. Occasionally during a deployment, he had shown his frustration to her on the phone but never directed at his son. Never. She tilted her head, softened her voice. "What happened this morning? Why didn't you call?"

His eyes wandered from the screen, as though he was talking to a stranger, a stranger he didn't even want to look at. "*I* had to go to physical therapy." He spat his words, boiling anger barely contained.

"On Christmas Day?"

Cheeks flushed, Mike focused on the screen again, leaned into the webcam and hissed, "You don't get it. You just don't get it, do you? I have to get this damned leg stronger otherwise they'll slap me with a medical discharge. Then how will you buy a pile of Christmas presents? Where'll the money come from if I'm out of work?"

Sarah straightened, backed away from the screen. "You told me the injury wasn't serious. What's the truth, Mike?"

His face blanked into a strained mask and he stared past the screen, into space. "I've gotta go."

"Wait."

The screen went dark.

<><><>

At four on Christmas afternoon, the front doorbell rang.

Sarah called from the kitchen, "Can you get that, Daniel? It'll be Rosa, Butch, and Noe."

Sarah was drying her hands at the sink when her friend came into the kitchen. Wearing a colorful, abstract-print dress set off with a yellow silk scarf, Rosa crossed the kitchen, gave Sarah a hug, and sniffed the air like a hunting dog. "Mmm. Smells so Christmassy."

Behind her, Butch filled the doorway. Sharply dressed in pressed blue jeans and a white short-sleeved shirt, a fresh dressing covered his right forearm. Pinkish skin, reminders of the burns he'd received in the rocket attack, distorted the Rosa tattoo on his biceps. Noe was balanced in the crook of Butch's other arm. In his onesie snowman suit, their one-year-old resembled a tiny stuffed toy.

"Merry Christmas, Sarah. Thank God you asked us for dinner," Butch said. "There's nothing to eat at home exceptin' baby formula and teething biscuits."

His soft Southern drawl brought a smile to Sarah's lips. She hooked Rosa's arm and pulled her back across the kitchen toward Butch, so she could wrap her arms around them both. Noe, sandwiched, turned big brown eyes on her, and she kissed the baby's head. "Thanks for coming, guys."

"Are you kiddin'? For turkey and trimmin's, I'd run five miles in combat gear." Butch's grin wrinkled the corners of his eyes.

Sarah stepped back so she could see his face. "I'm glad you're home."

Rosa squeezed her husband's arm and tilted her head, gazing up at him. "He was due at noon on the fourteenth. I stood in the rain at the airport till ten at night. Good ol' army—hurry up and wait." Butch dipped his head and placed a soft kiss on Rosa's forehead.

Sarah spun away, opened the oven, and basted the turkey. Her hands shook. Jealous heat pulsed in her cheeks, tears misted her eyes. She took a few deep, steadying breaths and wiped her face on the apron. When she turned, Rosa had drifted from her husband toward the kitchen counter, maybe aware how hard it was for Sarah to see them together when Mike was still overseas.

Rosa eyed the food. "Deviled eggs!" She popped one into her

mouth. "Damn, that's good. I wish I could cook."

"Me, too," Butch said.

Rosa narrowed her eyes. "Bite me!" She dismissed him with a wave.

Focusing on Butch, reading his face, Sarah asked, "Did you see Mike before you left?"

He shook his head. "Sorry. I was out of it for a couple days." He raised his bandaged arm. "When they discharged me from the field hospital, Mike had been air-lifted. But don't you go worrying, none. Lanstuhl has the best medics in Europe. He's in good hands."

Daniel, who had been standing behind Butch, squeezed under the big man's arm into the kitchen. "What happened to Dad?"

Sarah placed a hand on her son's shoulder. "Daniel, give them time to settle."

"Didn't he tell you?" Butch asked.

Sarah said, "Mike doesn't remember, or doesn't *want* to remember."

Rosa caught her tone and frowned a question.

Sarah shook her head—maybe later.

Butch covered Daniel's shoulder with a meaty hand. "I'll tell what I know, which isn't much. Mike, Yaz, and me were in my trailer. The Phalanx started firing. The next thing, a huge explosion like..." Head tilted, eyes scanning the ceiling, he searched for words. "... well, you know those Fourth of July noise makers?"

The boy nodded.

"Imagine ten of those goin' off right next to your head."

"Wow!" Daniel made a low whistle.

Butch nodded. "Air compressions rocked the trailer. The back wall shattered and came at me like a special effect in a movie... Pow! That's all I've got. I woke two days later in the field hospital hooked to a saline drip."

Butch fell silent, staring into the distance.

Sarah waited. Daniel glanced at her, clearly looking for guidance. Sarah turned to Rosa, but judging by her friend's face, this was news to her too.

Butch blinked twice before his eyes locked on the countertop. "Mind if I try a couple eggs?"

"Sure," Sarah said. But like Daniel, she wanted more, wanted to know everything. As though knowing would bring Mike closer.

"Butch, you were saying about the explosion."

"Oh, right. That's the damnedest story." He crammed an egg into his mouth and moved it to his cheek so he could talk. "When the medics cleared me, I went back—thought my gear might still be there—fat chance. The trailer was a burned-out shell. I couldn't believe anyone got out of that rubble alive. Josh, he lives four trailers over from us, told me after the explosion no one could get near because of the heat."

"What caused the fire?" Sarah asked.

"Iranian-built 107 mm rocket—blew a hole the size of a small car in the T-wall behind our digs. Concrete and shrapnel peppered the trailer and fractured the propane bottle in my space heater."

"So how *did* you get out?" Daniel asked.

"The damned robot dragged us out."

"Robot!" Sarah said.

Butch rubbed a hand across his cheek. "This is supposed to be classified, hush-hush an' all that crap—oops, sorry, Daniel."

Daniel grinned, and Butch winked at him. "Did Mike tell you what he was working on, Sarah?"

She shook her head.

"Well, it can't be too secret. Everyone at Camp Liberation saw it. So... just between friends, then?"

Sarah and Daniel nodded.

"VCOM. It's a prototype. What's the skinny one in Star Wars called?"

"3PO." Daniel's eyes glistened.

"Yeah, like him."

"Dad works with robots, like on a secret mission?"

"Yeah, your dad's real smart. He's military liaison for the field trials. He and this civilian contractor, Brian—regular brainbox— were testing the robot. Josh told me the VCOM dragged us out. I went lookin' for the geek—because he must have been drivin'—to thank him, an' all, but he'd shipped out." Butch shook his head. "A piece of the bedframe tore your dad's leg. Other than that, the medics said he seemed fine. Yaz was in pretty bad shape though— legs burned up."

"Poor Yaz," Sarah said. "Have you heard from him?"

Butch didn't seem to hear the question. His gaze slipped from Daniel's face and wandered across the room until it fixed on the window.

"How about a beer?" Sarah asked.

Rosa said, "Sounds good to me." Then she raised her voice, as though her husband were hard of hearing. "Butch, want one?"

Noe slid four inches down Butch's arm. Grasping onto his dad's shirt, he started to cry. Butch's focus remained locked on the window. Rosa plucked the baby from him. "Butch? Sarah asked if you want a beer."

Nothing.

"Butch!"

"Huh?"

"Beer?"

His eyelids flickered a few times as though waking from a deep sleep. "Sure." The easy smile returned.

Daniel tugged Butch's sleeve. "I got *Halo 3* for Christmas. Want to check it out?"

Rosa hooked Noe onto her hip. "You boys go ahead," she said. "I'll help Sarah with dinner."

When the women were alone, Rosa shook her head. "The medics cleared Butch, but I'm worried. Did you see how he goes away?"

"Maybe he's tired from the trip and the jet lag."

"He's been home two weeks, and it's getting worse. I don't know. Yesterday he was feeding Noe, and the bottle dropped to the floor, slipped from his hand. Noe was screaming, and trust me, he's got his daddy's lungs. Butch just stared at the wall. I had to shake him to, you know, bring him back."

"How long is he home?"

"He's due back on base next week. The unit deploys to Iraq again in four months. Butch shouldn't be in the rotation." Rosa rolled her eyes. "But we know how that goes."

"Give him time to rest. He'll be fine."

"I guess."

Rosa's tone and her furrowed brow made Sarah wonder what had remained unsaid.

FIVE

On the morning of January 2nd, 2009, Brian Matthews's cellphone rang as he climbed out of a taxi in downtown Atlanta. He answered the call. "Hi. Okay. Great. Yes." With three short words, he'd placed a deposit on a two-bedroom apartment in the heart of Raleigh, North Carolina. In a few weeks, his days of living like an impoverished student in a one-room rental would be over. All those nights spent perfecting the LightCube had paid off at last.

In the center of the sidewalk, Brian punched the air. Looking skyward, he turned a slow circle. Two men in pinstriped suits glared at him as they skirted past, obviously annoyed by his antics. A country boy at heart, the towering steel-and-glass buildings sent thrills through his chest—he'd finally *arrived*.

He strode into Militec's headquarters, heel clicks echoing across the cool marble atrium, and took the elevator to the twenty-second floor. A stunning blonde receptionist, wearing a dark-blue pencil skirt, cream blouse, and too-red lips, guided him to a conference room and pointed him to a tray of refreshments.

Pacing in front of the full-wall windows, Brian absorbing the cityscape as he sipped chilled Perrier.

At nine fifteen, Moshe Steinman, dressed in a gray suit and red silk tie, joined him. Brian was surprised to see the vice president in charge of the VCOM project. Militec's software team normally handled planning meetings.

"Brian, how are you? Did you have a good flight?" The executive crushed Brian's hand and waved him to the end seat of the long polished-oak conference table that dominated the room.

"The plane was late leaving RDU, but we made up time. Isn't George joining us?"

Steinman sat, spread his hands on the table, and focused on his fingers for a few seconds as though noticing something surprising there. Then he raised his head and locked lizard eyes on Brian.

"Before we start, I must commend your bravery. Pulling those soldiers from a burning building was heroic of you."

"Hardly heroic. I controlled the robot from five trailers away. I was in no danger. Even so, I've never been more frightened. Mike's the hero."

"Who?"

"Master Sergeant Mike Braeman. The trailer was an inferno, and he refused to leave until his friends were safe. He chose their safety over his."

Steinman offered a tight, disinterested smile. "Anyway, well done." He brushed a piece of lint from his tie then lifted his head and stared past Brian's shoulder, out the window. "Brigadier General Swain's chief of staff flew in from Fort Black this morning. You just missed him."

"Oh?"

His gaze sloped back to Brian's face. "There's no easy way to say this. The army has canceled VCOM."

Brian gave an involuntary, audible gasp. Blood thrummed through his eardrums, fast and loud. He opened his mouth. No words came. His right eyelid fluttered.

Steinman spread his hands, palms up, and shrugged his shoulders. "We were shocked as well. Didn't see it coming. Reports from Camp Liberation were positive, and then the rescue—"

"Was this because of the fire damage to the VCOM?"

"Good grief. No. Saving those soldiers worked in VCOM's favor. The army's decision is purely financial. Swain had been running the project from a discretionary fund. The field trial budget we requested exceeded fund limits. The general recommended continuation. Washington rejected. To further complicate matters, he's been reassigned to a new unit at Fort Black. As far as the army's concerned VCOM is back to square one."

Brian sprang to his feet. He turned away from the executive and paced along the table, using his hands for emphasis, talking to himself as much as to Steinman. "I can't believe it. VCOM's potential is enormous. It could save thousands of American lives. Controllers could fight from the safety of, well, far from IEDs, anyway."

"I agree. But, at our estimated production cost of five hundred thousand dollars each, VCOM doesn't fit with the military's new focus on budget reduction and downsizing. The mission has changed." He frowned, face dramatically serious to demonstrate genuine concern, as genuine as Moshe Steinman could manage. "You know, Brian, when we started this project the military was short of trained troops. VCOM was born in response to that challenge, but they solved the problem by lowering recruiting standards." Steinman shook his head. "Today, the army is struggling to *reduce* headcount."

Brian returned to his chair and tucked trembling hands under his arms. After hitting every milestone, he'd expected to negotiate an increase in his daily rate and a twelve-month contract extension. Cancellation hadn't occurred to him. "Will Militec continue the project? Maybe try for funding next fiscal year?"

"We'll make a pitch again in October when the new budgets are allocated. And if VCOM gets funded, you'll be the first to know. But until then, the project is frozen. I'm sorry, Brian. The best I can do is extend you thirty days while you handover to George's team. He's waiting on the sixteenth floor. Trust me, he's very upset."

Brian was sure that was true. George Stanislov was the yin to his yang. Brian's LightCube sent the commands, and George's software converted them and made the robot respond.

But George was a salaried employee of Militec. And George hadn't just put a thirty-thousand-dollar deposit on a shiny new Raleigh apartment. To stop the room spinning, Brian got up and opened another Perrier.

Moshe Steinman approached from behind, placed a hand on Brian's shoulder, and eased him toward the door. "Take that with you. I'll show you out."

If Militec's twenty-second floor was corporate chic, the sixteenth was frat-house grunge. No runway-model receptionist waited for Brian at the elevator; he knew the way.

George—phone clamped to his ear, leaning too far back in his chair, sneakers crossed on a cluttered desk—noticed him through the open door of his glass-walled office and waved. Brian signaled back. He padded down a three-hundred-foot-long central corridor that always reminded him of a scene in *The Matrix*. Either side, in dozens of soft-partitioned cubicles, hipster-hackers, ears stuffed with white buds, squinted at oversized screens. An occasional colorful poster brightened the blue fabric walls. A large, green, stuffed dinosaur poked its head over one divider. A helium-filled Happy Birthday balloon, cut loose, drifted against the ceiling. Carpeted floors and white noise deadened sound. Brian stretched his jaws a few times to pop his ears.

Mid-thirties, dressed in bleached jeans with designer rips and a sixties tie-dye T-shirt, George finished his call and met Brian at his office doorway. He ushered him in, closed the door behind them. And opened fire—both barrels. "Did Steinman tell you what that ass wipe from Swain's staff said?"

"They've canceled VCOM."

"They're idiots." George pointed to the seat next to his desk, and Brian sat. "We deliver the perfect ground force solution, and they get their calculators out and figure it's cheaper to kill American kids than to build robots." Brian opened his mouth to comment, but George had turned to stare out the window. "Or maybe the officers realized they wouldn't have a bunch of grunts running around following their stupid orders and stiffening their cocks with power trips." He spun and waved a hand in the air as though swatting the problem then took his seat and let out a sigh. "Sorry, dude. I know you're pissed off too. Three freakin' years. We built them the most beautiful interface known to man, and they can't see past their egos."

"So it's final, then?" Brian asked, still grasping.

"Done. No funding, and no further requisitions being submitted."

"Steinman said you'd try again in October."

George's eyebrows lifted. "Moshe's full of it. Not going to happen. Swain has already slinked off to manage a unit at Fort Black. I'm sorry for anyone in North Carolina that has to listen to that self-righteous prick."

Brian slumped lower in his seat. "Crap."

Twirling a pen, George leaned back in his chair and crossed his feet on the desk. "What are you gonna do?"

"I'm still in shock. My contract ran out in December. Steinman said he'd extend me one month while we clean up the documentation and do a handover."

George put down the pen. "What a tightwad."

Brian shrugged. His left eye twitched. He snatched a gulp of air and stared at the first drops of rain splattering the window. He felt George studying him.

"Look, if it'll help, I'll tell management we need sixty days to close the project."

George's kindness tightened Brian's throat. He feigned a cough and took a deep breath to steady his voice. "That would be great. I could use the time to look for something else. I was blindsided by this. Completely blindsided."

"Yeah, I know. We were too. Friggin' army." George bounced to his feet and wagged a finger at Brian as he paced in front of the window. "You know what you should do?" He didn't wait for an answer. "You should turn the LightCube into a game controller."

Brian gave an ironic laugh. "Yesterday, I might have agreed, but... want to hear about the icing on this cupcake?"

"Pray tell."

"This morning I put thirty thousand down on a condo in Raleigh. That'll teach me to count my money while I'm sittin' at the table."

"Brian, man. Come on! It'll take what, two, three weeks to mock up a demo?"

"Maybe."

"Pretend you're back in college. Close the curtains, drop Ritalin, and inhale coffee. You're the best coder I know." George waved an arm at the floor of technicians beyond his office. "There's fifty hackers out there. If I had five Brians, I could replace them all. Why'd you think I insisted you build the controller?"

Brian felt heat rise in his cheeks. Coming from George the compliment meant a lot. The Militec version of his LightCube was built on code he'd been improving for ten years: ten years of late nights and missed romantic opportunities. Most of the changes developed for the VCOM could be revised to drive a game instead of a robot. It might work.

But what if it didn't?

George wagged a finger at him across the desk. "You know what? I can get you into GameSoft."

"Really?" GameSoft was the top video game producer in the US.

"Yeah, really. My kid brother, Frank, went to college with Adam Barnes."

"The CEO?"

"Frank owes me more than one favor." George slapped two hands onto the table as he stood. The noise was loud enough to make Brian jump. He yanked a blue denim jacket off his chair back. "Come on. I'm taking you for coffee and convincing. Heck, I'll be your first customer. I'm sick of wearing out my thumbs on plastic knobs when I play *Call of Duty*."

On January 16th, Mike Braeman received permission to visit Mark Yazinski. With one arm braced on the bedrail and the other on his wheelchair, he eased from his hospital bed and maneuvered the three-quarter cast on his left leg onto a metal support. His bare foot stuck out like a battering ram.

He released the chair's brake and rolled past the other beds, nodding to those few soldiers who made eye contact. Nobody talked much on the ward. Everyone worried about being forced out of the army with a medical discharge—didn't want anything they said held against them, didn't want to show weakness.

After pushing through the double doors into the corridor, he stopped and drew a deep breath—disinfectant still, but mixed with sweeter air and a lower temperature than his stuffy ward.

A couple marines marching toward him broke formation and passed on either side. "Soon be back to killin' hajjis," one said.

"I—" Mike swallowed and tried again. "I sure hope so."

"Oorah," they said in unison and marched off.

Mike nodded. Those marines got it. Pity Sarah didn't. They had spoken this morning, and as usual, she complained because he wasn't lovey-dovey and emotional. What the hell did she expect? He was the breadwinner. If his leg didn't heal, what then? Was *she* going to sign up. Was she going to bring in a paycheck? This injury had made him realize what a stupid idea leaving the army was. What was he thinking? And then there was Daniel—*dad always said, spare the rod, spoil the child*—that boy would sample some tough love when Mike got home. And that pile of Christmas toys Sarah bought for Christopher. She thought money fell from the sky in Iraq. Things had changed in Fayetteville, changed for the worse. The sooner he returned home, the better.

He rolled along the corridor and called the elevator, a smile on his face—finally under his own power, instead of lying in bed answering stupid questions. Of course his frigging leg hurt.

At the sixth floor, he headed for the nurses' station. A male orderly looked up from his paperwork.

Mike asked, "Where can I find Staff Sergeant Mark Yazinski?"

"Friend or family?"

"Both." Mike pointed to his left leg. "We were hit by the same shell. Yaz is my battle buddy."

The man nodded and opened a drawer. He handed over a surgical mask. "He got out of ICU yesterday. Keep this on. He's at serious risk for infection right now."

"How is he?"

The orderly locked eyes with Mike. "It's been close, but he'll make it." He pointed to his right. "Take the first corridor on the left. Room six-twenty is halfway along."

Mike spun the chair.

"Mask!" the orderly barked.

"Ah, sorry." He hooked the elastic over his ears.

"Keep it on!"

Mike glared at him.

Unlike Mike's ward with rows of beds, Yazinski had a private room. A muted TV flickered on the wall. The bed tilted up so Yaz could watch, but his eyelids were closed and his head inclined to the side. A line of drool slipped from the corner of his mouth. Right arm hooked to an IV, Yaz's colorful tattoos clashed with the white covers. A frame tented the sheets over his lower body. Yaz's face was gaunt with dark circles below his eyes. He'd lost weight, a lot of weight. Guilt washed through Mike. He should have told Brian to get Yaz out of the trailer first. But he'd been amazed to even see the VCOM. Who knew Nerdman had it in him to rescue them. People were surprising, sometimes.

"Yaz?" Mike whispered, waited.

"Yaz?"

Yazinski's eyelids flickered then squinted open.

"Yaz. How ya doin', buddy?"

In slow motion, like a tank turret's turn, Yaz rotated his head. At first, Mike saw no recognition in his friend's face. Then a weak smile crept across his lips. He nodded and wiped his mouth on his shoulder.

"Hi."

The greeting sounded like a croak. He pointed to the water jug at his bedside and Mike poured for him. Yaz cupped the glass with two hands, childlike, sipped, then passed it back.

"What day is it?"

"Friday, January sixteenth."

"Damn. I missed Christmas. Forgot your present. How come you're still here?"

Mike slapped his cast. "I get this off on Monday. If all's well, I'll be heading home soon after."

"Lucky bastard." An attempted smile morphed into a wince.

Mike laid a hand on Yaz's arm. "Need something?"

"My foot burns, man. Hurts like crazy. Can't even rub it 'cause of this contraption." He gave the topside of the frame a light slap then reached behind him, snagged a call button suspended above the bed, and pushed. "Got a cute nurse though. Wait till you see." He grimaced again.

"Should I leave?" Mike asked.

"Hell no. I just need something for the pain."

The nurse blew into the room, all fresh air and efficiency. In German-accented English she asked, "You have pain, Sergeant Yazinski?"

"Left foot again."

"It's not quite time for your meds. Pain number out of ten?"

Yaz winced. "Twenty."

She frowned.

Yaz grinned. "Eight point five."

The nurse offered a sympathetic smile. "I think we can make an exception." She whisked around the bed: Cropped hair, square shoulders and face, she reminded Mike of an East German shot-putter from the seventies. Her nametag read *Anke*. "You have a visitor, Sergeant Yazinski."

"Good buddy of mine. Got caught in the same blast."

The nurse nodded to Mike. "It seems you were the lucky one."

Mike hadn't thought of himself as lucky. But compared with Yaz…Yazinski didn't look so good.

After measuring liquid into a hypodermic, she inserted it into the saline drip. Anke smiled at Mike. "This will make him sleepy." She took Yaz's vitals, marked his chart, and left with a curt nod.

"Want me to go?" Mike asked.

Yaz shook his head. "God, no. I've been in solitary. Haven't seen anyone without a white coat on since I got here."

"I tried, but no visitors allowed in ICU."

"S'okay. I don't remember much. They kept me busy with some hard core drugs—way better than we get at the front. I hope they don't pull me off cold turkey." Yaz's face softened. He drew a deep breath. "Christ, I want to walk to the head so bad. I hate pissin' in a bottle and shittin' in a pan. Maybe you can hep me." The words slowed and slurred, thick like molasses. "Heh, Mike. Thans for comin, dude." Yaz's eyes closed and his breathing deepened.

Mike sat with his friend for a few minutes, watching him sleep. He turned off the TV before leaving.

At the nurses' station, Anke was punching data into a computer. Mike cleared his throat and removed the mask. She looked up. "How is Sergeant Yazinski? I mean how long..."

She glanced at Mike's name badge. "He's your friend, yes, Master Sergeant Braeman?"

Mike nodded.

A smile softened her features. She lowered her voice. "His legs suffered fourth-degree burns. The field medics were very efficient. Sergeant Yazinski is lucky to be alive, but we could not preserve the limbs."

Mike gasped in a breath. "He lost a foot?"

"Both legs, Sergeant."

Heat pulsed into Mike's cheeks. His stomach swirled and swooped, ready to puke. He swallowed a few times. "Where? I mean how much." He pointed to his leg.

"Both above the knee."

Mike nodded, took a few seconds to gather himself. "But the pain. He said his left foot hurt."

"Residual feelings. Quite real, but not what he envisions."

"You mean he doesn't know?"

"He only transferred from the Intensive Care Unit yesterday. The surgeon will speak to him this afternoon."

"What time?"

"Afternoon." She turned up her palms and shrugged.

"I'll come back later."

She nodded, smiled, then turned back to her computer screen.

Pete Barber

SIX

Rosa leaned in to the vanity mirror on her bedroom dresser and applied a final touch of mascara. For the first time in weeks, her image smiled back at her. This morning, she'd packed Noe off to her mom's because Butch had agreed to a date night. One dinner out wouldn't fix everything, but it was a start. The family briefings she and Sarah had attended at the base said even spouses had to get acquainted again after a deployment. Although, Rosa had always assumed that meant *other* couples.

It was five of eight. Butch was downstairs, and she didn't want to keep him waiting, he was so quick tempered nowadays. She opened the bedroom door and wobbled on her heels—it was a long time since she'd dressed as a woman instead of a mommy, too long.

FOX Sports blared out of the TV. Smoothing the front of her dress, Rosa stepped into the living room, a smile on her lips and tingles in her belly, anticipating Butch's reaction to her outfit. He liked her in a dress and heels—hello sexy lady he always said before grabbing her in a bear hug and kissing her or mussing her hair.

"I'm ready, honey," she said.

Butch slouched on the sofa, head on the armrest, eyes on the TV.

She stepped in front of the screen. "What do you think?" The new dress—size eight, black with a white pencil trim and spaghetti straps—flared from the waist as she twirled.

Butch looked at her. No. Butch looked through her. Said nothing. Crushed her spirit like a bug underfoot.

"Butch, are you okay?"

"Tired."

Grubby and unwashed, a two-day stubble darkened his face. Yellow egg splashes stained the front of his T-shirt. His grimy old chinos bagged at the knees.

"Honey, it's almost eight," she said. "Our table's for nine. Why don't you wash, and change into a fresh shirt and jeans?"

Butch looked up with flat eyes and a slack face. "What for?"

Her jaw tightened, and she ground her back teeth. Last time he returned from Iraq, he couldn't get enough of her. That's how Noe happened. But this time? Five weeks he'd been home. Five weeks of tired and cranky and living like a slob. Five weeks and Butch hadn't looked at her in *that* way even once. After last night's drag-down fight, he'd agreed the date was a good idea. She'd spent an hour getting ready, she smelled good; damn it all, she looked good, too.

To hell with it!

One hand on her hip, Rosa pointed to the door and shouted, "Soldier, get up this minute and change. We're going out. We're going to behave like a happily married couple. I'm tired, too. Tired of your shit!" Tears were close. Rosa swallowed hard and pushed them away; she'd cried enough. Softer she said, "Butch, please try. Try for me. You promised. Only last night, you promised."

He waved a hand. "I want to see this replay. You're blocking the screen. Move."

Move? That was it? That was all he had? After the panic over the rocket attack—not knowing for three days if he was alive or dead. And the tiptoeing around since he returned home in case he *went off.* And forgiving him when he barked at her. And believing him when he promised it wouldn't happen again. And then, when it did, forgiving him again. Anger, boiling and bubbling and brewing inside her for weeks, erupted. "The hell I'll move!" she screamed. "Get up. Get changed. Or get out and I'll find a man who *will* treat me like a woman." As soon as she loosed the words, she wished she could take them back. Rosa didn't want anyone else. She wanted Butch. But he made her so angry.

Butch rolled into a sitting position. He glanced at his watch. "You're early," he said, a sly smile on his lips, "Fort Black whores don't start work till after nine."

Rosa staggered back as though she'd taken a pile driver to the chest. "Is that what you see here?" She waved a hand down her dress. "A whore. Is that what I am to you?"

"Whatever. I'm too tired. Go. Don't go. I couldn't care less."

Heat flooded her cheeks. Red fury swamped her mind. She took two steps, raised her hand, and slapped his face—full force.

Lightning fast, Butch sprang from the sofa and smashed his open palm across her left cheek. The blow spun her around, and she staggered into the TV, which toppled from its stand and squealed as it hit the floor. Arms windmilling, one heel snagged the carpet. Her ankle twisted. She lost her balance and sprawled on the floor with her dress hitched high, exposing the black garters she'd worn for him. He glaring at her, eyes low-lidded and laden with hatred, lips curled back in a vicious snarl. Her cheek pulsed and throbbed. Her heart slammed so hard against her ribs she couldn't catch a breath.

Butch straddled her, legs braced, thigh muscles bulging against his chinos. He lifted his gaze to the snowstorm on the television screen. Spittle sprayed her as he shouted, "Fuck it. I'm outta here. Stupid bitch!"

Sucking in a faltering breath, face inches from the floor, through tear-filled eyes she watched his boots leave the room. Blood dripping from her nose trickled down her lip, and she caught it in her hand to save the beige carpet. Her cheek stung and had swelled, narrowing her vision. The front door slammed. Something fell. Glass shattered in the hallway.

She scraped off her shoes and struggled to her feet on cotton legs. In the kitchen, she wet a towel and pressed it to her nose, tasting iron, gasping for air, breathing through her mouth. A buzzing started in her ears. She dropped the towel and gripped the counter with both hands. Running tap water echoed in the sink. Outside, a motorcycle roared. She panted and swallowed until the lightheadedness passed and her whole world centered on the throbbing pain in her cheek.

Rosa opened the trashcan and threw in the bloody towel. The lid clanged shut. Her home felt empty, cold, and foreign.

I have to get out.

After pulling on her old sneakers, she headed for the front door. Glass shards littered the hallway. Their wedding photo, dislodged from the wall when he stormed out, had smashed. Butch's face smiled up at her from the fractured frame. She stepped over the mess and opened the door. A blast of rain-laden wind wrenched the handle from her hand and the door cracked into her knee.

Butch had the car.

It was pouring down.

"To hell with it." Rosa lurched onto the front step and slammed the door behind her.

No key.

No phone.

No way back.

Her hip ached from where she'd collided with the TV. Her knee throbbed from the door. A rain and sleet mixture peppered her face, stinging her cheek where he'd hit her, and drenching her new dress.

She shuffled along the deserted sidewalk, bent into the wind like a hunchback.

Sarah and Daniel sat on the sofa giggling at Sandra Bullock's final scene in *Miss Congeniality*. When the doorbell rang, Sarah's heart pulsed and her stomach knotted. One hand went to her throat. Daniel's head jerked up; he stared, wide-eyed, at his mom.

Unexpected callers after dark were never welcome at the home of a deployed soldier. She forced strength into her voice. For Daniel's sake suppressing the fear. "Stay here. Finish the movie. I'll go." At the front door she called out, "Who is it?"

"Rosa."

Sarah slid back the safety chain and opened up. Strands of Rosa's long black hair plastered her face. A wind gust blew sleet into the hallway. Arms wrapped tightly across her chest, Rosa shivered in a thin dress so wet it hugged her body and showed her underwear.

Mouth open, Sarah stepped back. "Christ, Rosa. What happened? Come. Come in." Sarah glanced behind. Daniel stood at the living room door, watching. "Daniel, run upstairs and grab the white bath towel from my room." He sprinted away. "Get my dressing gown, too," she shouted after him, "the blue one hanging on the hook by the shower."

Her friend stepped into the hallway. "S… sorry, I'm dripping on the carpet." Her voice cracked. Sarah stooped low and snatched a glance at Rosa's face: drawn, stressed, frozen, and not all the moisture was from rain. She wrapped warm arms around her wet, trembling friend and pushed the door shut with her foot.

Daniel clomped down the stairs, three at a time, and held out the towel. "Hi, Mrs. Cassidy."

Rosa reached out a hand. Without meeting his gaze, she covered her head and rubbed at her hair. "Thanks, Daniel," she said in a tiny, high voice.

Before Rosa hid under the towel, Sarah noticed the swelling on her cheek. This was no place for her teenager. She took the housecoat from him. "Son, the movie's done by now. Why don't you head upstairs? Take a shower and change into PJs. You can play video games for an hour before bed. I'll be up later to check on you." When she nodded to him and widened her eyes, he got the message and left.

Such a good kid.

She parked Rosa on the couch and turned on a country music channel. "How about a cup of hot chocolate?"

Rosa's head nodded under the towel.

"Daniel's upstairs. The room's yours. Take off those wet things, dry off, and put on the robe. I'll be back in a five minutes."

When Sarah returned from the kitchen, Rosa had folded the towel on the back of the sofa and piled her wet clothes on top. The dressing gown swamped her. The collar, pulled high, covered her face. Sarah offered the steaming mug, but when she noticed the tremors in Rosa's fingers, she placed it on the side table instead. She knelt in front of her friend and stared into her face. Rosa's left eye glistened through a narrow slit. With one hand on Rosa's knee, Sarah asked, "What happened? Is Butch all right?"

She nodded and sobbed in a breath. "He's probably at The Blue Note."

"On Friday?" The local watering hole featured bands on weekends. The place would be hopping, full of single soldiers looking to score. And Butch had never been much of a drinker.

Rosa looked her in the eyes. "He goes every night."

Gently touching a fingertip to Rosa's swollen cheek, Sarah asked, "How did this happen? Did Butch hit you?"

"He didn't mean it. He bumped me as he passed, and I fell. My fault. I was standing in the way. It was accidental."

Sarah frowned but held back judgment; the fingermarks on her cheek didn't look like an accident. "Drink the chocolate while it's hot. I'll be back in a minute." Sarah went into the kitchen, wrapped crushed ice in a dishtowel, and brought it to her friend. "Here. This'll ease the swelling."

While Rosa held the compress against her face, Sarah sat next to her on the couch. "Where's Noe?" she asked.

"At my mother's. I… we thought being alone for a couple nights would give me and Butch time to reconnect. Time to discover each other again. But—" The dam broke and desperate sobs racked her.

With an arm around Rosa's shoulders, Sarah waited for the grief to soften before asking, "What's changed? You were so close. He seemed fine at Christmas, and I remember Butch after Noe's birth. He was crazy about the baby and about you. Said he wanted another when he returned."

Rosa shook her head. "He doesn't want me in *that* way nowadays."

"What? Why?"

"When he first got back, I—" Color rose in Rosa's cheeks.

Sarah massaged Rosa's shoulders. "We're best friends. You can tell me. I won't judge you, or Butch, and I promise it will go no further. Sharing helps. Rosa. Sometimes it's all we've got."

She nodded, eyes fixed on the floor. "When he came home before Christmas. When we climbed into bed, I was excited. You know, like a first time. Butch couldn't get it up. I told him it was okay. We cuddled. That was enough. To have him there beside me in bed, was enough."

That image lodged a lump in Sarah's throat. God, how she missed being in Mike's arms.

Rosa lifted her head. Tears welled in her eyes. "Later that night I woke and reached for him. Butch wasn't there. I thought maybe he went to the bathroom, but the house was quiet. I got up, walked around the bed, and about crapped myself. He lay on the floor, curled up, blocking the bedroom door, dressed in his cammies and fast asleep. I knelt beside him and whispered, 'What's wrong, *ma vida?*' He whipped around," she made a rapid sweep of her arm, "flipped me over, and started strangling me." Rosa tilted her head and revealed a long yellowing bruise ringing her neck.

"That's why you kept the scarf on Christmas Day."

"*Si.*"

"You should have told me." But even as she spoke the words, Sarah knew, were the roles reversed, she'd have done the same. Their men were under such pressure during deployment. It was a wife's role to protect them when they returned.

Rosa shrugged. "His eyes were crazy, far away. The madness only lasted a few seconds. I called his name, and when he looked at me, when he saw me, he begged for forgiveness. He didn't mean what he did. He didn't know where he was, or who I was."

Sarah patted her arm. "What happened then? Did he come back to bed?"

"Yes. I tried again. Tried to get him interested. I thought it might settle him. But he stopped me. Said he wasn't up for it." She pressed her lips together, shrugged. "And he wasn't. You know…"

This seemed odd. Mike was always horny when he came home from the field. "Was Butch like this after the last deployment?"

"No. I think the rocket attack… He talked about it on Christmas Day. It sounded like a big explosion. I've begged him to go to the doctor on base, but he says they checked him out at Camp Liberation and cleared him for duty. He won't go. Doesn't want to get labeled a faker."

Mike would think the same way. Warriors who complained were weak. No officer wanted weaklings in their unit.

"So did it help when you two finally had sex?"

Rosa sucked in a breath. "We haven't."

Sarah's mouth dropped open. "He's been home five weeks."

Rosa started to sob again.

"Sorry, Rosa. I didn't mean—"

"S'okay. I can wait. *That's* not the problem. Butch never used to get angry. He was my gentle giant. My mom said he spoiled me, treated me like fine china. Now all we do is argue. I can't do anything right. I try not to upset him, but… And when he's not mad, he sleeps on the couch. He sleeps all the time. When I ask why, he says I'm nagging. Says I don't understand. Says he has to catch up after Iraq."

"I'm sorry, Rosa. Can *you* talk to the doctor?"

Her head reared back. "Butch would kill me."

"What about Noe? Butch loves him so much. How is he with his son?"

Rosa shook her head. "Last week, he looked after him while I went to the store. When I got home, Butch was asleep on the sofa. Noe was in the kitchen." Her voice rose an octave. "My baby had climbed into the cupboard under the sink. He was playing with detergent and bleach bottles. What if he'd gotten a lid off, Sarah? My boy could have died."

Sarah swallowed the lump of fear that had lodged in her throat. Rosa must have been terrified.

"What did Butch say?"

"He said he only slept for two minutes and he was just about to get Noe. Told me I was getting hysterical for nothing. Then he stormed out and came back at three in the morning, drunk. I asked where he'd been, and he said—nowhere. I don't know what to think. Butch lies. He lies all the time."

"What are you going to do?"

Sarah passed a Kleenex from the box on the coffee table. Rosa's fingers trembled as she dabbed her eyes. "I can't go home, and I can't go to my momma's this late." She pointed to her face. "If Papa saw this I dunno what he'd do. Can I stay here tonight?"

"Of course. Christopher's staying with his grandma for a couple days. Let me change sheets, and you can take his bed."

"I couldn't, but maybe the couch?"

Sarah narrowed her eyes. Rosa was embarrassed enough, so she didn't press the issue. "Sure."

Rosa laid a hand on her friend's arm. "Thanks. I can't face another fight." She straightened and stared into Sarah's eyes. "Sarah, I don't know who he is. But I do know who he isn't. And he isn't my husband. Butch went to Iraq, but someone else came back."

Rosa buried her head in her hands and sobs shook her tiny frame.

"I'll get the covers and we'll make you comfy on the sofa. And I've got a sleeping pill with your name on it. Eight hours will do you good."

Upstairs, Sarah knocked on Daniel's door, and went in. "Finish that game and then turn in. Okay?"

"Is Mrs. Cassidy sick?"

"She'll be fine."

Daniel was waiting for more. But Sarah couldn't think what to say. If he still seemed concerned in the morning, they could discuss it further. Although what could she tell him?

As she pulled a comforter, sheets, and a set of her PJs from the hall closet, her mind was with her husband. She missed him so much, especially at a time like this. Butch looked up to Mike. When he got home, she'd ask him to help. If he were here, maybe Butch wouldn't be careening around like a loose cannon.

<><><>

After dinner, Mike climbed into his wheelchair and headed for the sixth floor. At the nurses' station, Anke told him the surgeon had broken the news to Yaz. Mike rolled along the hallway to his friend's room. How did you tell someone you'd chopped off his legs? How did a person do that? And how did Yaz react? How would *he* react? A sharp pain shot through Mike's calf. But at least he had his leg.

In the half-reclined bed, Yaz slept, mouth open, snoring—probably doped. Mike turned on the TV. For twenty minutes, he watched retired generals on CNN discussing Afghanistan and troop surges as though they knew what was happening. The Iraq war was, apparently, over—yesterday's war. Because the pols said the US was pulling out.

Yaz stirred and icicles skittered through Mike's chest. How did you talk to someone who'd just learned he had no legs? What did you say?

"Hi." Yaz slurred the word.

"How ya doin'?"

Yaz pointed with one finger, toward the bottom of the bed. "They tell you?"

"I'm sorry, man. I blame myself. I should have gotten you out faster. I should have moved, pulled the friggin' bedframe off my leg and got to you. I should have made Brian take you first."

"Dude. None of this is your fault."

Mike sucked in deep breaths, stared at the TV, and blinked to clear his eyes. "What did the doctor say?"

"He—" Yaz gave a half-laugh devoid of humor. He told me he'd amputated both legs. Said it was the only way he could keep me alive. I laughed, real sarcastic like. Didn't believe him. "Wrong room, Doc," I said. "I'm the guy with the painful left foot." His voice cracked. He pointed to his water glass. Mike tossed out the dregs and refilled it from the tap. Yaz sipped.

"So the doc pulled back the covers and told me to look." Yaz's face crumpled like a paper wrapper. Soft sobs shook his chest, then he squawked in a lung full of air and bawled like an infant.

Mike grabbed his friend's arm and squeezed. He wanted to say something, to comfort the man, but his mind was a blank wall. He stared at the bed. Below the cage, where Yaz's legs should have been, the sheets were flat. He hadn't paid attention when he visited earlier.

Yaz cleared his throat. "Sorry, man. I'm whining like a baby."

"You've earned that right, soldier."

He pointed down the bed. "Uncover them."

Mike shook his head.

"You need to, man. Otherwise, you won't get it."

Mike reached out. His fingers trembled as he pinched the corner of the sheet. "You sure?"

Yaz nodded. Mike rolled the covers off the cage. He winced and peered through narrowed eyes. He couldn't look. And he couldn't look anywhere else. Stinging tears spilled down his cheeks.

Where Yaz's legs should have been there were two fat bandaged stumps.

SEVEN

Brian Matthews trudged fifty yards across a rain-slickened parking lot to reach the entrance to GameSoft's five-story concrete and glass headquarters in Raleigh's Research Triangle Park. He took the elevator to the third floor. A friendly receptionist settled him into a conference room with coffee and a plate of Orio cookies. "Mr. Barnes is running late. Can I get you anything else?"

"Is this where we'll be meeting?"

"Yes."

"Then I'm fine, thank you. I need time to set up."

Brian synchronized his laptop with a projector positioned on a stand at the head of a small table. He clicked through his PowerPoint presentation once to make sure he had the correct version. Then he displayed the ten slides more slowly, mentally rehearsing his pitch.

When Adam Barnes arrived at ten thirty, Brian's stomach was churning, and he needed the bathroom. He'd never met GameSoft's founder, but the man's face was familiar. The twenty-four-year-old multimillionaire attracted plenty of publicity.

"Sorry to keep you waiting." The CEO extended a thin hand and Brian accepted a limp, warm handshake. Adam reminded him of a pale, bespectacled five-foot-tall marionette. A woman, also mid-twenties, accompanied Adam. He introduced Mia as a project manager. Both wore dark T-shirts and scruffy jeans—child prodigies could set their own standards. Brian felt overdressed in pressed chinos and a crisp white shirt.

"No problem. I'm grateful you could fit me in. I have a short presentation covering the LightCube technology. Then, if you wish, I can demonstrate an early version."

"The floor's yours." Adam and the woman settled at the table.

The familiar sales pitch calmed Brian's nerves. But with no questions, he finished the slides in under fifteen minutes. "If the

51

concept is clear, would you like to get hands-on?"

The CEO checked his watch, which did little for Brian's confidence. "I have until eleven."

"That'll work." Brian switched on his prototype LightCube—larger and thicker than the military version. Thirty seconds later, hundreds of thin beams projected upward from the device, forming a cube of light. Brian pushed the tablet in front of Adam and waved his fingers through the beams. "This is the controller." He plugged the viewing goggles and a headset into the side of the tablet. "I'd expect a production version to be more attractive." He grinned as he offered the CEO a black-rubber diver's mask he'd modified to build his heads-up display. The gear looked like a poorly executed science fair project. But the slick equipment that drove the VCOM in Iraq was US Army property and unavailable to him.

Adam positioned the goggles over his eyes and secured them with the strap. "Cool," he said, and extended his hands so his fingers interrupted the lights coming from the tablet. "Very cool. Wow!"

Brian said, "The demo is a primitive Mario-like simulation, but it should give you a general idea of the gaming experience."

Adam pulled on the headphones, and a wide grin cracked his face as his hands moved and flexed across the LightCube, controlling the images projected onto the inside of the goggles. Monitoring the man's hand motions, Brian visualized Adam's progress as his finger flicks maneuvered a cartoon character through a maze; the CEO was a quick study. Three minutes in, Adam's head jerked back. "Neat!"

Hopeful tingles surged through Brian's chest. Multicolored explosions had just filled the goggles, and Adam Barnes had enjoyed the experience. Brian had programmed the effect to illustrate the advantage of the retina display. The experience was immersive. Adam removed the headset, his grin still fixed in place. He handed the equipment to his project manager. Mia gave Brian a warm smile that reached her dark-chocolate eyes. She had perfect caramel skin and a cute button nose—totally out of his league.

"Can you restart it?" Adam asked.

"Sure. Just press the red button when you're ready, Mia."

Once Mia was up and running, Adam said, "Extraordinary software. Kudos. You've exceeded my expectations." Adam drummed his fingers on the table and fell silent for a few seconds before clearing his throat. "Honestly, Brian, I only met you as a favor to George's brother. He told me I owed him one. I probably owe him more than that." The sly smile that softened his face made him look even younger. "But after experiencing your… What do you call it?"

"LightCube."

"Huh. Not a fan of the name. No matter. I'm glad you brought it along."

"I'm a techie, not a marketing guy, but I think this interface could add tremendous value to your games, particularly a first-person shooter such as *Alien Smackdown*. The operator would be *inside* the battle zone."

Adam frowned, shook his head. "I disagree. LightCube is a different experience altogether. We code for Xbox, PlayStation, and PC so our graphics are optimized for delivery on a video screen. This is a paradigm shift. As with the change from 2D to 3D movies, the images have to be designed to leverage the 3D effects. Our hackers would have to code *for* your LightCube."

Brian's enthusiasm evaporated. His left eyelid fluttered. His voice dried up. He had no argument to contradict the man's assessment because Adam Barnes was right. The LightCube was a disruptive technology—the most expensive kind. It required goggles and a three-dimensional light-sensing display, and a new coding approach. The technology was exciting, but the business challenge of bringing it to market was enormous, and expensive.

The CEO sprang to his feet. He tapped Mia's shoulder, and she pulled off the goggles and headset and laid them on the table. Adam offered his hand. "By the way, George told me how you used the LightCube to rescue those soldiers in Iraq. Three of them, right?"

"Right. I—"

"How are they doing?"

Heat blistered Brian's face. He'd been so self-absorbed since leaving Iraq, he hadn't inquired about Mike and his team. "Two are hospitalized in Germany. The third only suffered minor burns. I don't have an update on their recovery."

Adam nodded. His eyes far away, mind probably focused on his next meeting. "Good. Anyway, thank you for the demonstration. Give me a couple days to think it over?"

"Sure. I appreciate the opportunity."

They shook hands, and Adam and Mia left, closing the door behind them. Brian sighed, packed his kit, and headed for the exit.

Back to square one.

An hour later, back home in his one-bedroom rental apartment in downtown Raleigh, surrounded by boxes—he didn't close on his new apartment until January 30th, he kicked himself again for putting such a large chunk of escrow down on the condo. The realtor had told him with multiple competing buyers, the juiciest down payment usually won. The realtor had been right, but the realtor didn't have to make the mortgage payments.

Brian logged on to his email and fired off a "How are you and the guys doing?" message to Mike Braeman.

"Better late than never," he said to his reflection in the window, although the words did little to convince. What if one of the guys was seriously injured, or even dead? How would he feel then? *Like shit.* The new apartment and the VCOM cancellation had filled his mind. And once George had set up today's meeting, he'd burned up the keyboard to create the demonstration for GameSoft—another waste of time and money.

His laptop beeped. Mike had replied. "Yaz is pretty bad off. We're both still in Landstuhl Hospital, but I ETA Fayetteville next week. Butch is home. Let's meet so we can thank you for saving our butts."

The message did nothing to ease Brian's guilt—some friend he turned out to be—his financial problems were inconsequential when compared to what Mike and Yaz and Butch had faced in Iraq.

EIGHT

Sarah came downstairs a little after seven to an empty couch. The bedcovers, neatly folded, were stacked on the back. In the kitchen, Rosa, still dressed in the blue robe, slouched over the table, head in hands. When Sarah coughed, her friend looked up and pointed to a cup of coffee. "I hope you don't mind."

"Course not. You should have woken me."

"I haven't been up long." On her left cheek, a blue swelling trimmed with yellow and black edges distorted her features.

"Did you sleep?" Sarah asked.

"On and off. You?"

"Fine." Sarah poured coffee. Actually, she'd lain awake for hours worrying about her friend, and then fighting off more worry about Mike. Was he really *recovering* in Landstuhl? He'd been strained on their Skype calls and brusque on emails. She suspected he was more severely injured than he had told her. That would be typical of Mike—not wanting to bother her, taking the responsibility on himself.

"Where are the boys?" Rosa asked.

"Daniel's sleeping, *of course*. When Noe grows up, you'll see, that's what teenagers do—eat and sleep. Christopher's at my mom's."

"Sorry, you covered that last night."

"Christopher and I both needed a break. You know how it gets when it's just you and them all the time. Look. We're not big on breakfast. How about a slice of toast?"

"Thanks, but I better get going. I tried to wash the dress, but—"

Wrinkled and forlorn, Rosa's little black dress draped the back of a kitchen chair.

"Aww, Rosa. You shouldn't... How stupid of me, I never thought. I'll find something for you to wear. What are you, size

55

ten?"

"Eight."

"Good for you! Luckily, I have a few wishing clothes." When Rosa raised her eyebrows, Sarah said, "Wishin' I was a size eight again. I kept them for motivation." She patted her stomach. "Didn't work, but you'll look great in my skinny jeans. Come upstairs and pick something out. You can use my bathroom to freshen up."

Thirty minutes later, Rosa came downstairs, hair wet, wearing Sarah's jeans with the bottoms turned up and a black sweater, sleeves bunched to make it fit. Sarah had a plate of buttered toast and a fresh pot of coffee on the table. She pointed to the seat opposite.

"I don't know how to thank you—" The words caught in Rosa's throat.

"That's what friends are for. Now grab a slice and tell me what you plan to do."

Rosa nibbled at a piece of bread and stared at her hands. "I've been thinking. Perhaps I overreacted. Butch was tired. I should have asked him when he came home from work if he still wanted to go before I got dressed up. Perhaps he forgot the arrangement. He does forget the damnedest things."

"Or he's being selfish. If this was the first time he'd lost his temper, maybe, but from what you told me last night, this is your new normal."

Rosa winced.

Sarah leaned across the table and laid a hand on her friend's arm. "Whether he forgot or not, I think Butch should talk to a doctor and find out what's *really* going on."

Rosa's chin trembled. She wiped at her eyes.

"Rosa, Butch is a good man. Wouldn't harm a fly. First to volunteer if someone needs help. My kids love him, and they're no pushovers. That's not the person you ran from last night. This sudden change can't be just your fault."

Sarah got up, stepped across to the kitchen counter, and riffled through a drawer. She brought back a Military Community Awareness pamphlet titled *Homecoming* and laid it in front of Rosa. "Read through the bullet points—the warning signs for combat fatigue. Aren't these things happening to Butch?"

She pushed the flyer away. "I know this, Sarah. You and I

attended the briefings together, remember? But what's the point? He won't report sick. It's a sign of weakness. It'll reflect badly on him. Three guys from the last deployment got booted out with other-than-honorable discharges. They lost everything—healthcare, pension. Everything."

Rosa took a deep breath and let it ease out. "And to be honest, I'm scared too. While he was in Iraq, we discussed him leaving the service. He's missing out on Noe. Even with a big cut in income, at least he'd be home more. It's tough enough for ex-military to land a civilian job, but without an honorable discharge, it'd be impossible." Rosa stood. "Thanks, again, but I've got to go. Mom will be expecting a call."

"I'll come along."

"No need. I'm fine."

"Oh, yeah? Even though you're locked out and I have the spare key to your house?" Sarah grinned, tried to make light of the situation. She wouldn't let Rosa walk into God knew what at home. At least this way, she could get her there safely. And if there *was* more trouble from Butch, she could offer an escape route, or call someone.

Rosa shook her head, but a smile tweaked her lips. "Okay."

After leaving a note on the fridge for Daniel, Sarah found an old parka for her friend; the hood hid Rosa's bruises. The rain had stopped, but the damp cold had a raw bite. They drove the four blocks in silence with Rosa twisting at the hem of the parka, rolling and straightening it in her lap.

When they pulled up outside Rosa's home, she jolted upright and grabbed the dashboard. "The car's not here." Her voice was thick with panic.

What thoughts must be racing through her friend's head. Sarah gritted her teeth and choked down her own fears. Good job she'd insisted on coming. Rosa needed her support. What the hell was Butch thinking? Thank heavens Mike never pulled stunts like this.

They walked up the path together. Sarah handed over the spare key, and Rosa opened the front door. "Wait here while I check upstairs."

Standing in the hallway of the empty house, Sarah studied the broken glass on the floor and hoped the picture had just fallen and not been thrown. Doors opened and closed as Rosa moved through the bedrooms. Seconds later, she appeared at the top of the stairs, wide-eyed. "He hasn't been home."

"You sure? Maybe he fell asleep on the couch." Sarah beat Rosa to the living room, but Butch wasn't there. Rosa grabbed her purse and tipped the contents onto the table. She snatched up her cell phone. "I've got a voicemail. Five a.m. Oh, God!" Her hand trembled as she punched in her password. She pressed the phone to her ear and her eyes filled with tears as she listened.

Sarah waited, expecting the worst. Butch was showing symptoms of battle fatigue. At the base briefings, the presenter, a psychiatrist, had discussed self-inflicted harm—a cry for help, he'd called it. He'd talked about suicide, listed the warning signs. Sarah had heard the words but never connected those symptoms to Butch. They were other people's problems. A wave of nausea churned her stomach, and she steadied herself against the back of the sofa. What if Butch had hurt himself? What if...?

Rosa lowered her phone. Her face was pale as paper. "He's been arrested. I have to pick him up from Fayetteville Police Station. He called," tears spilled down Rosa's cheeks, "and I wasn't here for him."

Sarah put an arm around her friend's shoulders. "Come on. At least we know he's safe. What happened?"

"Driving While Impaired. He still sounded drunk on the message. Wait—" She held up a hand and spoke into her phone, "Call Butch."

"I'll be outside in the car." Sarah hurried from the room.

Her friend followed a few seconds later and climbed into the car.

"Did you speak to him?"

"No. The phone's turned off, or dead, because he didn't pick up."

They drove to town. In front of the police station, Sarah slowed. Butch sat on the sidewalk, slumped against the building's brick façade. Chin tucked into his collarbone, his head lolled to one side. His left knee showed pale through a bloodied rip in his jeans. Rosa jumped from the vehicle before it stopped. She ran to her husband and knelt next to him. Sarah followed but held back, gave them space. The crumpled man her friend was hugging resembled a hobo not the reliable family man Sarah knew him to be. What a mess. How Sarah ached for Mike to be home. Butch would have been his responsibility. But, as with everything else, she had to handle both sides of the marriage during deployment.

Only when Rosa tried to haul Butch to his feet did Sarah move closer. They each took an arm and helped the big man stand. He stared at Sarah for a second. Then his gaze sloped away.

"Where's the car, Butch?" Rosa asked. He stood there, swaying, stinking of alcohol, tobacco, and body odor. Rosa had a tight hold of Butch's arm, struggling to keep him erect. Her eyes were full of tears; her lips twitched; Rosa was cracking.

Sarah said, "Let's get him into the car before he falls over, then I'll ask the cops where they found him."

The desk sergeant, stern-faced and balding, checked the arrest record and gave Sarah the car's location. "Paul Cassidy's a lucky man," he said.

"How so?"

"If he'd taken a swing at me, I'd have charged him with assault."

"He was violent?"

"Officer Wilson brought him in, and if he hadn't ducked, the haymaker that young man threw might have knocked his head off."

"I don't understand?" Sarah said.

"Me either, but Wilson's a former marine. Luckily for Mr. Cassidy, *he* does understand. Get him home and make sure he doesn't drive again. His license is revoked." He opened a desk drawer, pulled out a flyer, and handed it over. "Here, this explains the legal process."

Back at the car, Sarah handed the leaflet to Rosa. Butch sat in the rear. No one spoke during the fifteen-minute drive to The Blue Note. When they arrived, the Toyota was the only car in the bar's parking lot. "Apparently," Sarah said, "the police stopped him before he reached the road."

"Thank God. Driving that drunk, he could have been killed."

"Or killed someone else."

Rosa glanced at Sarah and she immediately regretted the words. Her friend needed support, not more guilt.

They helped Butch out of the back seat and he stood, unsteadily, while Rosa searched his pockets for the car keys. Once he was loaded into the Toyota's passenger seat, Rosa reached out of her driver's window and squeezed Sarah's hand. "Thank you," she whispered.

"Sure you'll be all right?"

Rosa nodded. "I'll put him to bed. Mom'll keep Noe while we sort through things. I don't know what—" Her voice cracked and Sarah waved her away.

"No problem. I'll follow you home, just in case."

When Rosa pulled into her driveway, Sarah waited in the road, not wanting to interfere. Her friend was embarrassed enough. At the front door, Rosa turned and waved. Sarah shouted out the passenger window, "Call me and let me know how things go. I'm here for you, okay?"

Rosa opened the door, and Butch stepped through. His feet crunched glass shards into the carpet, and he bent to pick up their broken wedding photo.

He spun around. "What happened?"

Before she could speak, he brought his hand up and caressed her bruised cheek with the back of his fingers. "Who did that to you? What's going on, Rosa?" Concern filled his eyes.

"Don't you remember?"

Butch shook his head, innocence, and bafflement on his face.

Rosa closed the door, took a deep breath, and faced him again. "You hit me, Butch." She pointed to her face. "Then you stormed out and slammed the door so hard the picture fell and broke."

Butch's mouth opened. He reached out and gathered her in. She pressed into his chest and sobs shuddered through her. Butch murmured into her hair. "I'm sorry. I don't remember. I'd never hurt you. I love you, Rosa. I—"

He held her shoulders and eased her away, stared into her eyes. "Noe? Did I hurt Noe?" He sucked in a breath and a huge man-sob shook his chest.

She stroked his cheek. "Hush, now. Noe's with my mom. He's fine." She took his hand and led him into the kitchen, sat him at the table, put on the kettle, and spoke in a soft voice with her back to him. "Butch. Noe's fine. I'm fine. The wedding photo can be repaired. But you're not fine." She faced him. "Butch, I want you to get help."

Shoulders rounded, head lowered, he stared at the tabletop. Whatever demon he was fighting, the battle was over. The demon had won. Her warrior was defeated, broken. A shroud of sadness numbed her mind. She ached for him, ached to help, ached to fix what was wrong. But this enemy was beyond her, beyond them both. Butch had never raised a hand to her, hardly ever raised his voice. But since his return from Iraq, he frightened her. Three years ago, she fell in love with his gentle nature, his powerful body, his Christian values. In a matter of a few weeks, her hero had transformed into a drunk who slapped her face, flew into wild rages, endangered his son, stormed out of the house, and remembered none of it. What the hell had happened after he left home last evening? Did he know? Could he know?

She sat at the table and tipped his chin up so she could meet his eyes. "I understand why you don't want to report this... problem. But how can the army make things worse than they are? You can't go on like this, not remembering what you do, hurting those you love." She leaned in, stroked his arm, and whispered, "Neither can Noe. Neither can I."

"You're right. I'll go to the primary care manager and ask for help." Butch stood and turned to leave.

She laughed. "Hold on, big man. First, you need to shower and change. Can't go out in public looking and smelling like a vagrant."

He nodded again. "I'm sorry." He snatched a glance at her, then averted his eyes and padded upstairs like a whipped puppy.

As Sarah pulled into her drive at home, Daniel, dressed only in a T-shirt and jeans, was shoveling slush and ice from the front path.

She jumped from the car and ran to her son. "What are you doing? It's freezing out. Leave that. Get in the house."

He glanced up—face and neck blotched red, eyes bloodshot—shook his head and went back to work. She grabbed his hand and stopped him scraping. "What's the matter? What is it?"

"Dad's here, and he's mad because the place looks so messy." Her son's chin quivered; he was close to tears. "Dad called me a lazy bastard. Mom. I'm sorry."

"Mike's home?" Why hadn't he told her he was coming? And

why shout at Daniel. Nerve endings, exposed and raw from the Butch incident, ramped up her heart rate. She shivered, not with the cold, not with anticipation of his homecoming, but with uncertainty. What the hell was going on? She prized the shovel from Daniel and laid it on the lawn. "Leave this. Come in and get warm clothes on, and I'll handle your dad."

"You go first," he said in a shaky voice, fear in his eyes. In the hall, Mike's kitbag leaned against the wall. A clattering of dishes came from the kitchen. A voice she hadn't heard in the home for over a year, a voice she'd longed for, shouted, "Friggin' mess!"

She whispered to Daniel, "When did he get here?"

"Thirty minutes ago."

"Go to your room. Now. I'll deal with this."

Whatever this is.

Daniel thumped up the stairs two at a time. The noises in the kitchen stopped. Mike shouted, "You wait there until I inspect that path, my boy! You can't slack off with me. I'm not your mother."

Daniel kept moving. His bedroom door slammed.

Sarah stepped into the kitchen. Pots and pans and dishes and canned food cluttered the countertops. Every cupboard gaped open, empty. Mike, still dressed in cammies, held a saucepan in each hand and glared at her. "This place is a pigsty."

"Honey. I didn't expect you. Why didn't you tell me you were coming?"

"So I could see what you've been doing. Or *who* you've been doing while I was fighting for your freedom. And it doesn't look as if you've been doing much of anything except spoiling my sons." He slammed the pans down on the table. One rocked and clattered to the floor. He swept his arm at the room. "And serving them food from dirty plates. I want all of this washed, and these cupboards cleaned, ASAP." He glared at her.

Something had happened to cause this, but he was home. She'd waited so long for him to return. "We can get to that, Mike. It's so good to have you back. She moved to him, wrapped her arms around his waist and pressed her cheek into his chest, warm and strong. I missed you so much." He remained rigid, arms at his sides.

"I see that." He pushed her away. "I've been traveling twenty hours. I'm going to shower and rest. Get this mess cleared up. Then we have some serious talking to do." He grabbed an aluminum walking stick off the chair, limped from the room, and clomped up the stairs with his kitbag.

Sarah scanned the wreckage of her kitchen. For weeks, she'd envisaged Mike's homecoming: she'd cook his favorite spaghetti dinner, wear a nice dress, get her hair and nails done. Then, later, soft candlelight in the bedroom.

Slumped in one of the kitchen chairs, her head sank into her arms. Last year when he returned, Mike had been so happy to see her and the children. He couldn't keep his hands off her, even embarrassed Daniel with the way he touched her and kissed her and held her hand as though they were on their honeymoon again. This homecoming wasn't part of her fantasy. Disappointment coiled around her chest and squeezed. Silent tears trickled, pent up from Rosa's terrible night, and now this. Her bedroom toilet flushed. Shower water ran through the pipes. She crept up the stairs, tapped on Daniel's door, and went in. Daniel, bent over his computer with his back to her, jerked upright and spun around. Sudden fear in his eyes softened to relief. He must have expected his father. This wasn't the homecoming he'd envisioned, either.

"Look, Daniel, your dad's been traveling for twenty hours. I guess he got wound up. He'll be okay once he's had a rest."

"He called me a bastard."

"Dad didn't mean it. You'll see."

"What about the front path?"

"I'll handle that. Did you eat?"

"I had cereal while you were out."

"Good. Play online for a while. I'm going to check on him."

He nodded, but his eyes were wary. She closed his door and headed for their bedroom. Mike was toweling off with his back to her. A glimpse of his broad shoulders and tight buns sent heat flooding through her belly. She watched his biceps flex as he pulled the towel back and forth. "I could help with that," she said, her voice husky with need.

He stiffened. She swallowed. Was still angry? But when he turned, a familiar smile lifted his face and softened his eyes. "I'm sorry about—" He finished the thought with a wave of his hand. "I guess I was upset you weren't here when I arrived."

"You should have called, Mike. I had a special homecoming planned for you."

Anger ghosted across his face for a second. He took a deep

breathe, steadied himself. "I'm not due home for two days, but when the medics released me, I hustled and found Space-A on a supply plane."

"Well, you're here now, and that's what matters." She pointed to the ladder of red stitch marks on his left calf. "How is it?"

"It'll always have limited motion, but they cleared me to rejoin the unit."

She moved to him and laid a hand on his bare back. "Why don't you finish drying, then climb under the sheets. Let me shower. I'll join you in two minutes?"

He bent and kissed her forehead. Shivers trickled down her neck, spiked her nipples, and stole her breath. After closing the bathroom door, she yanked off her clothes and tossed them in a pile.

Showered and perfumed in ten minutes flat, she snuck back into the bedroom, slipped naked under the covers, and snuggled against his chest, feeling the warmth of her man for the first time in over a year. She kissed his neck and dragged fingertips across stomach muscles still taut from active duty. Why couldn't they lie here forever? Mike pulled away from her. He seemed about to speak, but then he grabbed her shoulders, flipped her over, and took her from behind. Roughly, satisfying an animal need. He finished fast, way before she was ready, then his breathing slowed and deepened and sleep took him.

Feeling used and unsatisfied, she rolled over and propped up on an elbow, studying his face. The lines around his eyes, on his forehead, and at the corners of his mouth were new. White streaks peppered his sandy hair. This last deployment had aged him five years. Was there something else? Something he and Butch had both suffered? Had it been the rocket attack? She would never ask, and probably never know. Mike would handle it. This army wife understood *that* unwritten rule of combat.

Sarah kissed his cheek and slipped from the bed, leaving him sleeping. Between the exhaustion and jetlag, who knew when he'd wake. Now he'd released his anger and frustration, she'd give him the homecoming she'd planned. When he woke, they'd forget about the kitchen incident and start over.

She showered and dressed. On her way downstairs, she knocked on Daniel's door, poked her head in. "Dad's asleep. He'll be more himself when he's rested. Don't hold a grudge, Daniel.

Forget earlier—scraping the path and the shouting. Okay?"

"Sure."

"Good boy. I'm headed to the grocery store. Spaghetti Bolognese for dinner?"

"Cool."

She smiled, closed his door, and skipped down the stairs, humming to herself. It took a few minutes to find her purse buried under the chaos on the kitchen table. *I'll fix this when I return—needed a spring cleaning anyway.*

Pete Barber

NINE

The elevator doors opened on the sixth floor, and the young woman Brian met two days earlier at Gamesoft's HQ smiled at him and offered her hand. "Thanks for coming at such short notice."

Brian found her Hispanic features especially attractive. Her broad white smile, long black hair, and chocolate eyes sent a heat wave tingling through his cheeks. He cleared his throat and stepped out of the elevator.

"Mia Hernandez," she said. Brian shook her hand—small, soft, warm.

"Nice to see you again. Working weekends, I see." The call he'd received last night from Adam Barnes had shocked him—nine p.m. on Friday. Apparently, rumors of the CEO's workaholic tendencies weren't an urban myth. Adam liked the LightCube. He wanted to meet and discuss the possibility of hooking it to a GameSoft product.

She started walking. "If you work with Adam Barnes, you work all the time. He does."

"Are you tech or marketing?"

"I'm a technical project manager, but let's wait for Adam to explain." Nervous energy skittered through Brian's belly. This could be his big break

At the end of the hallway, she opened a door and let Brian into a corner office. Floor to ceiling windows overlooked an ornamental lake at the rear of the building. Adam rolled his chair away from an uncluttered desk, stood, and reached across to shake hands.

"Thanks for coming, Brian." He pointed to a conference table set against one window. "Why don't we sit. Do you need anything? Coffee? Water?"

"No, I'm fine."

"Excellent."

They settled around the table and Adam said, "Mia is project manager for a game we're developing. So new it doesn't have a name. We call it Soft16. It's a first-person shooter slated for delivery in—"

He turned to Mia who said, "Twenty months."

"Right," Adam said. "Soft16 will be our first 3D game. Or at least that was the plan, but after your demonstration, Mia and I discussed the possibility of packaging Soft16 with your LightCube."

"Wow! That's exciting," Brian said.

Mia, smile gone, face and tone all business, said, "On the positive side, the 3D capabilities fit well with the immersive nature of your retina display. However, GameSoft has never delivered hardware before, and we'd have to develop and package the cube and the heads-up display."

Adam smiled. "No offense, Brian, but something a tad more appealing than black swimming goggles."

Brian laughed. "I understand. The army's version resembled a pair of designer sunglasses—far cooler."

"Right," Adam said. "Which brings up a major concern. Do you own the code?"

"Absolutely. The demo you saw is built on code I have written over the past ten years. The US Army owns a version I modified for them to control the VCOM. But—" Brian tapped a finger to his forehead. "The knowledge of the changes we incorporated lives here."

A smile passed between Adam and Mia. The CEO rubbed his hands. "Excellent. So here's our proposal. Mia will provide access to the Soft16 code and technical support to help interface the LightCube. How long will that take?"

Brian eased back in his chair. "Without seeing your code, that's difficult to estimate."

"Finger in the air, Brian. I won't hold you to it. Years? Weeks? Months? Days?" Adam leaned in. "Minutes?" Sharp eyes pierced Brian's, and his scalp prickled. He didn't want to hang a long estimate on the work and kill the project before it started, nor did he want to be overoptimistic and disappoint by missing the deadline.

"Based on my experience working with Militec, four to six months."

Adam's gaze switched to his project manager. "Can you staff it,

Mia?"

She nodded, and Brian quietly let out the breath he'd been holding.

The CEO pressed her. "Without delaying Soft16's 3D implementation?"

She smiled and shook her head. "Nice try, Adam. We can support him to build a prototype. To repackage and deliver Soft16 with marketable hardware is a different discussion."

"Understood." Adam refocused on Brian. His stomach churned. Things were moving fast. "That leaves just one question. Do you want the project? You'll have to work on site. I can't allow GameSoft code to leave the building even on a remote link. We'll provide a workspace and computer access. You'll bring your existing code and modify it here. If the prototype is successful, we'll want to negotiate an exclusive license for the LightCube, right, Mia?" Adam glanced at his project manager. She nodded her approval. Adam, grinning, faced Brian, and waited.

He tried to clear his mind. This was a huge opportunity, but he'd jury-rigged the demo. The LightCube needed work, a lot of work—at least three months of sixteen-hour days. How would he live, and how would he pay for upgrades to the hardware? Damn it all. If he hadn't bought the condo. But if GameSoft funded him, he'd surrender ownership—he'd just be a paid contractor. Whereas, a licensing agreement with one of the biggest gaming companies in the world would mean a perpetual royalty on every game. And, if Soft16 was successful, on future games as well.

This was the brass ring—not the time to chicken out. He'd figure out the money, somehow.

When Brian raised his hand it appeared to travel in slow motion, but when Adam Barnes clasped it, Brian squeezed and shook and smiled and said, "When do we start?"

Pete Barber

TEN

On her way to the grocery store, Sarah called Rosa. "Hi, guess what?"

"Go on."

"Mike's home!"

"Wow, that's terrific. You didn't tell me he was coming so soon."

"Didn't know. He surprised us."

"Men! I'm happy for you. Say hi from me, okay?"

"Sure. Hang on a sec." Sarah turned in to a parking space at the front of the store and switched off the engine. "How's Butch?"

"I dropped him off at the base. He has an appointment with the doctor to talk about, you know. The temper and forgetting stuff."

"That's good, right?"

"I hope so. Butch is nervous about going, but last night scared him. He'd blacked the whole thing out."

"They'll know what to do. He's not the only one suffering. At the seminar they encouraged us to come forward, right?"

"Uh huh." Rosa didn't sound confident.

"He'll feel better getting it out in the open; you'll see."

Inside the store, now, Sarah grabbed a shopping cart. "Look, Rosa. I've gotta go. Tell me what happens, okay?"

"Sure. And, Sarah."

"Yeah."

"Thanks again. You know, for being there."

"Of course." She hung up and scooted along the aisle, swerving the cart for fun and singing along with the piped music. After gathering the ingredients, she splurged on a bottle of Chianti to complement the Bolognese. They'd have a family dinner, and then tonight, in bed, she and Mike would take it slower. Excitement tingled her thighs and made her shiver.

On her way home, she called her mom. "Mike's back."

"That's wonderful news, honey. When?"

"This morning. Do you mind bringing Christopher back this afternoon? He'll be excited to see his dad. Better yet, why don't you and Pops both come, stay for dinner. I'm making spaghetti. There'll be plenty to go around."

"That's sweet, but you need family time."

"Don't be silly. You *are* family. Mike'll be delighted to see you."

"Well if you're sure. Can I bring anything?"

"Just your appetite."

When Sarah arrived home, Mike and Daniel were sitting on the sofa, their backs to her, playing *Halo*. She stopped in the hallway and watched through the door as their blond heads moved in sync with the game. Funny how such a simple thing as two people playing a video game could be so special. For a couple minutes she remained in the doorway silently absorbing the fact that their family was finally back together.

Although she worked hard to fill the void while Mike was deployed, there were certain things only a dad could do for a son. With a smile on her face, she headed for the kitchen and started to clean up the mess from Mike's impromptu spring-cleaning.

"Left! Look out on your left!" Mike's voice boomed through the house.

The place was so quiet when Mike was away.

"No. No! God damn it, Daniel. Too slow. You're dead, boy. Dead!"

Sarah's mouth dried up, and she turned to stone in the middle of the kitchen with a pack of ground beef in her hand. She held her breath, listening, waiting. The harshness in Mike's tone was beyond game play. Daniel's sneakers slapped against the wood flooring in the hall. He flashed past the doorway and stormed up the stairs. She rushed into the hallway. "Daniel?"

On the landing, Daniel stopped and glanced down. His face was crimson, eyes filled with tears. He turned away. The bedroom door slammed behind him.

She marched into the living room. Mike sat alone on the couch, still working the controller. "Mike, what's wrong? Why'd you shout at him?"

He paused the game and turned to face her, arm on the back of the sofa, eyes narrowed. "Daniel has to learn. Slow reactions get people killed!"

"Mike, it's just a game. You've upset him. He's missed you so much."

"Daniel's got to stop being a mommy's boy. And when did he last get a haircut? I've seen neater hippies." He spun away, grabbed a can of Bud off the coffee table, and took a slug before picking up the game controller. An alien exploded and showered the screen with virtual blood and guts.

A vehicle pulled into the driveway. She raced to open the front door. Christopher sprang from the rear of his grandpa's car and tore along the path toward her. Eyes wide and cheeks flushed, he shouted, "Is Daddy home?"

She signaled with her thumb, and he ran past her into the living room. She heard him scream, "Daddy, it's you!"

Sarah stiffened, teeth clenched, waiting, unsure.

"Come here, you monster. Holy moly, you've grown three inches. Mom's feeding you too much."

When she heard Mike's rumbling laugh mixed with Christopher's giggles, she rotated her jaw and took a deep breath. Her mom stood on the doorstep, staring at her, reading her face. "You okay, honey?"

Sarah smiled. "Yes, of course." Her dad came up the path and gave her a hug. "Glad to have the man of the house back?"

"You can't imagine."

He smiled and handed her a bottle in a brown bag. "A little something for the homecoming."

"Thanks. Go on in. I'll put this in the kitchen."

Christopher shouted, "Grandma, Grandpa, Daddy's home!"

"So I see," Grandpa said. "Hi, Mike. Welcome home, son."

Sarah strained to hear an answer that didn't come. Instead, the TV volume increased until the game's explosions and gunshots filled the kitchen. Her mom joined her, carrying a bunch of cut flowers. "These'll need to go in water. They won't last, but I thought they'd look nice on the table."

Pops came in and stood with his arm around her mom's waist.

"Is Mike all right?" he asked.

"Why?"

"He didn't even say hello. Just turned up the TV."

Sarah said, "I'll talk to him. He's wrought up. I think the journey—"

Her mom laid a hand on Sarah's arm. "We'll just go, dear."

"No, Mom. It'll be fine."

Tightening her grip, her mom shook her head. "Really. Let the poor man settle in. There's plenty of time to get together later." She took a step back. "Come on, Pops. I've got a list for the grocery store."

He pecked Sarah on the cheek. "Call if you need anything," he said. "Anyway, where's Daniel?"

"In his room." Heat rushed to Sarah's face.

Pops patted her shoulder. "We'll catch him later in the week. Enjoy your family. You've waited long enough to get them together again." He stroked her cheek and whispered, "Love you, kid."

"Love you too, Dad." Tears misted her eyes as her parents walked away. They shouted a goodbye to Mike through the living room door, but he didn't answer. The front door clicked shut, and all that remained was the noise of the video game, and a band of anxiety squeezing Sarah's stomach. For a fleeting moment, she wished the home could be back the way it was.

Before Mike had returned.

In the waiting room of the base medical center, Butch scanned a magazine. After reading the same paragraph three times and not following a word, he tossed the book back on the table. Hanging on the opposite wall, a life-sized schematic of the human body depicted the nervous system as a mass of snaking green and red lines. Hard to believe that stuff was all inside of him. A nurse appeared from the rear office. "Sergeant Cassidy?"

He sprang to his feet. "Yes, ma'am." His voice came out sharper than he intended.

She smiled, didn't seem to notice how jumpy he was. "Come on through."

Butch followed her into a small examination room, and she

pointed to a chair. He sat while she took his vitals. As she coiled up the blood pressure cuff, she said, "The doctor will be in directly. Just wait here, please, Sergeant." She closed the door behind her.

The same chart of the nervous system hung on the wall to his left.

A squat man with a balding head and salt-and-pepper beard came in and introduced himself as Dr. Wainwright. Butch stood and they shook hands.

The doctor dragged a second chair across the room and positioned it so they sat four feet apart, facing each other. "You wanted to talk about some unusual behavior."

Butch took a deep breath. Was he doing the right thing? The doctor had a laptop open on his knee. Whatever they discussed would go on Butch's record. But he'd hurt Rosa. He winced, shook his head.

"Sergeant?" The doctor was staring, head tilted, face open, questioning.

He had to decide.

For Rosa and Noe. Butch clenched his gut and committed. "I've been getting dizzy. Sometimes I have to sit or I'd I fall over. And I've been forgetting stuff. Not like my keys. I mean big things I shouldn't forget. And—" He lost his train of thought. His chest tightened and his throat closed. For a few heartbeats, he forgot how to breathe.

The doctor nodded. His face stayed expressionless, but open, not judgmental; at least Butch didn't think so. His voice stayed low and calm. "How about if I ask questions and you answer?"

"That would be easier. Thanks. Shoot."

"When did you get back from Iraq?"

"December fourteenth."

Wainwright typed in the date. "How long was your deployment?"

"Eleven months, this time."

"And the time before?"

Butch looked at the ceiling while he tried to remember. "About the same, I think. It'll be on my record."

"Last time you returned, did you have any of these symptoms: dizziness, memory loss?"

Butch shook his head. "Not that I recall, and Rosa, that's my wife, would have said."

"Good. So let's focus on this deployment. While you were in Iraq, did you experience a powerful force or blow to your upper body or head? You may not have been physically injured. Does any event fit that description?"

"There was a rocket attack."

"When did that occur?"

"Few days before I came home."

"Tell me what happened?"

Butch frowned, squeezed his eyes shut for a second. Fear flooded in and made his stomach pucker. He sucked in deep breaths and rubbed at his cheeks. He needed another shave. Had he remembered to shave? He wasn't sure.

Wainwright smiled. "Take your time. Why not step me through it. What were you doing five minutes before the attack?"

That was easier. "It was evening, just getting dark. Me and Yaz, that's Sergeant Yazinski, we were playing Xbox in my trailer—*Need For Speed.* Yaz had just wiped out, again. We were laughing about it when this huge explosion happened. The noise was deafening—so loud it hurt. It came from all around. The TV was against the back wall, and the trailer's paneling just blew in." Butch pulled a handkerchief from his pocket. His face was hot. He mopped a slick of sweat from his brow. Except on Christmas Day at Sarah's, this was the only time he'd spoken of the incident. He tried not to think about it. Although he woke up in that trailer nearly every night.

The doctor cleared his throat. "So there was a loud noise, and the panels collapsed. What happened next?"

"The back wall slammed into the TV and the TV hit Yaz in the chest and he flew across the room. How you'd see it in a movie, you know, as though a magic force tossed him aside like he was made of paper."

The doctor was typing up a storm. He stopped when Butch fell quiet, and asked, "What happened to you?"

Butch strained, squeezed his eyes shut, tried to remember. But came up blank. He shook his head. "Sorry, Doc. I got nothing."

"That's okay. Try to picture yourself as Yaz flew across the room. Were you still seated?"

"Yes. Oh, that's it, I flipped backward in the chair. It felt as though someone slammed a sandbag into my chest and dropped me. I remember watching the ceiling fan. A rock fragment smashed into the fixture, ripped the whole fan, blades and all, from the roof." Butch's voice cracked.

"Would you like a drink of water?"

He nodded, and the doctor got up and filled two plastic cups at the sink. They sipped. "Thanks," Butch said.

"Okay, so you saw the fan. You were on your back, then? On the floor?"

"Yes."

"What's the next thing you remember?"

"When I woke. In the field hospital."

"How could you tell you were in the hospital?"

"I was lying down. I sat up. You know, fast. The room spun, and I flopped back and realized my legs and belly were strapped to a gurney. When the dizzy spell passed, I looked around. The guy beside me was sitting on his bed, knees dangling over the edge, staring. I asked where we were and he told me Camp Liberation Field Hospital."

"How did you feel?"

Butch held out his arm. "This stung like hell. I got a burn." Butch ran a hand along his forearm.

The doctor pointed to the still-pink skin. "How is that, now?"

"Fine, thanks, Doc. No problems there."

"Did you talk with the soldier in the next bed?"

"Yeah, I asked him three or four times what happened to Yaz and Mike, and he didn't answer. I wondered if he was a hajji."

"Why? Did he look like a local?"

"No. 'Cause he looked blank, couldn't understand what I was saying. Then I figured it was me. The words got stuck somehow, you know, as if I had cotton in my mouth or something."

The doctor nodded and smiled. "What time was this?"

"Huh? Not sure. I lay back down because the room started spinning. Later, when a medic came in the door, I saw it was light outside. Sunrise was around seven, so it was after that. I reckoned I'd been out all night. But when they released me I found out it was two full days."

"What caused the explosion?"

"A rocket slammed into the T-wall behind my trailer. If the barrier hadn't been there, I wouldn't be talking to you right now."

The doctor nodded. "What time did the attack happen?"

"Hmm, okay, Brian arrived at the trailer about eighteen hundred hours, and the Phalanx fired up soon after. He went outside to see what was up, and then the rocket hit."

"What did the medic do?"

"Who?"

"You said a medic came in to the field hospital."

Butch noticed a low buzz in the quiet room. The chart behind the doctor's head pictured a male subject. He wondered if the nerves were different on women? He squinted and traced a red line that began below the man's left ear but he lost track as the lines bunched at the neck. Although he traced it again, and again, Butch couldn't keep it in focus.

"Sergeant?" An urgency in the doctor's voice caught Butch's attention.

"Yes?" The doctor's left eyebrow lifted, waiting. He must have asked something. "Can you repeat the question, please?"

"I asked what treatment the medics gave you in the field hospital."

"Ah, sorry. He checked my vitals. Asked me how I felt."

"What did you tell him?"

"That my arm hurt like hell." Butch grinned and raised his arm to show the doctor his scar.

"But that's okay now, right?"

"Fine, thanks, Doc. No problems there."

"Hmm. What about the dizziness?"

"Yeah, I was still dizzy. Not dizzy. Lightheaded maybe. Like after a couple beers."

"Had you been drinking?"

"No. Never was much of a drinker." Heat rose in his cheeks. When had he changed, then? Because he sure was a drinker now.

"Did the medics ask questions as I'm doing now?"

When the room fell silent, Butch realized the doctor had asked another question.

"Sorry, what?"

"The medics, did they question you like I'm doing now?"

Butch shook his head. "I asked them about Yaz and Mike, they were both in the trailer with me when we were hit."

"And did the medics understand what you were saying?"

"Not at first. I had to speak real slow. Yaz and Mike were hurt bad. They were airlifted to Landstuhl, Germany. I was lucky, the medic said."

The doctor glanced at his screen. "So, Sergeant, correct me if

I've got any of this wrong. You were relaxing in the evening, playing a video game when an enemy rocket exploded close enough to your trailer to blow in the rear wall and throw you and Sergeant Yazinski across the room. You received burns on your arm and lost consciousness for two days. Does that sound accurate?"

Butch nodded.

"Okay, now we know what happened. Tell me why you asked to see me."

Compared with this question, the other stuff had been easy. Butch's mouth dried up. He swallowed. "Rosa, that's my wife—" The words got stuck. He coughed. Tried again. "Rosa went to a seminar on base, and the presenter talked about personality changes and such."

"And have you noticed changes?"

"I guess. I keep forgetting things. And I get angry a lot. I've been going out to The Blue Note."

"Let's take this a piece at a time." The doctor looked up from the laptop and softened his voice. "Sergeant." He smiled. "Look. I know this is difficult. Remember I'm not here to judge, just to help. Okay?"

Butch nodded and rubbed his sticky palms against his jeans. A sweat droplet trickled down the side of his face. He pulled out the hanky to mop his forehead again and squirmed lower into his chair. His heart slammed and bumped and thrumming in his ears as though he were jazzed and ready to go into battle.

"Let's talk about your memory first."

Butch breathed out. That was easier. He rolled his neck and heard a click. Maybe the memory loss was more important than the other stuff.

Wainwright cleared his throat. "Can we, Sergeant?"

"Yes, sir."

"So, tell me something you've forgotten since you came back that your wife thinks you'd have remembered before you were deployed."

"There's lots."

"Tell me the worst one. What brought you here, for example."

If he told him, it couldn't be taken back. This went on his permanent record. Butch swallowed the rock lodged in his throat. "Well, the other day, while Rosa was at the store, I was watching Noe, my son."

The doctor smiled. "How old?"

"He's just turned one."

"They're so cute at that age."

"Yes, he is. Anyway, when Rosa came home, I'd fallen asleep on the sofa, and Noe had wandered into the kitchen and gotten into stuff in the cupboards he shouldn't have. I didn't watch him good enough. Rosa was hoppin' mad, and quite right, too. I told her I'd only just nodded off, but the truth is, I didn't even remember he was there."

"You mean you forgot that you were minding him?"

"No. When she asked where Noe was, I didn't know who she meant. I mean I'd forgotten that was our son."

The doctor held up one hand. "Give me a few seconds." He typed for a little while. Then he looked up and said, "What else?"

Butch's heart slapped against his ribs. "Isn't that enough?"

"The more you tell me, the better chance I have to help. Was that the incident that persuaded you to see me?"

Butch sighed. "No. That happened last night. I hit my Rosa." His throat locked up again, and he sucked in a few breaths and dug his nails into his palms. He damn well would not cry. What the hell was wrong with him? "Doc, I love my wife. She's everything. I'd never harm her. But when I saw her this morning. When I saw her face all bruised. I asked her how it happened. She told me I did it. I don't remember touching her, but she's telling the truth."

"When did she say this happened?"

"Last night before I went to the bar."

The doctor nodded and typed. He smiled. "You're doing well, soldier. I know this is tough. Hang in there. We're nearly through. Tell me, how are you sleeping?"

"I kinda nap. I'll drift off, then wake. Sometimes I throw off the covers, sweating like when I was back in the field in Iraq, or else I'm shivering, freezing, as though I have the flu."

"Do you have any aches and pains, other than the burn?"

"Headaches. Real bad. Feels like my brain's trying to squeeze outta my eyes."

"How do you deal with that?"

"Tylenol."

"Does it help?"

He shook his head. "Not much."

"How frequent are the headaches?"

Butch opened his mouth to answer, but he couldn't remember. "Often," he said.

"Okay. Let's backtrack to Iraq. How long were you in the field hospital?"

"On the third morning, I got up."

"And?"

"I told them I was feeling fine."

"Were you?"

"Yeah, a bit shook up, you know. But I wanted to find out about Yaz and Mike."

"Did they clear you for duty?"

"Yeah, but I was kept around base, just hangin' out because I was rotating out three days later."

"Okay, Sergeant. I've got everything I need." He clicked and tapped the keyboard a few times. "I'm prescribing antidepressants and anti-anxiety pills. You take them in the morning and at night. They'll help with the surges of anger. And I'm giving you something stronger than Tylenol for the headaches; only use these when needed. None of these drugs mixes well with alcohol. Can you stop drinking?"

"I never used to drink. Never liked it much. I can stop."

"Good. Alcohol might appear to help, but it's a mood depressant. Drinking will make things worse. Trust the medication." He clicked again, and a printer on the far side of the room hummed. Then he closed the laptop, spread his hands on top, and made eye contact with Butch. "When the human brain is subject to a violent shock it rattles about and gets bruised. This leads to what used to be called a concussion. Nowadays we prefer the term traumatic brain injury or TBI. The symptoms you've described—anger, change of personality, problems sleeping, and memory loss—are common in TBI sufferers."

"Can you fix it?"

"These drugs will treat the symptoms, but only time will affect a cure. Your brain is bruised and swollen, like any bruise, it needs time to shrink and heal."

"How long?"

"I afraid I can't be precise. Maybe weeks. Maybe years. Some symptoms may last indefinitely."

Butch hadn't known what to expect from the doctor, but learning he might never recover hadn't occurred to him. His heart fluttered and accelerated, trying to burst from his chest again. He wiped his hankie across his forehead again, blew his nose. He had no words. How would he tell Rosa? Well he wouldn't. He'd figure this out himself. He stood and offered a hand.

"Thanks, Doc. It's not the kinda news I expected or wanted, but at least I'm not going crazy. I hope the pills help."

The doctor stood. "They will."

"One more thing," Butch said. "Will my command hear about this?"

"Of course. But General Swain is fully cognisant of these types of injuries. There's no reason you can't remain a useful member of the unit provided we handle the worst symptoms. Sergeant, you did the right thing coming in. We can't fight an enemy if we don't know he exists. Can we?"

Butch nodded. "Thank you, Doc." He closed the door behind him and made his way out of the building. Once outside, he called Rosa to pick him up. Not having a driver's license sucked.

ELEVEN

When the front door closed behind Sarah's parents, Mike yelled, "Good riddance." Seated on the sofa with Christopher pressed against him he asked, "Ready for the next level?" Christopher nodded. Mike clicked the controller and engaged the enemy. Sarah was speaking. He sensed her standing in the doorway but blocked her out. More nagging. Since he got home: nag, nag, nag. The house was filthy. Daniel looked and acted like a spoiled brat. Even Christopher had needed a few sharp words to bring him into line. He glanced down at his son and ruffled his hair. "But you'll be okay, now Daddy's home. Right, Chris?"

His son stared at the TV. "Yes, sir."

See, it doesn't take much to get respect.

Sarah moved in front of him, blocking the screen, hands on hips. He paused the game. "What?"

"Yes. What?" she said. "What the hell's the matter with you? You chased my folks away. You've upset Daniel. You're playing video games and—" She picked up the plastic rings from the six-pack of beer he'd finished. "— getting drunk in the middle of the day. We've waited a year for you to come home and this is all you care."

Christopher wriggled, and although Mike tried to hold him, he squirmed off the couch and ran to his mom and buried his face in her belly.

This wasn't the homecoming Mike wanted either. He'd seen enough on Skype to suspect the place had gone to shit without him, but things were worse than he'd feared. He sprang to his feet, stepped forward, looming above her, faces inches apart. Their son, sandwiched between them, started to cry.

Sarah met his stare, ready for battle.

What was the point?

He was worn out from fighting—fighting the hajjis, fighting the

German medics, and now fighting this bullshit in his own home.

He shouted in her face, "I didn't sign up for this. I'm outta here, and you'd better adjust your attitude by the time I get home." Waving a hand around the room, he said, "Clean this place up. Then remind your sons they should respect their father." Mike put a hand on her shoulder and pushed. She staggered back a step, flinched, and wrapped her arms around Christopher. "Didn't see that coming did you? Now shape up. And make sure dinner's ready when I get back."

He grabbed the car keys from the hook in the hall, snagged his leather jacket, and slammed the front door behind him. On the path, he stopped and pulled sharp, fresh American air into his lungs. "Ah. So good to be out of the dust, and sand, and heat." He drove four blocks to Butch's place. No one was home, so he headed for The Blue Note. At least there, he could talk to soldiers who understood what the hell was going on in the world.

The bar's parking lot was mostly empty. It was only two fifteen, a little early for the evening crowd. No problem; he needed time to himself.

Time to think.

At the bar, he took a stool and ordered a Wild Turkey and a Bud chaser. He downed the shot, ordered another, then phoned Butch but got voicemail. After leaving a message telling him to come to The Blue Note, Mike scrolled through his contact list, stopped at Brian Matthews's name, and called.

Brian was playing what-if with a budget spreadsheet when his phone rang. He'd been massaging numbers since he returned from his meeting with GameSoft, and there was no way he could fund the project. He didn't want to talk to anyone right now, but the call was from Mike, so he answered.

"How're they hangin', Nerdman." Mike's words were slurred, celebrating his homecoming, maybe? Although the sergeant had never taken more than a couple beers while they were in Iraq.

"I'm doing fine, thanks. How's the leg?" Memories of the screams in his headset when the VCOM tore Mike's leg away from the broken bedframe sent a shiver snaking down Brian's spine. It must have hurt like hell.

"They patched me up pretty good. Out for my first night of freedom, and I'm looking for someone to show me what I've been fighting to preserve in the good ol' US of A. Why not join me for a beer?"

Brian's gut reaction was to decline. Then he scanned the spreadsheet again and a black cloud descended. The LightCube was his chance to stop workin' for the man. Instead, it looked as though he'd have to run to Adam Barnes, cap in hand, and admit he couldn't deliver. "Shit."

"What?"

"Sorry. Yeah. Aw, hell. Why not? I can be in Fayetteville in ninety minutes. Where are you?"

When Brian arrived at The Blue Note a little after four, Mike, standing at the bar with a group of guys dressed in cammies, noticed him and gave an exaggerated wave.

The men made room and Mike shook Brian's hand. "This is the guy I was tellin' y'all about. Brainiest dude I ever met. What'll you have, Brian?"

"Michelob Ultra, thanks."

Mike bought a round of beers for the group and a bourbon for himself. The bar crowd was noisy, with everyone forced to shout over a heavy metal number booming from the jukebox. Even so, Mike's voice was louder than needed. "These guys," he pointed to four of the soldiers, "are shippin' out in the a.m.—first tour. They'll be stationed at good ol' Camp Liberation. Got any advice for them, Brian?"

"Take a sand pail. You'll need it. That place is like the surface of Mars."

Mike laughed and slapped Brian's shoulder hard enough to buckle his knees, and way more enthusiastically than Brian's comment deserved. The men exchanged glances, and over the next five minutes everyone sidled off, leaving Brian and Mike alone.

He regretted coming. Babysitting a drunk wasn't much fun. Perhaps if they shifted from the bar Mike would calm down. "How about sitting where it's quieter, and you can catch me up on the guys."

The words flipped Mike's serious switch. His face flattened to a grim mask. He frowned, nodded. "Let's do it."

They carried their drinks to a four-top in an alcove. Mike positioned his latest bourbon shot precisely at the center of a beer mat and stared at the drink.

"So how are Butch and Yaz?" Brian asked.

Dragging his attention from the table, Mike looked up and sighed. "Butch is fine. He's home. I left him a message earlier. He'll probably come by. Heh, wait. I'll tell him you're here."

Before Brian could protest, Mike called and left another message.

"And Yaz?" Brian asked. "You guys were in Germany before I got discharged from the field hospital."

Mike turned his head, took a few deep breaths. When he faced Brian again, his eyes were full. "Yaz lost both his legs."

Brian exhaled with a whoosh as though punched in the gut. He clamped both hands on the table's edge to keep his balance. Mike reached out and patted him on the arm. "I know—shocking as all hell. You've been there. You understand. Most of these." Mike waved a hand at the crowd. "Well, the ones who haven't been posted, anyway, just don't get it." Mike locked his eyes on Brian's. His speech no longer slurred, his words more carefully chosen. "It sucks, but Yaz and me and Butch have to look at the positives. If you hadn't driven the VCOM into the trailer when you did, we'd all have burned up for sure. Yaz nearly didn't make it, anyway. The medics told me it was close. He lost so much blood they worried about brain damage. Because of you, he's alive."

"Have you talked with him? Is he, you know—"

"Yeah, he's crazier than ever. Yaz is strong. He'll strap on a pair of artificial limbs and hike downtown to get another tattoo."

Brian went to speak, but no words came. He drained his beer. "I'll get us a drink."

Mike shook his head and pointed to his half-full shot glass. "I'm good." He waved Brian away. "Go ahead. You've got catching up to do."

When Brian came back from the bar, Mike told him Butch was on his way. "Gave me some bullshit about not coming. But when I said you wanted to see him, he changed his mind."

<><><>

By the time Mike had told his Landstuhl escape story, bragging how he conned his way onto a cargo flight to get home two days early, Butch arrived. Mike jumped up and hollered across the crowded bar. Butch spotted him and headed their way. Walking behind, Brian recognized Rosa from the family photo in Butch's trailer. That picture, taken right after Noe's birth, didn't do her justice. The puffy face and paunchy belly were gone. She wore a white blouse and tight jeans. Tanned skin stretched like silk over high cheekbones. Another woman, a taller blonde, came in with Rosa and followed her to their table.

The men shook hands, but when Brian turned to Rosa, she pushed his arm aside and hugged him. She whispered into his chest, "Thank you for saving my Butch." She pronounced her husband's name with an exotic Spanish lisp—*Booch*. Brian's face pulsed with heat. He gave her a small squeeze and felt her softness, smelled her hair, something musky, but with a citrus edge— whatever perfume she wore, it suited her.

"Okay you two, break it up before I throw a bucket of water over you," Butch said. Rosa laughed, pulled back, and her brown eyes sparkled up at Brian.

Mike stepped toward the second woman and placed a hand on the small of her back. He sounded oddly formal, unsure of himself, when he said, "Brian, I'd like you to meet my wife, Sarah."

She returned Brian's firm handshake. With blue eyes and an honest, open face, Sarah was an attractive woman except for a worry-frown that seemed permanent. Her grip and the steel behind her eyes gave Brian the impression she was a woman to be reckoned with.

"Pleased to meet you at last, Sarah. Mike spoke of you so often in Iraq, I feel I already know you."

Mike put his arm around her, turned her from the table, and whispered into her ear. Brian didn't catch the conversation, but he heard Mike say, "Sorry."

After finding a chair and seating Sarah next to him, Mike hailed the server. "What can I get you guys?"

"Coke for me," Rosa said and fixed her gaze on Butch.

"Same," he said.

Mike raised his eyebrows. "Really?"

"I'm taking medication. Doesn't mix well with booze."

"Brian, ready for another?" Mike asked.

"No thanks. I'll make this the last. I have to drive back to Raleigh."

"Budweiser, honey?" Mike asked his wife.

"Sure."

He placed the order and smiled at Sarah. A look Brian couldn't fathom passed between them and made him feel he was intruding.

"Brian?" Rosa, sitting opposite, fixed him with chocolate eyes. He thought he might melt into them. "Butch told me you drove the robot and rescued him and Mike and Yaz. That was very brave."

He pursed his mouth. "Not really brave. The robot went into the trailer. I operated it from a hundred yards away. Mike was the hero."

Sarah's head jerked up. She stared at Mike who became engrossed in arranging four beer mats into a diamond shape on the table.

"You never told them?" Brian asked.

Mike shrugged and mumbled, "I just got back."

Brian focused on Sarah. He couldn't meet Rosa's gaze without getting flustered. "When I first got the VCOM into the trailer, Mike was farthest from the fire. I couldn't see the others through the smoke, so I headed for him, but he pointed to Butch and ordered me to get him out first. After I'd dropped Butch outside, when I went back, the flames had gotten worse, but Mike waved me off again and told me to get Yaz—" Brian's voice caught in his throat. He remembered Yaz's burns, the blackened and crusted flesh. A wave of nausea washed through him and sweat moistened his brow. He took a swig of beer and fought for control. "What Mike did was the bravest thing I've ever seen."

Rosa reached out and laid one hand on his arm and one on Mike's.

Mike's cheeks were red. He cleared his throat. "Butch, have you heard from Yaz?"

Butch shook his head. "You?"

Mike glanced at Brian, blew out his cheeks, and then took a deep breath. "I saw him in Landstuhl. No easy way to say this. Fourth-degree burns. He lost both legs—amputated above the knee."

Sarah's hand went to her mouth.

"Damn," Butch said. "How's he handling it?"

"A lot better than I would. You know Yaz, always sees the rainbow not the rain. He reckons if they fit him with a pair of those spring legs, like that South African sprinter, he'll be able to jump high buildings."

Butch sniggered, then laughed; Mike joined in; Brian caught it, too. The women remained solemn-faced. Rosa's eyes brimmed with tears. Sarah's gaze locked on her husband. When the men's knee-jerk hysterics faded, the table fell silent long enough to create distance between them all.

Finally, Mike said, "But, you're right, Rosa. Brian here, Nerdman to his friends," Mike gave Brian a friendly arm-punch, "saved our asses."

Butch said, "No shit, dude. Did you see the trailer the next day?"

Brian nodded. A draft from the ceiling fan chilled his face. He remembered the burned-out shell—nothing but ashes.

Rosa gave Brian's arm a tiny squeeze before she withdrew her hand. "Thank you both, anyway, for Butch." Where she'd touched him, his skin pulsed.

"So, Brian," Mike said, lifting his voice, shifting the focus, "how's VCOM?"

Brian shook his head. In a voice still deadened by memories of the blackened trailer he said, "Canceled—lack of funds."

Mike's head pivoted. His eyes widened and his neck and cheeks flushed. Brian eased back in his chair. The man looked as though he was about to come across the table, to strike out, to explode. He roared, "You've got to be fuckin' kidding me!"

"Heh, dude, watch the language—ladies present," Butch snapped.

Mike shouted at Brian, spittle spraying. "The demonstration was perfect. This is asshole Swain's fault. He fucked up, didn't he?"

Butch's right hand snaked out, and he grabbed Mike's wrist. Knuckles blanched from the pressure he was exerting, he spat words from between tight lips. "My wife is at this table, soldier. Mind your mouth."

Switching the focus of his anger, Mike glowered at him.

Sarah jumped from her seat. Her chair scraped backward and tipped over, clattering to the floor.

A group of women standing close by edged farther into the bar. The bartender craned his head to see over the crowd. With one hand on Mike's shoulder and the other on Butch's, Sarah said, "Come on, guys. Don't bring the war home." She smiled at Butch and waited.

"Sorry," Butch said. He released his grip, leaving white finger marks on Mike's skin.

Brian stood. His hand trembled as he retrieved Sarah's chair. He'd spent six months with these men in a combat situation and never once seen them come close to blows. Sarah threw him a thank-you smile and sat.

Into the silence hanging between Mike and Butch, Brian said, "It wasn't Swain. He recommended continuing the project. The appropriations committee voted him down. They balked at the cost of the production version, especially in light of the planned troop reductions."

Sarah asked, "What will you do next, Brian?"

"Ha. That's a one-hundred-thousand-dollar question."

Mike stared at the table. Butch still had eyes locked on the top of Mike's head. The danger hadn't passed.

"What do you mean?" Sarah raised her eyebrows and flicked a look at the two warriors. She wanted him to change the tone.

"Well, on Tuesday, I showed the LightCube to Adam Barnes."

That got Mike's attention. "The GameSoft whiz-kid?"

"The same. I went to their offices yesterday to discuss a potential business cooperation. They're interested in licensing the LightCube for one of their games."

Butch stopped glaring at Mike, reached across the table, and thumped Brian's back. "That's great news, dude. Heh, don't forget your poor army buddies when you move onto millionaires' row."

"Fat chance of that," Brian said.

"Which game?" Mike asked.

"A new one, 3D, scheduled for release in a couple years."

"Cool."

The tension had lifted. Sarah smiled, and Brian thought she winked at him, although he couldn't be sure. He laid his hands flat on the table. "Sorry to disappoint, but it's a no go, I'm afraid." Brian recognized the look that passed between Butch and Mike. To these men of action, he was brains heavy, but balls light. He spoke quickly, determined to prove them wrong. "Come on, guys. It's not that I don't want to. Hell, this could be the biggest break of my life. But the US Army owns the rights to the device we used in Iraq. I have to start over with the primitive version I had before VCOM, and I can't afford to build what GameSoft needs. I'm going back Monday to ask Adam to hire me as a contractor to do the work."

"Well, that is a more secure approach. Isn't it?" Rosa said.

Mike slapped the table. "Except GameSoft will own the controller, right?"

Brian nodded and delivered a watery smile. He didn't want to talk about this. He wouldn't have mentioned it if Sarah hadn't begged with those big blue eyes. Crap.

"How much do you need?" Mike asked.

"Like I said, it's a one-hundred-thousand-dollar question."

Mike looked over at Butch, who gave a small nod. "What if we could raise the money?" Mike asked.

Rosa's face switched from calm to alarm. Her voice lifted an octave. "We don't have that kind of money."

Mike waved an arm to the room. "I'll wager every guy in this bar plays video games, and they have more money than you'd think, especially the ones returning from overseas. Most of them lock away the hazard pay they receive while they're deployed. Can't spend much in Camp Liberation anyway, right, Brian? And Sarah and me have equity in our home." Mike stared at Sarah. Brian couldn't read her expression. Intensely focused on her husband, her cheek twitched. She ran a hand through her hair.

Brian's ears and face were burning, and he knew they'd be beetroot red. "Guys, that's… well… an estimate. In software there are no guarantees. Timescales always overrun. But I'm honored you'd even think this way. Thank you."

Sarah completed her visual examination of Mike and returned her attention to Brian. She tilted her head to the side. "Tell me about this LightCube?"

Brian sipped his drink, and before he could speak, Mike answered for him, talking fast and using both hands. "You know how we hold the thumb controllers to play video games?" He mimicked the action.

"*Sí,*" Rosa said. She smiled at Brian and set his pulse racing again.

"Well," Mike said, "Brian has a better controller. It's like a cube of light that projects from a tablet. He waves his fingers around and controls what the robot does. Or, for GameSoft, it would control the game so there'd be no need for the thumb controller."

"And you don't need a screen," Butch said. "The images project onto the inside of a pair of cool glasses. Right, Brian?"

Sarah shook her head. "I don't understand—" Mike opened his mouth to explain further, but she held up her hand and stopped him. "*I* don't understand, but if Adam Barnes only needed three days to decide, that means a lot."

Butch asked, "What did Barnes commit to?"

"Not much. Access to his gaming software, and technical assistance with the interface. I have to create a working prototype before they'll license the controller from me. Of course if that happens; once I have a contract with GameSoft, I'll be able to raise funds for production. Or, they may go exclusive because it'd be a real market differentiator—a breakthrough, like Sony's Wii." Brian heard himself and realized he didn't have a chance of accomplishing what he'd just described. "But, honestly, guys. I'm out of my depth here. I think it's better to—"

"I'd like to see this LightCube," Sarah said.

"Me too," Rosa said. They all stared at him until he said, "Really? Okay. I can drive down with the demo tomorrow if you're that interested."

They finished their drinks and walked as a group into the parking lot.

The others had already driven off when Sarah started her car, but Mike grabbed her hand before she shifted. He leaned across and with one finger pressed to her cheek, he turned her to face him. The intensity in his eyes sent ants crawling through her stomach.

"Sarah, I love you more than life itself. You gave me Daniel. You gave me Christopher. You're a perfect wife to me, a perfect mother to my boys. I can't explain why I've behaved like I have since I got home. But it stops here. I'd like to start over. If you'll allow me."

When she arrived at the bar, Mike had apologized for his behavior, but she couldn't tell if he was talking or the booze. Now she was sure. And something snapped. From deep within her came an involuntary wail. A piercing sound fermented from the pain and fear and confusion she had contained, held back, bottled up since

Christmas: all the excuses she'd made to the children after Mike's emotionally distant Skype calls, all the anguish she'd hidden when he came home, screamed at her boys and disrespected her parents. Her walls broke and grief burst through and she flung both arms around her warrior's neck and clamped on, hanging from him as though he were a lifesaver in a hurricane. Headlight after headlight from cars leaving the parking lot raked the windshield and played against her closed eyelids, and still she held tight.

When she finally released him, his cheeks were wet with tears.

Mike straightened in his seat.

Head bowed, chin on his neck, he whispered.

"Thank you."

Pete Barber

TWELVE

The following morning, while Christopher *helped* Sarah prepare Sunday breakfast, Mike sat with Daniel in the living room and apologized for his behavior since returning from Iraq—the talk was Mike's idea. After ten minutes, they came into the kitchen. Mike, arm looped over his son's shoulders, said, "Are we ready to feed this growin' boy?" Sarah smiled. The house was a home again. Last night, in bed, she and Mike had made love. Her man had been passionate but also careful to see to her needs, and afterward she'd fallen asleep nestled in his arms, safe, secure, and sated.

After breakfast, the kids went to play and left her and Mike, sitting at the kitchen table.

"Should I call your folks?" he asked.

"I don't think that's necessary. They understood that you were tired and stressed after the long trip from Germany. But thanks." She reached out and squeezed his hand. Mike smiled and seemed calm, but she wondered how he might react to her next suggestion. *I can't live life in fear of sending him into a rage.*

Sarah took a deep breath. "What do you think of me asking Pop for advice about the LightCube investment?" She waited, stomach clenched, steeled for another angry outburst.

"Good idea," Mike said. "I think Brian's technology is amazing, but you're the accountant, and Pops has run his plumbing business for thirty years. It can't hurt to get his opinion."

Before Christopher, Sarah had worked full time in Fayetteville General Hospital's finance department. She still filled in occasionally when they were shorthanded. When Mike welcomed Pop's input, it increased her confidence that the considerate, supportive man she had sent to Iraq was finally home.

Sunday afternoon, Brian brought the LightCube and swimming goggles to their house. Butch, Rosa, and Noe joined them in the living room, and the adults took turns driving the Mario demonstration. Even Christopher tried, squealing with delight when Mario danced to the beat of his fingers. It proved impossible to pull Daniel away.

How much Brian's project had helped to snap Mike out of his funk, Sarah couldn't tell, but perhaps her man needed to see a way forward that didn't involve him being the breadwinner in the US Army. When deployed, he shouldered a huge responsibility. And the staff cuts weighed on his mind. They'd even discussed not re-enlisting this summer.

Pulling equity from the house to invest in a software project was risky, but Mike admired and trusted Brian. Others made big money in technology. Heck, some were just kids—why not her and Mike? One thing was for sure, if Daniel's response was any barometer of success, Brian's LightCube would sweep the nation.

Brian was teaching Daniel a few nuances of the device when Sarah said, "Brian, can you excuse us for a few minutes?"

A doubtful look crossed Brian's face when he saw his potential backers leaving. "Sure. I'll be fine here."

She led Butch, Rosa, and Mike into the kitchen, and they hunkered around the table. "Well?" Sarah said.

No one answered. Then Mike and Rosa both spoke at once. Mike waved for Rosa to go ahead.

"I think it's magical," she said.

Sarah grinned. "I felt I was inside the game, not sitting on a couch controlling it. Butch, what about you?"

He shook his head. "It's nowhere near as good as the version Brian had in Iraq. How do we know he can improve it?"

Butch's flat affect and dull voice tempered Sarah's enthusiasm. "We'll ask him how long it'll take. But, Butch, don't you think if we showed this to the guys in the unit they'd be impressed?"

"I guess."

Rosa chucked her man under the chin. "Don't mind Grumpy. He got outta bed on the wrong side."

"The device he had in Iraq *was* way better," Mike said, "but Brian explained he had to start again from the original code. Rosa and Sarah have only seen this version and you're impressed, right?"

They nodded. "Okay, we're agreed on the technology," Mike said. "Sarah talked to her pop this morning and got pointers about equity. Everyone okay with her taking the lead?"

All three stared at her, and Sarah's heart played out a fast drum beat. Saying you will do something and doing it, are very different things. But if they took this leap, she couldn't put the burden of responsibility on Mike. He had enough to deal with. "Okay," she said. "Bring him in."

Sarah and Rosa organized coffee, and Mike pulled Brian from the other room. They sat around the kitchen table with a plate of cookies between them. Sarah unfolded a page of notes she'd made while on the phone with her dad. "Brian if we can fund this project to the tune of one hundred thousand dollars. What will the money be spent on?"

He reddened and cleared his throat. His left eyelid fluttered. Brian was thirty-five, Mike's age, yet he acted like a nervous schoolboy. Rosa had confided that she thought him cute—not Sarah's type, though, too skinny and cerebral.

"Well, I plan to work full time on the project. I'm talking sixteen-hour days, seven days a week. I have to eat and pay my bills. Unfortunately, I blew my savings on a condo in Raleigh." His face glowed red. His neck was blotched like a map. "Believe me, guys, if I'd known GameSoft was happening, I'd still be living in my cheap and cheerful one-room rental. *And* I didn't expect VCOM to be canceled. I assumed... Well you know what I assumed."

Mike tapped Brian on the shoulder. "We understand. You need to deal with the situation at hand, not the one you wish was here, right?"

Brian nodded. "So I estimate three thousand a month to gas the car, pay the bills, and buy food. I won't have any business costs because I'll work at GameSoft's offices."

Sarah asked, "How long will it take to build the LightCube?"

"Four to six months."

Sarah jotted a figure. "That's eighteen thousand dollars operating expenses. And the rest?"

"That's for the fabricators to build a new LightCube and heads-up display. Adam Barnes wasn't too impressed by my swimming goggles." A smile crept into the edge of his mouth.

Rosa laughed aloud. "Oops. Sorry!" she said. "They are kinda clunky."

Brian raked fingers through his hair. "I plan to contract with the same company that built the army's version, but I can't use the VCOM design specifications, so I have to recreate them. Militec spent two hundred fifty thousand to create the equipment I used in Camp Liberation."

"Wow!" Mike said.

Sarah's eyes widened. "So how come yours will be so much cheaper?"

"Partly because everyone overcharges the US Army, but mainly because they've built the LightCube before."

Sarah frowned. "But you can't use that work."

"Right, but imagine you wrote a report then had to reproduce it a few months later. Second time would be easier and faster. Same thing applies for the hardware manufacturers. The build will be quicker and cheaper. As Rosa pointed out, the swimming goggles are the biggest obstacle. I asked George—he's my opposite number at Militec—and he felt sixty to eighty thousand would be enough. By the way, George wants to participate if there's equity available."

"He runs Militec's software development division, right?" Sarah asked.

Brian said, "George is chief technology officer."

Sarah glanced at Mike and widened her eyes. He nodded back at her, clearly thinking the same thing she was--if the head of tech at Militec wanted in, that was a huge positive.

"Okay, Brian." Sarah fixed him with a businesslike stare. "Now for the one-hundred-thousand-dollar question. How much equity are you offering your investors?"

Brian smiled. "When my dad was alive, he had a saying: 'One percent of something is always more than a hundred percent of nothing.'" Brian opened his palms face up on the table. "I'm not a businessman, but I am a terrific hacker. I know how this technology should be developed, so I won't give up control. But, you're taking a risk, and I'm honored you are. How about thirty-three and a third percent?"

Sarah fired back, "Why not forty-nine percent? That'll still give you control."

Mike's head snapped up. Rosa's mouth dropped open. The kitchen fell silent. A car horn sounded outside.

Brian took a few seconds before he answered. Face flushed and the tips of his ears bright red, he said, "I can't bring money to the table. I wish I could. *But* I have spent ten years building what you saw today. In time and materials, I've got over three hundred thousand dollars invested. And don't forget, the thirty-three percent is founder's stock. We'll need a second round of funding after the prototype is ready. Venture capitalists will fight for a piece of the action once GameSoft commits. So in six months, your founder's shares will be more valuable."

Rosa frowned. "So we can sell our shares at a profit?"

"Exactly," Sarah said. "Once Brian has the prototype built, other investors will want in because the risk will be lower. Pops told me a second round typically goes for three to six times the first."

"So each of our dollars will be worth six?" Rosa asked.

Brian nodded. "You won't *have* to sell, but you could take money off the table. Maybe cash in enough to recoup your investment. So you're playing with house money."

Sarah asked, "Any more questions?" No one spoke. "Okay, let's take a vote. Who's in favor of investing in Brian's LightCube?" Rosa raised her hand. Butch looked at her with deadened eyes and raised his. Mike followed, so did Sarah. She delivered a beaming smile.

"Brian. You've got a deal."

Pete Barber

THIRTEEN

Brigadier General James Swain's five-foot putt flirted with the edge of the cup on the eighteenth hole and rolled three feet past. He scowled.

His opponent, Dr. Philip Wainwright, placed his golf ball in front of the marker he'd left nine inches from the flagstick and tapped in for par. He offered his hand. "Looks like drinks are on you." He laughed when he saw how pissed off Swain looked. "Don't be such a rotten loser, James."

"All right for you to say, but this is becoming a habit."

"Twice in a row is hardly a habit, and one stroke is hardly a massacre. Come on. It's too cold to stand here arguing. I'm ready to thaw out in front of the clubhouse fire."

"Pah!" The general stormed off the green. Wainwright shook his head as he picked up the flagstick, replaced it in the hole, and followed his pouting playing partner.

By the time they'd changed shoes and stored their clubs in the locker room, Swain's temper had subsided. The officer's lounge was empty except for a couple of folk at the bar. They sank into red-leather easy chairs set either side of a low table in front of a blazing log fire. The steward took the general's order for two scotches. "Put them on my account."

"The spoils of war, sir?"

"No need to remind me."

The steward chuckled and strode away.

The friends were on their third drink when the doctor said, "Saw one of your guys this morning. Got caught in that December rocket attack at Camp Liberation. Weren't you over there at the time?"

"I left a few hours earlier. Knowing the hajjis, the missile was a stray. Those incompetents couldn't hit a barn door from ten feet."

"*He's* struggling, though."

101

"Was he seriously injured?"

"Not physically. Well, he had first-degree burns on his arm, but that's not his problem. He's showing classic TBI symptoms."

Swain frowned. "Name?"

"You know I can't tell you that."

"Sergeant Cassidy?" The general leaned forward in his chair. "Paul Cassidy?"

The doctor sighed. "Not much gets by you, James. He's disoriented, anxious, having problems concentrating and sleeping. He may have been lucky to avoid a direct hit, but the blast knocked his brain about. Why?"

"Why? Because it's a crock. That's why!"

The doctor straightened. "Excuse me?"

Swain waved his hand as though shooing a fly. "It's horseshit. Cassidy was picked up for DWI two nights ago. Point-two blood-alcohol level. Drunk out of his mind. Fortunately the cops pulled him over before he killed someone."

"Any prior instances of substance abuse?"

"Don't start that psycho-babble with me, Philip. I heard about his behavior at The Blue Note. It wasn't an Iraqi rocket that made him slug a six-pack and eight shots of tequila. Paul Cassidy made that choice."

"Substance abuse, especially if it's out of character, is a classic symptom of trauma. You know that, James."

The general grunted. The leather creaked as he sank back and sipped his whisky. "All I'm saying is he didn't have a TBI or PTSD or any of your other trendy acronyms before he got busted for drunk driving. That soldier's conning you. How come these—" Swain winced as though his words tasted unpleasant. "—*symptoms* conveniently appeared right after he screwed up. I've seen this too often. It's no coincidence. And I won't tolerate malingerers in my unit." He wagged a bony finger at the doctor. "As far as I'm concerned, Cassidy, and anyone else who steps over the line, is taking the place of a good soldier."

"What will you do about the DWI?"

"I've started the paperwork for a Chapter Fourteen discharge."

Wainwright shook his head and leaned back. "Dishonorable? He'll lose everything: benefits, medical follow-up, access to the VA, pension."

"Not my problem. I didn't ask him to get trashed and drive

drunk. I can't take a soldier like that into the field. He'd be a danger to those around him."

"I plan to recommend him for medical discharge, pending a more thorough evaluation."

Swain angled forward, back erect, eyes blazing. "For Christ's sake! Have you seen this unit's records? The last five soldiers you recommended are still on roll, one of them from fourteen months ago. The processing takes forever. You know my orders. I have to reduce headcount. We redeploy this summer. Should I lay off a good soldier instead of this drunk? No. Men like Sergeant Cassidy are taking up space, leaving me short of real warriors."

Wainwright narrowed his eyes and studied the general. The man was convinced. This was a big problem. Paul Cassidy displayed classic symptoms resulting from traumatic brain injury. He needed medical care, psychological attention. But Swain was a stubborn old buzzard when he set his mind to something. "I could recommend a transfer to a Warrior Transition Unit."

"Even if you could find him a place, which I doubt, you may as well save the ink. I won't sign off on the request. Sergeant Paul Cassidy's not injured. He's a liability."

The doctor glared at the stern face of the man opposite him. He knew his friend was under extreme pressure. Although it was outside of Swain's control, the decision to cancel VCOM had negatively affected his credibility. The general's recommendation to proceed, although based on results, was shortsighted. He had failed to take into account the changing political wind. But the ease with which the general had just dismissed Wainwright's medical expertise was tough to swallow. How would Swain react if a doctor told him how to run the damn unit? Maybe the top brass were right. Maybe Swain had been promoted beyond his competency.

Swain met the doctor's gaze, unyielding. Wainwright gripped his thighs and bent forward. Unable to control his anger, he hissed, "This man suffered a severe trauma to the head. The explosion blew out the rear walls of his trailer. The blast was less than six feet away. If he's suffered a TBI—" Swain tried to interrupt, but the doctor raised a hand and cut him off. "If he's suffered traumatic brain injury, he's going to need treatment, now, and for the foreseeable future. You can't take that away from him over one disciplinary transgression."

"That's his story. Cassidy wasn't alone in that trailer. Sergeants

Braeman and Yazinski *suffered* too. They aren't looking for an excuse." Swain reached forward and slammed his thick-bottomed crystal glass on the table, hard enough to splash the dregs. "Yazinski lost both legs for Christ's sake. Last week, he petitioned for a return to active duty once he gets used to his prosthetics. Now that's a soldier."

The general wagged a finger. "You don't get it, do you? Cassidy's read the literature. God knows we could paper the mess hall you're your pamphlets and DVDs. He's attended your feel good seminars. PTSD is an open-book exam. You've given him the answers to your damn stupid questions. Hell, I could ace the test. I could get a free ride because I have angry outbursts and headaches or whatever else he's whining about." He eased back in his chair and let out a sigh. "I know you mean well, Philip, but he's pulled the wool over your eyes. It's time to teach a lesson to these slacker soldiers."

Wainwright slugged the last of his whisky and stood, glaring at the general. "I'll fight you on this one, James."

The general waved him away with a dismissive flick of his wrist.

Wainwright was furious, but the determination in Swain's eyes, stoked by three scotches, made him defer the battle. Officially, the doctor's first step was to lodge a complaint with the unit commander. Problem was, he'd just played golf with the unit commander. "I'm leaving," he said.

A victorious smile crept across Swain's lips and he signaled the steward.

"Drive carefully. I think I'll have one for the road. See you next Wednesday for revenge."

FOURTEEN

Rosa pulled the Toyota into her driveway. Normally, they walked to the Braemans'—it was only four blocks—but Rosa wasn't sure Butch could make it. He climbed out of the car, leaving the passenger door wide open, and lumbered along the path. She unhooked Noe from his seat and closed the car doors with her butt. Her husband stood on the front step, staring straight ahead, waiting, childlike, for her to open up.

Antidepressants, anti-anxiety pills, and painkillers. Taken together it seemed a lot to handle. Still, *she* wasn't the doctor. The warning instructions on the pills described every possible side effect—as though the manufacturers were only interested in covering their asses. She had nowhere else to turn. Other soldiers must be struggling like Butch, but their wives wouldn't help. No one wanted to discuss her man's problems. No one wanted to admit weakness in case it got back to command.

Maybe once he got used to the pills, he'd become Butch again.

She missed his smile.

With Noe balanced on her hip, she reached past her husband, turned the key, and pushed open the front door. "Come on, Butch. You're tired out, aren't you?"

Two steps into the hallway, he stopped so suddenly that she ran into his back. He stood, blocking her path, arms dangling by his sides, shoulders drooping, and nodded.

"Why don't you head upstairs and get ready for bed. I'll give Noe his bath and settle him. Then I'll bring you a warm drink. Off you go."

He paused, as though the instructions were complex and required time to process, before plodding up the stairs. For a while, it seemed, she had two children to take care of.

Later that night, Sarah hummed as she toweled off from the shower. Skin tingling, heart racing, she dressed in a skimpy black outfit Mike had bought her a couple Valentine's Days ago. She had never felt glamorous enough to carry off the lacy bra, tiny panties, and sheer negligee. But the first time she wore them, Mike brushed her embarrassment aside when he said, "You're a real woman, not airbrushed to perfection, but all mine, and smokin' hot." And she did feel sexy when he wrapped his arms around her, cupped her butt, and pushed his hardness into her. The outfit had certainly added steam to their lovemaking that night—phew!

Sarah hoped the black lace would work its magic again tonight. The day he arrived home, Mike had *taken* her. Although she had understood his need, she felt cheated. Last night, though, was lovely. The afterglow had stayed with her. Today, he'd rebuilt trust with her and Daniel and Christopher. Tonight was about Mike. She planned to show him what he'd been missing.

After spraying on a liberal dose of perfume, she took her gold locket from its special place in the bathroom cabinet. The memory of the first time she'd worn it, the night before he deployed, warmed her belly—she didn't need the sexy outfit that night. Sarah peeked around their bathroom door into the bedroom. Mike's back humped toward her under the covers. She tiptoed across the room and stood on his side of the bed. His eyes were closed, so she stroked his cheek with the back of her finger and whispered, "I've got something for you, soldier."

As though he'd been waiting to pounce, coiled and ready, Mike flung back the bedclothes, sprang from the bed, and roared like a bull—the sound so loud and so sudden it hurt her ears. She leapt backward and raised her arms, protecting herself from the blow that seemed inevitable. Face inches from hers, teeth bared, the rage in his eyes made her stomach clench and forced bile into her throat.

She swallowed and coughed and staggered back. Her left foot caught in the rug and sent her tumbling into the dressing table. Her flailing arm caught on the alarm clock, clattering it into a vase filled with the flowers her mom had brought, which hit the wall and shattered. She scrabbled for support and ended sprawled on the floor with her head jammed against the bottom dresser drawer. A sharp pain shot down her neck. Mike bent over her, fists balled tightly, thigh muscles bulging out of his jockeys. He screamed,

"Get up! Raise your weapon, soldier. Return fire. That's an order!"

Sarah stared up at him, terrified, unable to speak, unable to think. Silent seconds slipped past before recognition registered, and his face changed. He straightened, brushed invisible crumbs from his bare chest and hissed, "Sarah, what the hell are you doing sneaking up on me?"

She swallowed and spoke in a tiny voice. "I put this on for you. I thought—"

The bedroom door banged open and Daniel burst in. High over his right shoulder he held his baseball bat, poised to swing.

Mike rotated and locked laser eyes on his son. "Don't you dare barge in here!"

Daniel's mouth dropped open when he saw his mother sprawled on the floor. Sarah whipped an arm across her chest and covered her nipples, hard with fear, and clearly visible through the sheer material. She scrambled to her feet. With one hand covering herself between her legs, she turned from her son's wide-eyed gaze, ran into the bathroom, and slammed the door.

In the bedroom, Mike and Daniel bellowed at each other. Sarah couldn't focus on the words. Eyes squeezed shut, panting for breath, she prayed for it to end before Daniel got hurt. Why had she run away? Her son needed her. Grabbing the housecoat from its hook, she covered herself and gripped the doorknob.

And froze.

The noise had ceased. She pressed her ear against the door.

Thwump. Thwump. Thwump. Thwump went her heart.

When the bedroom door slammed, she squealed and jumped with fright.

Hand still on the doorknob, she strained to hear. Mike was moving around the bedroom, pacing, like a big cat. Then the bedsprings creaked. He wouldn't go back to bed without talking to her.

Surely not.

The house fell quiet. She waited—silence.

"You can do this," she whispered. But her voice lacked the conviction of her words. She was living in a nightmare of uncertainty, living with a Jekyll and Hyde. Over dinner and all evening Mike had been, well, Mike. But now?

Sarah turned to the sink and swilled her face. When she straightened, the mirror told its tale: bloodshot eyes, pale hollow cheeks, forehead lined with worry. *No time to feel sorry yourself.* She clenched her teeth, grabbed the doorknob, and turned.

The hinges squeaked. Sarah peered into the bedroom. Mike was under the covers. When he didn't stir, she crept across the room. As she eased the bedroom door open, something sharp stuck her in the heel. "Ouch." She held her breath, never lifting her gaze from the shape of Mike's shrouded shoulders. He didn't move. She picked up her locket. The chain must have broken when she fell.

After slipping out, she quietly closed the door and tiptoed to Daniel's bedroom. Pausing with one hand hovering over the doorknob, she shook her head. What could she say? How could she explain Mike's outburst, explain something she didn't understand? Better postpone that discussion until daylight. She crept downstairs, hesitating at each creak as though she were burgling her own home.

As she stirred sugar into a mug of hot chocolate in the kitchen, Sarah again caught sight of herself in the mirror. She looked old and worn. Hands cupped around her drink, she headed into the living room.

Tonight it was her turn to sleep on the couch.

FIFTEEN

Mike's cell phone woke him. He grabbed it from the bedside table and answered.

Yaz said, "Hi, Mike, how're you doin', dude?"

"Great." Mike squinted at the clock on the nightstand—six a.m. "Yaz? Where are you?"

"Fayetteville's own Holiday Inn Express."

Mike glanced at Sarah's side of the bed. Empty. Good. "When did you get in?"

"Last night."

"You should have called. Who picked you up?"

"I'll tell you about it sometime. Listen, Mike, I need a ride to base?"

"Sure thing." Mike headed to the bathroom with the phone to his ear. "Eaten breakfast yet?"

"Nope, just got up."

"Give me thirty minutes, and I'll buy you an egg."

"Last of the big spenders. There's a Waffle House next door. Meet me there."

"Roger that."

Mike washed, dressed, and crept downstairs; he wanted to avoid another nagging session from Sarah. The living room door was shut, so he assumed she was in there. He slipped out the front door and closed it quietly.

At the diner, he found Yaz sitting in a booth, a wheelchair folded beside him in the aisle.

Mike grasped his friend's hand and shook it. "Damn, you look great. What'd they feed you in that hospital? You've put on twenty pounds since I last saw you."

Yaz beamed. "Been working out." He flexed his biceps.

"Impressive!"

"I need the guns. With no legs I do a lot of liftin' and haulin' of the rest of me."

Mike shook his head. "You should've called. I'd have come to the airport for you."

"I guess I needed to do it myself."

Mike smiled. "You managed, obviously."

Yaz grinned. "I manage more than you know. Mostly I wanted a solid night's sack without nurses waking me to take pills and vitals and such. Anyway it was a great flight."

"How so?"

"Met this marine on the plane—Irish—true to form, he had a fifth of Jim Beam in his kit. First drink I'd seen or smelled for months. I got so soused, I even let the grunt carry me down the steps after we landed."

"I hope he didn't drive you to town."

"Naw. No way he could've gotten behind the wheel. His family picked him up."

"So who'd you ride with?"

"Damnedest thing. A dozen of us bummed the plane ride from Germany. On the tarmac, I held back, you know while the wives did their huggin' and stuff. When I rolled through the gate, two old guys were waiting for me. Gave me a crisp salute and welcomed me home. Even thanked me for my service."

"Nice."

"I thought so. Said that no one met them when they came home from 'Nam, and they didn't want that to happen to me. Real nice guys. They drove me here, even stopped along the way to buy me a soda and a sandwich."

"Good to know there's still folk like that around."

"Damn right."

"Anyway, how's your mom?"

Yaz rotated his coffee cup, pressed his lips together. "Good, I think."

"How's she handling—"

"I didn't tell her, yet."

Mike's voice lifted an octave. "She doesn't know you were wounded?"

"Well, yeah. I told her that. She doesn't know about these." He pointed under the table.

"Dude, she's gonna find out."

"I thought I'd get the prosthetics, then visit Texas. It'll be easier for her to handle if I'm walking."

"I guess." The waitress hovered, so Mike ordered a coffee. "How's the pain?"

"Crazy thing is I still have cramps in my feet. Go figure. Phantom pains they call them. Better every day though. How's Sarah and the kids?"

Mike screwed up his face. "They're fine, but things have sure changed at home."

"How so?"

"Meh, I'll catch you up another time. Let's order."

Yaz stared at the server while she shouted their orders aloud to the cook even though he stood only ten feet from her. "Ya know," Yaz said. "Before I deployed I never even noticed they did that—weird."

"Did what?" Mike made a performance of looking around as if he'd missed something.

"Really?"

Mike grinned, and Yaz gave him a deprecating look. "You shouldn't mock the crippled." Yaz let the words hang for a couple seconds before reaching across and thumping Mike's arm. "Just kiddin'. But it's the little things you miss when you're away."

"Like a dumb Waffle House tradition of callin' out the order? Uh huh."

"Whatever, dude. *You* haven't changed, anyway."

Mike pointed to the wheelchair. "What's the news on borrowing a gently used pair of Forrest Gump's magic legs?"

"The base medical unit will hook me up. Sooner the better, too." He slapped the chair. "That contraption's a PIA."

The food arrived. Yaz cut into his steak and eggs and crammed a few pieces into his mouth. He groaned and rolled his eyes. "Can't get grease like this in Germany."

Mike smiled and nibbled a square of toast. Lately, he had no appetite.

Yaz chipmunked his meat into one cheek and said, "Seen Butch?"

"Yeah. He got back before Christmas—hardly a scratch on him. Had a run-in with the law last week though."

"Oh?"

"Got busted for DWI trying to drive home from The Blue Note at three a.m. Didn't even get outta the parking lot."

"What an asswipe."

"Lost his license."

"Ouch."

"He's been in to see Wainwright."

"For drinking?"

Mike shrugged. "Rosa's idea. The doc thinks he's got a TBI."

"From the rocket attack?"

"I guess. He's on antidepressants, pain meds, and anti-something else. Half asleep most of the time. I don't see how that helps."

"Is he still on the booze?"

"Can't drive to The Blue Note without a license."

"Bummer. What other uplifting news you got?"

"Wait till you hear this one. Remember Brian Matthews?"

"Nerdman?"

"The same. Butch and Rosa, me and Sarah are going into business with him."

Yaz raised his eyebrows and made a come-on signal with his hand.

"He's working at GameSoft, building a new LightCube. Only instead of controlling VCOM he'll be running one of their games."

"Cool. So how are you *in business*?"

"Equity partners. He needs capital to build the hardware. You want in?"

"And if I hadn't come home when were you going to share this opportunity with me?"

"We were going to email you."

"Sure you were."

"No, really. We need more partners."

"How so?"

"Butch and Rosa are going all-in with their savings, twenty thousand. Well, Rosa is. I don't think Butch knows his ass from his elbow."

"He that bad?"

"Was last time I saw him."

"What about you and Sarah?"

"She's for the idea."

Yaz narrowed his eyes. "And you?"

"I think the LightCube is the bomb."

Yaz nodded. "No shit. I told Brian a dozen times, I'd be first in line if he hooked that cube up to *World of Warcraft*. How much does he need?"

"A hundred thousand."

He whistled.

"The guy who runs Militec's software division is putting up twenty thou, and he's got an inside track."

"Not too shabby."

Mike leaned in, lowered his voice. "Brian's the smartest guy I know, but he's no businessman. If he can't raise the money he'll give the cube to GameSoft, just work for them."

"That's crazy."

"That's what I think."

Yaz swallowed his last mouthful of food, drained his coffee, and waved the empty cup at the server. "Hit me again, honey." She winked and refilled his mug.

Yaz focused on Mike. "Look, I didn't spend shit in Iraq, and I've been laid up for three months in Germany. I have thirty thousand, sitting in the bank gathering dust. I was planning to buy a Mustang." Yaz pointed below the table. "Gonna be awhile before I'm driving anywhere, though, and I'll have to live on base."

"We can borrow thirty against the house." Sarah had told Mike she didn't want to chance over ten, but how would she feel watching the others get rich, especially since this was his idea? Mike offered his hand across the table. "Dude. If you'll put in thirty, I'll match it. With Butch's twenty and the guy from Militec, we won't need anyone else—keep it in the family, right?"

"Right. What about Sarah?"

"She'll be fine with it."

Yaz grinned, grabbed Mike's hand and crushed it. "Deal."

After dropping his friend at the base, Mike stopped by the bank and signed papers to move thirty thousand dollars from the credit line into their checking account. He told the clerk Sarah would drop by later in the day. The bank needed both signatures.

When he arrived home, he found Sarah in the kitchen balanced on a set of steps, clearing out the top cabinets. He stood in the doorway for a few seconds, admiring the view. Perhaps they could get her folks to babysit and have a date night, soon. Yeah, he would run that by her. Because of the kids, things had been tense since he returned. A nice meal out would do them both good.

"What're you up to?" he asked.

She shrieked, grabbed the wobbly ladder, and climbed down. "I almost had a heart attack. Don't sneak in like that."

He laughed. "Sorry." Her hair was mussed, and she had a black smudge below her left eye.

"You've got something here," he said, touching his cheek.

She glanced in the wall mirror and rubbed at the dirt with a cleaning rag.

"Guess who I just drove to the base?" he said.

She faced him, hands on hips, face flat, waiting.

"Jeese. Looks like you've got a flea in your panties." *When did Sarah become Mrs. Grumpy?* "Yaz. He called this morning, and I met him for breakfast."

Her face lit with a smile he had seen little of lately. "When did he get back?"

"Last night. I gave him a hard time for it, too. Told no one he was arriving and took himself to a hotel for the night."

"How is he?"

"Better than I'd be if I'd lost both legs."

"No shit, Sherlock."

A tidal wave of anger tore through him. "What the hell's that supposed to mean?"

They locked eyes. Silence descended. The kitchen clock's tick filled the chasm between them.

"Nothing." She sighed out the word. "I need to get this finished. I have to drop by the store to pick up dinner before Christopher gets out of kindergarten." She turned her back on him, climbed the steps again, and resumed her cleaning the cupboard.

Here we go again with frosty Sarah. "Yaz is coming in on the LightCube deal. He's putting up thirty thou."

She stopped working but didn't turn. "He must be sure, then."

"It's a safe bet. Look, Sarah, the Militec guy is in for twenty, so is Butch. Yaz brings thirty. And so should we. I dropped by the bank and filled out the forms. They're waiting for your approval. Why not drop by and sign the papers on your way to the store."

She stepped down again and turned to face him. "You're certain, then?"

"Of course. We agreed. Why?"

Sarah put her hands on her hips. "Why?" Her lips were a thin white line. "Let me see: You hardly ever want sex. You can't stand the kids. You fly off the handle at every opportunity. You're drinking during the day. Mostly, you wish you were still in Iraq with your buddies. Does this sound like a good time to start a new venture that puts our home at risk?"

The muscles in his jaw bunched. His heart rate spiked. Blood whooshed past his ears. Why was she goading him. "The forms are waiting for you." He stepped toward her, backing her into the steps. He took five fast breaths before he trusted himself not to lash out. "For once, Sarah, do things my way." He raised his hand and she cringed. He wagged a finger in her face, emphasizing each word. "I'm the breadwinner in this house, and we will not pass up this opportunity. Got it!"

She ducked under his arm and ran out the door.

I don't know what's wrong with her, but it'd better be her time of the month. I can't put up with this drama every time I open my mouth.

Mike grabbed two beers from the fridge and hunted through the cupboards until he found a bag of chips. In the living room, he sank into the sofa and tuned to a First World War documentary on the History Channel.

The front door slammed. Then Sarah's car started, and she burned rubber backing the damn thing out of the driveway. Anger surged; she didn't give a shit that he'd be the one to pay for new tires when she tore those up.

He muted the TV and phoned Brian, who didn't answer. Mike left a message telling him about Yaz and how they'd raised eighty thousand between them.

He signed off with, "Better get codin', Nerdman."

Pete Barber

SIXTEEN

Sarah pulled over outside Rosa's house. Butch's car was in the driveway. She ran up the path and rang the bell. Rosa opened the door with Noe balanced on her hip.

"Thanks for making time. It's just—"

Rosa put a finger to her lips. She signaled for Sarah to follow, led her into the kitchen, and closed the door. "Butch is dozing on the couch; he hardly sleeps at night, and he just nodded off. The rest will do him good. He has orders to report to General Swain this afternoon."

Rosa slipped Noe into his highchair and shook Froot Loops onto the tray. The boy snatched up a handful and giggled as he poked them into his mouth. A couple, one pink one blue, hung on his chin, and when he grinned at Sarah she laughed. Her cheeks felt stiff. The act felt foreign. Damn, was it that long since she'd laughed?

"Coffee?" Rosa spooned grounds into the filter.

"Great. How is Butch?"

Rosa switched on the coffee machine and joined Sarah and Noe at the kitchen table. "Honestly, I don't know how to answer. The drugs make him so dopey he sometimes nods off in the middle of a conversation. I can't trust him to hold Noe."

"What about his temper?"

"He's too high to get angry." Rosa shrugged. "But nothing's fixed. I mean if he comes off the pills won't he be the same?"

A wet blanket of disappointment pressed Sarah's shoulders lower. If the drugs had helped Butch, then maybe they could do the same for Mike. But it sounded like Rosa was living with a zombie. If that was the only cure, did she even want it for her husband?

Rosa poured their drinks then filled Noe's Tippy Cup with juice and handed it to him. He giggled at Sarah again—showing off.

Sarah sucked in a deep breath, stared at her fingers. If she didn't share she would burst. Sharing was all she had.

"Mike threatened me last night."

Rosa lowered her cup. "Mike?"

"We had a terrible scene. I'd dressed for bed in a sexy outfit." Sarah's eyes remained fixed on her hands.

"It's okay. I understand, Butch likes me to dress kinky for him too. At least he used to."

"Mike must have fallen asleep, and when I woke him, he flew at me. Knocked me to the floor." She raised her head and looked into her friend's face, relieved to see concern not judgement. "Rosa. His eyes. I thought he would kill me. He didn't know who I was. Called me *soldier* and ordered me to return fire. I knocked over a vase. The noise brought Daniel into the bedroom. He was protecting me. And me dressed like a hooker. I was terrified for us both. It was awful."

Rosa reached across and laid a hand on Sarah's arm. "Mike?" she whispered. "I can't believe it."

"Me either. What the hell happened out in Iraq that no one is telling us?"

Rosa frowned. "Take my advice. Don't ask. I did and got my head bitten off. Butch said nothing happened, but if nothing happened, why the hell did he get so mad when I asked?"

Sarah stared into her friend's eyes. "Rosa, I'm scared. When I turn the key in my front door lock, I don't know who will be home. Will it be the Mike I fell in love with, or the crazy person who attacked me last night?"

"I know what you mean."

The conversation stopped. Rosa stared at the wall; Sarah watched Noe eating cereal until he threw his cup on the floor and broke the silence. Sarah gathered it and placed it back on the tray. "You said Butch has to see General Swain. What about?"

"Who knows? The captain called earlier. Butch said it's just procedural bullshit."

"When does he see Doctor Wainwright again?"

"That's the thing. As far as the medics are concerned, they gave him pills, so he's cured."

"Rosa. I can't live like this. I'd hoped... If Butch was..."

"I know. Maybe it'll settle down once they've been back awhile. Remember in the briefings they said to expect a readjustment period."

"God, I hope so. But there is some good news. Yaz got home yesterday. Mike spent the morning with him and took him into the base."

"How is he?"

"Apparently, he's the same old Yaz."

"Fun guy. I always liked him."

"Me too. He's investing in Brian's LightCube project."

"That's great."

"Mike said you and Butch are putting up twenty thousand dollars. Is that true?"

Rosa nodded. "I got to thinking, perhaps the military won't work out for Butch after this last deployment. If this game controller is as good as the guys expect, in six months our twenty could be one hundred twenty. Then maybe Butch could resign. You know, get a regular job."

"Yaz is investing his savings—thirty thousand."

"Wow! Then again, he's single, so why not? What about you and Mike?"

"He wants to match Yaz, but I'm scared. If it doesn't work out, we could lose our home. I couldn't bear that. We've worked so hard to get where we are." She drained her coffee. "Look, I have to stop at the grocery store before Christopher gets out of kindergarten." Sarah got up. "Thanks for listening."

"Ditto."

They walked in silence to the front door so they didn't disturb Butch. Rosa closed it behind Sarah with a quiet click.

Pete Barber

SEVENTEEN

Christopher ran toward his mom, waiting at the school gates. He thrust a sheet of paper into her hand—a crayon drawing of Mike, her, Daniel, and Christopher standing in descending height order and holding hands.

"Lovely colors, Christopher."

"Can we put it on the fridge?"

"Sure."

On the drive home, approaching their bank her foot eased off the gas. She glanced in the driver's mirror at her son. How could she risk his security, his happiness when things were so uncertain at home? She accelerated and drove by. Next time Mike was calm, she'd talk it through with him again.

As she opened the front door, Christopher dashed past her, shouting, "Daddy, Daddy."

"In here," Mike called from the kitchen.

Sarah's stomach clenched, waiting for an outburst. None came. When she peeked into the kitchen, Mike, knees bent, arm around his son, was admiring Christopher's picture. Sarah smiled. Mike was such a good dad. Rosa was right; he just needed time to readjust. He stuck the artwork to the center of the fridge door with a couple magnets.

"Hi, honey." She put her purse on the table. "Nice to have an artist in the family."

Mike looked up. "Did you go to the bank?"

Her mouth opened. No sound came. An invisible hand clamped her throat and squeezed.

His eyes darkened. "Well?"

She swallowed and croaked, "Let's talk later. I have to fix Christopher a sandwich." Sarah placed a hand on Christopher's back. "Come on, young man. Let's see if SpongeBob is on." He ran into the living room. Mike straightened, glaring at her, fists

121

clenched. She spun away and followed Christopher, positioned her son in front of the TV, and switched on cartoons. "I'll be in the kitchen, okay?"

Eyes locked on the screen, he didn't answer.

Sarah took two paces into the kitchen and stopped. Her husband hadn't moved. The muscles on his arms were twitching. Purple veins stood out on his neck. Body torqued. A trap, set and ready to snap shut, Mike screamed, "You don't get it! You don't get it!" He pummeled his right fist into his palm. The violence made her heart lurch.

She tried to swallow the dry rock in her throat.

Her husband slammed his fist again. Two hundred twenty pounds of pure hatred dominated the far side of the room, glaring at her with the same vicious eyes she saw last night in the bedroom. An icy shiver trickled down Sarah's back. She was a stranger, an intruder in his space.

Mike broke eye contact. Stiffly, like an automaton, his head swiveled, scanning the kitchen. Target obtained, he flexed his knees, and with his left hand snatched up a kitchen chair. Holding it by one leg, he swung the heavy oak above his head as though it were weightless, roared, and smashed it onto the kitchen counter.

He glared at her again. Spittle sprayed from his mouth as he screamed, "Now do you get it?"

Sarah froze. Unable to comprehend Mike's fury, she was terrified to move or a make a sound that might further enrage him.

He hoisted the next chair and crashed it onto the sink. A tap snapped and water spouted three feet in the air. The chair stayed whole, so he swung again and again and again. Breakfast dishes, still stacked on the draining board, shattered and bounced. Porcelain shards rattled off the cabinets, scattering and spinning across the tiled floor. A sharp splinter spiraled through the air and stung as it nicked her cheek. Her hand covered the spot and came back wet and red.

"Mike. It's okay, honey. Breathe." She tried to keep her voice steady, but she was hardly breathing herself.

From ten feet away, icy assassin's eyes locked on her again.

"Momma?" Christopher grabbed the back of her skirt, his voice high and shaky. The touch of his tiny fingers on the back of her leg twisted her gut.

Sarah spoke fast, chanting her words, too terrified to turn, as though her gaze, locked with Mike's, was all that held him at bay. "Christopher. Go to your room. Now! That's an order, young man." She prayed her voice sounded firm, not fearful. When she felt Christopher leave, Sarah stepped back and gripped the frame of the door leading to the hall, one hand each side, legs braced, blocking the way.

A veteran's wife whose husband had struggling with PTSD had spoken at a briefing she and Rosa had attended. She shared stories of violence in the home. Sarah had felt sorry for her, but never considered the information relevant. Mike wasn't violent. Before last night, he'd never raised a hand to her. Sure, he'd been ill tempered since he returned.

Could he really hurt her?

Could he hurt the kids?

The back door opened—Daniel, arriving home from school. He stepped into the kitchen and stopped dead behind his father. Rail-thin, almost as tall as Mike, he looked around the kitchen with wide eyes, taking in the chaos, then peered past his father. In a shaky voice he said, "Mom, Dad. What's going on?"

"Daniel!" Sarah pointed at the wall phone, to Daniel's right. "Call 911."

Mike's head rotated like a gun turret. He lunged across the room and using the single stubby leg—all that remained of the chair—as a club. He smashed the phone. Plastic splintered. The body of the device buried into the drywall, and the handset rattled to the floor and hung there, suspended from the coiled cord.

As though the violence had triggered it, Sarah's cell phone rang in her purse on the table. Mike snatched the bag and tipped it upside down. The phone dropped out. A picture Rosa and Noe filled the screen. Mike raised his weapon and slammed it into the device, crushing it. He struck again, trying to drive the phone through the tabletop. Pieces of shattered metal and plastic spiraled across the room.

Sudden silence filled the space. Blood pounded in her ears. Mike's breathing sawed and rasped. Water sprayed and splashed against the window. But the violence had stopped.

Mike's fist opened. The chair leg clattered to the floor. With arms drooping by his sides, her husband's face slackened, and he straightened to his full height.

Four paces away, towering over her, his eyes went wide and

glassy.

And he laughed.

Not her husband's deep-throated belly laugh. Not an embarrassed *I'm sorry* laugh, but a high-pitched crazy-person's laugh.

His hyena grin, the tears tracking down his cheeks, and the snot bubbles at his nose triggered a primal response in Sarah. Her body vibrated; her mind blanked. One thought remained.

Save the children.

Sarah made a *come on* hand signal to Daniel who stood, rigid, behind his father. His gaze darted around the room, seeking a route through the carnage of broken chairs and dishes and phones.

As though dodging bullets, Daniel ducked low and ran past his father. When he reached her, she enveloped him, pulled him close, and hissed in his ear, "Go to Christopher's room and lock the door."

He shook his head—*No.*

Sarah pulled back so he could see her eyes. "Daniel, go!" Then softer, she whispered, "Protect Christopher." She swiveled and pushed him through the doorway into the hall. He ran up the stairs.

The sound of Christopher's bedroom door slamming shut sent a shudder through Mike. As though woken from a trance, he charged toward her.

Sarah cowered and tensed, but no blow came. Instead, he brushed past and through the door, clipping her shoulder as if he didn't see her standing there. The sharp stink of his sweat filled her nose.

Christopher. Daniel.

Mike took the stairs three at a time, the leg injury forgotten, or masked by his fury.

She raced after him and screamed. "Mike. No!" But he bypassed Christopher's room, and from halfway up the stairs, she saw the door to the master bedroom slam shut.

The boys were safe, for now.

Sarah pressed a hand to her chest. Her heart threatened to burst through her ribs. Dropping to her knees on the stairs, she slumped forward and rested her forehead on the carpet. What to do? How could she get help without a phone? She couldn't leave the children.

"Momma. Momma!" Christopher's cry snapped her into action.

Get them out of the house.

Sarah climbed the stairs and tapped on her son's bedroom door. "Daniel. Open. It's Mom."

The lock turned. The door opened a crack. Daniel peeked out—must have been standing there, waiting. Christopher pulled the door wide, pushed past his brother, and wrapped his arms around her legs, squeezing so hard she had to grab the doorframe to prevent a fall.

She peeled Christopher's hands back, crouched, and whispered, "Daddy's upset, okay. So I want you and Daniel to run to Aunt Rosa's house and stay there a while." She looked up at Daniel and said, "Tell her not to come here. Tell her—"

I can't turn Mike in. It'll be reported to his command. It'll go on his record.

"Tell her not to call 911 until I've spoken to your dad, okay."

Christopher twisted his hands in the material of her T-shirt and sobbed into her breasts. She hugged him but focused on Daniel. "Take him. Now. While Dad's in our room."

Daniel puffed out his chest. "I'm not leaving you."

His jutting chin, balled fists, and determined face brought prickling tears of pride to her eyes.

"I'll be fine. I need you to do this for me, son. It's important."

Daniel held his pose for four beats of her heart then nodded once and grabbed his brother's hand. "Come on, Chris. Let's see whether Aunt Rosa has baked cookies."

Sarah stood and kissed Daniel's head, spoke into his hair. "Good boy."

When the front door closed behind them, and only the hissing water in the kitchen broke the silence, she moved toward their bedroom.

Her hand trembled as she grasped the knob, turned, and inched the door inward. "It's just me, Mike." She sang the words.

No answer.

She eased open the door, braced for an attack.

"Just me, Mike. I'm—"

As the door swung ajar, one hand shot to her mouth. A squeak escaped her lips. Mike sat on the bed facing her, eyes open but unseeing.

The muzzle of a thirty-eight revolver, shoved three inches into his gaping mouth, rested on his lower teeth, angled up.

He held the weapon in both hands, left thumb resting on the trigger.

Sarah lowered her hand, tried to slow her breathing enough to speak in a calm voice, to mask the terror. A sudden move could end her husband's life, could change her world forever. The balance was that precarious. "Mike," she whispered. "Mike, honey. It's Sarah, your wife. I love you, Mike. Can you hear me?"

Saliva dribbled along the gun barrel and dripped from the trigger guard, forming a dark patch on Mike's jeans. His hands and body remained stiff. Locked and loaded, unmoving. But when she spoke, he blinked. His eyes moved a fraction, focused on her. Pity filled her heart and flushed her fear.

Her left leg weighed a thousand pounds. She lifted it and stepped forward. Then froze. Face screwed tightly, squinting though her eyelashes, she waited for the deafening sound, waited for her husband's blood and bone and brain to blast the ceiling.

Breathe. She whispered. "Mike. I love you. I'll help you."

A sob wracked his body, and his hand jerked as he took a faltering breath. She slammed her eyes shut and covered her ears. Two long seconds passed.

"Take it away, Sarah."

She opened her eyes a crack and peeked through. Spoken around the barrel, his words were difficult to distinguish.

But he'd used her name.

"I will, honey. I'll take it away." She took another step, paused, then another, paused, until she stood three feet from him.

In slow motion, she lifted her right arm, keeping the rest of her body rigid. Jaw clenched, she touched one finger to the back of his trigger hand, feather light.

And stopped.

His eyes lifted to hers. "Take it away." His voice sounded tiny, far away.

"I will. I promise, but you have to help me, baby." She waited for his eyes to acknowledge her intent before wrapping the fingers of her right hand around the gun's stock. Reaching out, she laid her other hand on his head and smoothed his hair.

"I've got your six. I've got your six, my husband. Let me help. Let me take it away."

His grip eased, and she felt the heft of the weapon. As the weight transferred, the gun dipped, and she winced. But his thumb slid from the trigger, and his hands flopped, boneless, onto his leg. Sarah lifted the weapon, fell forward, and wrapped him in her arms, holding the gun behind his back.

Mike roared into her neck like a wounded animal. It was the most chilling sound she'd ever heard. Her head shook, too heavy to support; she felt her control slipping and forced herself back to the now, away from his terror. She needed to be the strong one.

Peering over his shoulder, she opened the gun's cylinder. With trembling fingers, she tipped the weapon and emptied five shells onto the bed. Then, as Mike had taught her, she pressed the ejector rod to release the round from the top chamber.

Where it waited.

Ready.

And so nearly spent.

Daniel shouted from downstairs, "Mom?"

His voice was high and tight with tension.

"Momma. Are you okay?"

Sarah eased away from her husband and stared into the face of a boxer beaten in the last round after giving his all, hopeless, full of despair. Large pupils swamped his blue irises, welling tears leaked unchecked down his face. Sarah kissed her husband's forehead and whispered into his hair, "I have to check on Daniel. I'll be back in a minute."

He didn't acknowledge her. As she straightened, Sarah hid the weapon with her body, so he didn't see her tuck it in the front waistband of her jeans.

Leaving the bedroom door open, she stepped onto the landing. A rearward glance showed no movement from her husband.

She shouted, "Stay there, Daniel. I'm fine. I'm coming."

Her son stood at the foot of the stairs. As she descended, his eyes widened and locked on the gun. He held out a cell phone. "Aunt Rosa wanted to call 911. I told her not to."

"You did good."

"Is Dad okay?"

Shaking her head, she said, "Better, but he's had some kind of breakdown. We need to get him help."

The base's medical team would know how to handle Mike. But if she took him there, it was the end of his career in the army. He'd be marked as unstable, untrustworthy, and cast aside like so many others. That wasn't a choice she alone could make.

Sarah took the phone from Daniel and dialed Fayetteville General Hospital, asked to speak with Eddie in the ER, and prayed he was on duty. Not a friend, just a work colleague, but Eddie was a Vietnam vet who understood combat; he'd struggled with "the demons," as he called them, for years. Her heart flipped when she heard his voice. Eddie asked whether she needed 911. "No." Was Mike violent? "No." If she told the truth, the police would come, and who knew what effect their uniformed presence might have. They might set him off again. "I'm bringing him in. We'll be there in twenty minutes," she said. "But, Eddie, he's really confused."

Eddie asked what drugs Mike had taken.

"None so far as I know."

Eddie softened his voice. "Don't worry, Sarah. Get him here and we'll take care of him. I'll be watching for you. Drive careful, now."

The compassion in his words forced a sob from her throat. She hung up, couldn't even say goodbye, couldn't think beyond the next step.

Daniel put a hand on her arm. She jumped at the touch before pulling him in, hugging him, needing to feel him—to know this struggle was worthwhile.

The gun, still in her belt, dug into her belly. She released Daniel, ruffled his hair, and slipped the revolver into the top drawer of the small chest in the hall where they kept the phone books.

"We need to get Dad into the car. Follow me upstairs. But Daniel—" She handed him the phone, then gripped his shoulders and stared into his eyes. "If I tell you to run, run as fast as you can to Aunt Rosa and call 911."

He nodded but looked away, so she grabbed his cheeks in both hands and forced him to face her. "Promise me."

Daniel held her gaze and gave a firm nod. "I promise."

She ran up the stairs, Daniel right behind her. Through the stair rails, she saw Mike still sitting at the bottom of the bed where she'd left him, slumped, head in hands. When they reached the landing, she held up one finger to Daniel and whispered, "Wait here, and remember your promise."

Sarah stopped in the bedroom doorway. "Mike? It's Sarah. I need you to come with me."

He straightened and faced her: Cheeks gray and in need of a shave, hair tousled, eyes hooded and unfocussed, her warrior

128

looked so lost she couldn't be certain he'd heard her words.

Going to him, she placed one hand under Mike's arm and pulled. "Come on you big lump. We need to get going."

His hand flopped onto his lap, body limp. She was five foot five, one hundred forty pounds—no way she could move him, even with Daniel's help. Not daring to press, Sarah covered her face. Her tears finally came. If she called the police, Mike might react. But how else could she do this without help?

Through sobs, she begged, "Come on, Mike. Please, honey. Please."

Nothing.

When Daniel spoke from behind her, she gave a start, hardly recognizing her son's voice because of the tone.

"Master Sergeant!" Daniel commanded, "the Delta Force convoy is waiting. We need to get to the vehicles. Now. Move it, soldier."

As she turned to Daniel, Mike sprang to his feet, rushed past her through the door and stopped on the landing, casting around as though he'd never seen the house before.

Mouth open, she stared at Daniel who held up one hand to her—wait—and used a stage whisper to direct his father. "The building's clear, Master Sergeant. Our vehicle's in the garage. You take shotgun. Let's move. Go. Go. Go!"

Mike ran for the stairs, Daniel on his heels, and Sarah followed. She found her keys on the kitchen floor, and delayed long enough to shut off the water under the sink, so the house wouldn't be flooded when they returned. When she reached the car, Daniel was in back, Mike in the passenger seat, safety belt on. She raised the garage door and reversed out.

On the drive to the hospital, to Mike every pedestrian was an enemy combatant. He cringed each time they passed a parked car. He grabbed an invisible steering wheel and his feet manipulated nonexistent pedals. At one point, he slammed his hands against the car's roof, screaming, "Hostiles, hostiles on the roof."

Daniel shouted from the rear, "Raven sweep confirms our route is clear. Ground assets are in place. Stand down, soldier."

For twenty minutes, Sarah drove Mike through enemy territory, her heart slamming and hands white-knuckled on the steering wheel.

When they stopped outside the ER, she honked her car horn. A dark-skinned medic in a white coat and wire-rimmed glasses hustled out of the electronic doors. A shiny stethoscope hung from his neck. Behind came Eddie, rolling a wheelchair. A vet, she hoped, would understand.

From the back seat, Daniel said, "Master Sergeant, you've taken friendly fire. Go with the medics. Get patched up. We need you back in the field. Delta Force will collect you on our return sweep."

Mike climbed out and sat in the wheelchair. Eddie, bent low, whispering in her husband's ear, pushed him into the ER.

Sarah parked then hurried back to follow her husband. Daniel jogged beside her. She tapped her son's shoulder. "How did you know to do that?"

"What?"

"To talk to your dad like that. To get him to follow instructions."

Daniel shrugged. *"Call of Duty.* Dad and I used to play all the time. That's how they talk in the game."

As the automatic doors opened for them, Sarah grabbed Daniel and hugged him. "Thank you, Daniel. Dad'll be okay now. The doctors will know what to do."

He pulled away, shaking his head.

"Dunno, Mom. I'm pretty sure Dad thinks he's back in Iraq."

EIGHTEEN

Sarah followed signs to the hospital reception and spoke through a letterbox-slit in the glass window. "I'm with Mike Braeman."

Behind the desk, an overweight woman in scrubs pushed a clipboard through the gap below the security screen. "Fill this out, please."

"I need to see my husband."

The receptionist softened her voice. "He's with the doctor in the ER. I need the paperwork so we can treat him correctly."

Sarah took the forms and filled out their insurance details. Normally, she'd check *no* in the boxes asking about prior conditions, but today she had to mark *yes* to depression, anger, lack of sleep, and suicidal tendencies. A sickly feeling crept through her gut. Was this the right thing for Mike? Were her answers labeling him crazy?

Was he crazy?

Daniel touched her shoulder and she jumped.

"Sorry, Mom. Can I have a soda?"

She handed over a couple dollars, and he headed to the machines.

A series of crashes sounded from behind the door marked ER, followed by angry voices—men shouting, sounds of a fight. Mike's voice was the loudest. Sarah dropped the clipboard, rushed to the doors, and yanked the handles—locked.

The receptionist shouted across, "Ma'am, you can't go in there."

"But that's my husband. What's going on? I need to be with him."

Behind the doors, a pitched battle raged. Then a sudden silence. Sarah pressed her ear to the wood. The voices adopted a lower register. She heard, "Okay, one, two, three, lift. Lock those restraints tightly."

Daniel returned with sodas. "What happened?"

"I think Dad had another episode."

Sarah returned to the registration window. The half-dozen folk in the waiting room ignored the muted TV on the wall and stared at her instead. "You need to let me though there," she said, pointing at the ER. "I can calm him."

The receptionist raised her voice. "I'm not authorized. Please, Mrs. Braeman, fill out the forms. The doctor will be out soon to speak with you."

Deflated, powerless, Sarah returned to her seat. Daniel's wide eyes searched her face and brought her back to reality. She squeezed his knee. "Your dad will be fine. He's in the best place. The doctors will take care of him, son."

He nodded and sipped his soda although the worry remained in his eyes.

Forty minutes after she'd handed the completed forms to the receptionist, the man with the white coat and stethoscope, whom she'd seen when they arrived, came out of the ER. Two men in security uniforms flanked him. "Mrs. Braeman?"

Sarah sprang to her feet and rushed toward the man who took a step back so the guards were in front. "I'm Sarah Braeman. Can I see my husband?"

"This way." He pointed to a door at the back of the waiting area. Eddie, with a fresh Band-Aid stuck to his forehead, came out of the ER and joined them. At least he smiled at her.

She told Daniel to wait and followed the three men into a small conference room. Eddie brought up the rear and closed the door.

White Coat said, "Mrs. Braeman, I'm Doctor Mahmud. Your husband has suffered a psychotic break with dissociative disorder."

"What does that mean?" She searched their grim faces, finally lighting on Eddie's.

In a voice softened with concern, Eddie said, "He's had a flashback, Sarah. Mike thinks he's in a combat situation in Iraq."

She shook her head. "That's what Daniel said." The men all stared at her. She felt accused, guilty, but of what? "How do we bring him back?"

The doctor snapped, "Are you the caregiver?"

His thick accent threw her. It took a couple seconds to decoded the words. Sarah's mouth dropped open. Caregiver was a new term for her. Was she? If not her, then who? "Yes."

Wagging his finger at her, the doctor said, "Your husband attacked me." She stared at the man: five foot three or four, black hair, dark skin, scruffy beard, his nametag—Dr. Mohammad Mahmud—pinned to his lapel. "Your husband is homicidal. Does he have a history of attacking people of Middle-Eastern descent?"

Sarah's head whirled. What the hell could she say to that? "Look! I brought my husband here because he tried to commit suicide. I get that he's having a flashback. My fourteen-year-old son worked that out. Shouldn't you be helping him, not accusing him?"

"Your husband is a racist."

Sarah locked her jaw and glared at the man. Never had she wanted to punch someone as much as she did right now. She spat words from between clenched teeth. "My husband is an active duty soldier who just returned from Iraq. He wasn't on a Middle-Eastern vacation! He was fighting for your freedom. If he thinks he's back at the front, I expect a man called Mohammad Mahmud coming at him with a hypodermic needle *would* seem like an act of aggression. My husband was defending himself."

She took a step toward the doctor who backed up and waved his hand as though swatting away a bug. "I can't deal with this aggression." He spun around and marched from the room, leaving Eddie and the two guards.

"What the hell does he expect, Eddie?" Sarah swiped the back of her hand over her eyes. She would *not* give that little prick doctor or his bodyguards the satisfaction of seeing her cry.

Eddie touched her arm. "Hold on." He turned to the men. "She'll be fine, now. You guys head off." They didn't need a second invitation. Once she and Eddie were alone, he said, "Mahmud went nuts when Mike called him a fuckin' hajji." He grinned, and she choked back a laugh.

"It's not funny, Eddie."

"Yeah, I know, but it was. You should have seen the doc's face."

She shook her head.

"Look, Sarah, they can't handle Mike here. He's sedated, but he was out of control for a short while. If we hadn't grabbed him before he reached Mahmud, he might have snapped him in two."

"I hear that. Wouldn't mind poppin' the self-righteous asshole myself."

"They want to send him to a rehab center. The place handles addiction, but they're equipped to handle post-traumatic stress disorder. It's a lockdown facility. They'll put him in a room where he can't hurt anyone, including himself. Once he calms, staff will work out a treatment program. As his caregiver, you must sign to agree."

"Mike doesn't have PTSD." But as she spoke the words, she knew it was a lie. Since the night of the rocket attack, Mike had been a different person. She'd been in denial. PTSD happened to other women's husbands.

Eddie said, "I'm no doctor, so I can't diagnose, but I've seen this movie before. Whatever label you want to use, Mike needs help."

"But a nut house? They're sending Mike to an asylum?"

"It's not a bad place. And they'll take Mike's Tricare health plan." Eddie looked at his shoes. "Five years ago, that was me strapped to the gurney. Rehab saved me, saved my marriage. It's that, or they'll call a police crisis team to take him away. And his command will find out—he'll lose his security clearance."

"That means the end of his army career."

"Trust me. Rehab is better."

Sarah's ears buzzed, and the room swayed. She grabbed a chair and sat, heavily, elbows on the table and head in hands. Eddie touched her shoulder. "It's your decision, Sarah, but I think you need to make it soon. I know what Mahmud wants. Mike gave him a real scare."

"Can I see him?"

"Sign the papers so they can arrange transport, then I'll take you through. Does Mike have any leave due?"

"Ten days."

"Well then?" Eddie raised an eyebrow.

Sarah signed release papers and Eddie took her and Daniel through the ER to a curtained-off area. Sarah sucked in a sharp breath when she saw Mike secured to a gurney with straps around his legs, chest, and neck—tied down like a dangerous animal. His hands, locked at his sides, had a couple Band-Aids on the knuckles and his left eye was puffy, but he looked peaceful.

She bent, kissed his lips, and put her hand on his forehead. "You've always been there for us. Now we're here for you, big guy."

Standing beside the gurney, she watched his chest rise and fall in an even rhythm. Their breathing synchronized. Eddie tapped her arm and whispered. "I'll make sure he's loaded. You should go home and rest." He widened his eyes and nodded toward Daniel, whose face was gray.

"Thanks, Eddie. I don't know what we'd have done without you."

"Come on," he said, "I'll walk you to your car." On the way, he talked of his flashbacks from Vietnam. "They understand PTSD more now than back then. The docs at the rehab know their stuff."

"How will I get in touch?"

"They'll call you. It may be a few days. They'll stabilize him first. Trust me; it's for the best."

Trust him. What choice did she have? Sarah drove home, empty, impotent. She'd let her husband down. Why didn't she see this coming? The warning signs were there. Rosa was the better wife, the better *caregiver*; she'd gotten help for Butch before the shit hit the fan. Never had Sarah felt such a failure. She detoured, stopped at the bank, and signed the loan papers.

If she'd done that earlier, perhaps this wouldn't have happened.

Pete Barber

NINETEEN

Three months later...

From the street, Sarah honked her car horn and Rosa came out of her house, running, head bent against the rain. Butch stood in the doorway, but when Sarah waved, he averted his eyes and closed the front door.

"If this is spring, summer can't get here fast enough. Damn weather," Rosa said as she dived into the vehicle.

Rosa had called that morning desperate to meet for lunch. "How come Butch is home?" Sarah asked.

"Ah. let's save that for later. How's Mike?"

"Oh, you know. Some days, when he smiles or laughs at something Christopher does or says, I think it'll be all right. Then a car backfires and he ducks for cover and screams at me for fun." Sarah took a deep breath. "Sorry, I didn't mean to dump on you. You've got your own problems with Butch. Look, it's not all bad. Mike hasn't had a serious outburst for over a week. The biggest challenge for me is accepting that he'll never be the man I married. But, I'll learn to love this version." Sarah shook her head. "Ha!"

"What?"

"Listen to me. I sound as though I've swallowed one of those 'Living with PTSD' brochures."

"Any news about the LightCube from Brian?" Rosa asked.

"Not since last week's email. You saw that, right?"

Rosa nodded.

"It sounded positive. The only good thing to come out of Iraq if you ask me. I think we'll make money soon, don't you?" Sarah asked.

"Brian didn't say when though."

Sarah smiled. "But no bad news. He still thinks we're on track for late summer."

137

Rosa fell silent. Sarah glanced across. Something was going on. She opened her mouth to ask, but because of the frown on Rosa's forehead and her friend's faraway look, she elected to wait.

They parked in the mall's underground lot. At the food court, they grabbed a couple slices of pizza and Rosa led them to a corner table.

Sarah let Rosa swallow a mouthful before firing her question. "Okay, give. What's important enough to require an emergency ladies' lunch?"

Rosa took a deep breath. "Swain has Chapter Fourteened Butch."

Pizza slice halfway to her mouth, Sarah froze. "Wh… How? Why?"

"Swain started proceedings right after the DWI."

"Rosa, why didn't you tell us? Maybe we could have helped. Mike will vouch for him, and Yaz, I'm sure."

Rosa began to cry. Sarah reached across, held her friend's hand until she gathered herself. Through sobs she said, "I only found out this morning. That's why he's home. He was dishonorably discharged yesterday."

"That can't be right. It takes months."

"Oh—" She pulled in a faltering breath. "—he's known for months, just didn't tell *me*."

"Shit, Rosa. What'll you do?"

"That's why I wanted to meet. We need our money back from Brian?"

Sarah's head was spinning. A million guesses about the reason for lunch today wouldn't have brought her to this. "What about his health benefits?"

"He's lost everything. I'm frightened, Sarah. Without pills, without therapy, what'll happen to him?"

Sarah shook her head, struggling to grasp the consequences: no medical coverage, no pension, no pay packet coming in, and a dishonorable discharge on his work record—a huge black mark, even in the civilian world. "Can he appeal?"

"If he'd told me months ago when the process started, maybe then. But he didn't. We had a big argument this morning. That's why I had to leave."

"But *why* didn't he tell you?"

"Butch loves his country. He would lay down his life for

America. And he loves the military. The US Army has been his family for longer than Noe and me. Right until the end, he couldn't believe his family would turn their back on him. He's been in denial." Rosa took a deep breath and looked into Sarah's eyes. "I'm frightened of what he might do. You know?" She lowered her voice, leaned in. "Like Mike."

"Is Butch suicidal?"

"I don't think so. But neither was Mike. You didn't see that coming, right?"

Sarah winced as Rosa's words brought to mind that day when she'd found her husband with a gun barrel in his mouth.

"Butch has stopped taking his pills, says we can't afford them. If we can just get the money back, it'll give us breathing space— time to think and plan. Sarah, will you talk to Brian? I can't handle it. I'll just—" And the tears started again.

"Of course."

When Mike got home from work, she settled him in his armchair and brought a cup of coffee. She'd learned not to spring surprises on him, so she eased into the Butch and Rosa situation.

"I had lunch with Rosa today," she said.

"How is she?"

"Not so good. Butch was Chaptered-Out yesterday."

"I know. It sucks."

Sarah jerked upright. "You knew? You knew and didn't tell me!"

Anger flashed in his eyes. Mike put his coffee down and balled his fists. He took a series of deep breaths, one of the coping strategies they taught at the lockdown facility. She stayed quiet, waited.

Will I have to walk around on eggshells forever?

The tension in Mike's body ebbed. He sighed out one final breath. "Butch didn't want anyone to know," he said.

"Maybe you or Yaz could have helped."

Mike shook his head. "You don't get it! Swain has Chaptered-Out eight soldiers from our unit this year. His mission is to reduce headcount. Yaz can't afford to get involved. Swain's wait-listed him for a Wounded Warrior Unit. There's competition for places. Yaz doesn't want to mess up his chances. And if they find out about my... breakdown, they'll get rid of me, too. I can't raise any red flags."

Sarah reached across, laid a hand on his arm. "But Butch has a traumatic brain injury. It's not his fault he got the DWI."

"Not how Swain sees it. He's an SOB, but his command loves him—he's beating his headcount targets, and most are Chapter Ten or Fourteen discharges—not paying benefits is cost-effective for the military."

"Good God!"

Mike shook his head. "God can't help."

TWENTY

At four p.m. on April 29th Mia popped her head around the corner of Brian's work cube on GameSoft's fourth floor. Her normal friendly demeanor and sweet smile were noticeably absent. Voice sharp, all business, she snapped, "Adam wants you in his office."

"And good afternoon to you. Just let me finish this edit."

She shook her head. "He needs you now!"

Brian smiled. "Is this a prank?"

"I wish." Her voice softened. "Come on, Brian. Adam's pissed off. Don't keep him waiting."

And she disappeared. The fifteen-second exchange was surreal. GameSoft was a laid-back place to work, and Mia was an easygoing person. As he headed for the elevators, his mind jumped and jerked around. What the hell had he done to make the CEO angry? His project was on schedule. The fabricators had delivered the prototype LightCube and heads-up display. Adam loved it.

Mia held the elevator door. He stepped through and she pressed *six*.

"What's this about?"

She shook her head. "Adam will tell you."

In silence, he followed Mia along the hallway to the CEO's office. She knocked, opened the door, and waited for Brian to step through before closing it behind them. Adam met them halfway across the room. He pointed to the conference table, and they sat. In his hand he held an envelope. He pulled out the letter and slid it over the table to Brian.

The correspondence was addressed to Adam Barnes on letterhead from the United States Justice Attorneys General. Brian looked up. "What is this?"

"Read it. Then you tell me." Adam's face was an unreadable mask. His eyes burned into Brian's. The hairs on the back of his neck lifted. He'd never seen the man so intense.

In the second paragraph, the JAG demanded that GameSoft cease and desist using software illegally obtained by Brian Matthews from a classified US Army robotics project. The letter claimed GameSoft had infringed US Army copyrights. The army intended to seek punitive damages.

Brian lifted his head. The CEO's stare hadn't softened. His eyes searched Brian's face as though he could see the truth written there.

"This isn't correct," Brian said. "The code is mine. I spent years building it before my contract with the army. I used my code as a basis for their VCOM project, but my terms of employment with Militec stated the original code was my property. Heck, I had to give *them* authority to use it."

Adam glanced at Mia, whose gaze never left the tabletop. She looked drawn, shaken. Maybe her job was at stake. The CEO locked lasers on Brian again and said, "Prove it."

Mia's nervousness was contagious. Brian's head shook. Under Adam's scrutiny, it took long seconds to organize his thoughts. "A copy of my original code is held in escrow by the JAGs in Washington—the same code I demonstrated when we met in February. Before starting the VCOM project, they insisted on receiving the code on CD, flash drive, and a hard copy which I signed on each page. At the time, I thought it was a stupid bureaucratic make-work project. In hindsight, perhaps not."

Adam's face softened. He pointed at the letter. "So why send this?"

Brian studied the letter heading. "Huh. This comes from Fort Black. I guess their right hand doesn't know what their left hand is doing. May I have a copy?"

When Brian looked up again, Adam was nodding his agreement. "Keep that one. Okay, Brian. I believe you, and I'm relieved. Nevertheless, I will not get into a pissing match with the US Army. The LightCube project stops until you bring me a letter from these guys," Adam tapped the document with his index finger, "rescinding this claim of copyright infringement."

So much for being on schedule. But Brian swallowed his objections; there was no point; in Adam Barnes's position, he'd do the same.

Barnes stood and held out his hand. Brian shook it. "Don't take too long. I can't keep resources locked up on the LightCube indefinitely, okay?"

"I'm on it. Thank you."

Mia escorted him out. While they waited for the elevator, Brian said, "Sorry if I got you in trouble with your boss."

She blew out her cheeks. "You don't know the half of it. I've never seen him so livid. He'd cooled off by the time you got here." She locked soft brown eyes on his. "Can you fix this?"

"Sure. I know people at Fort Black. I'll head there right now and find out who pressed the panic button."

The elevator came, and he climbed in. She threw him a sweet smile and a wave as the door closed. He stopped by his desk to grab his jacket and laptop, made copies of the cease-and-desist letter then headed to his car.

What the heck is going on at Fort Black?

Sarah received Brian's call a little after five p.m.

"You must be psychic. I planned to call you this evening."

"Oh? Just hold that thought, Sarah. Something has come up. We need to meet. Can you get Rosa, Butch and Yaz together?"

"When?"

"Today."

"What's wrong?"

"Ah. Difficult to explain over the phone. I'm on my way to Fayetteville. I'll be at your home around six thirty. It's important."

"Mike and I are here. I'll call the others."

"Thanks, I'll see you soon."

Sarah hung up. Mike stared at her, studying her face. "What?"

A chill of loneliness washed through her. Before this last deployment, they'd been a team. But now? Brian's call sounded like trouble, and she had to keep that to herself, carry that worry alone. Mike could only cope with sanitized snippets of problems. As though he were a petulant child ready to fly into a tantrum, or worse still, primed to retreat into his inner space. Juggling jelly was simpler than the balancing act she performed with him, and *between* him and the children. Her husband was here, physically in the same room, but *she* must handle Brian's problem, whatever it was. Caregiver, the doctor had called her; it went way beyond that.

She sighed. "Brian has something he needs to discuss," she said. "He's on his way. Give me a few minutes. I need to call Yaz and Butch."

Mike stood, too quickly. He wobbled and grabbed the back of the sofa to steady himself. After his breakdown, he'd spent five days in the lockdown facility. He was discharged into the care of their local GP. Each visit cost a co-pay, but Mike insisted they not use the base's medics. He couldn't risk being labeled weak or damaged. In response to deepening depressive episodes, the doctor had prescribed a new antidepressant. He warned it might leave Mike lightheaded until he built up a tolerance.

The drugs reduced Mike's temper tantrums. There had been no further talk of suicide. But she ached to have her strong, supportive husband back to share the load.

"It must be serious if he's coming on such short notice," Mike said.

She made calming signals with her hand. "Not necessarily, he might have a new demonstration to show us. We'll find out soon enough. Honey, you look bushed. Why not lie down and try a nap, so you'll be rested when the others arrive?"

Mike nodded. "Maybe I will. These new pills are dragging on me."

"You're due to take one, remember. Here." Sarah retrieved his pillbox from the bureau drawer, opened today's segment, selected the large yellow capsule, and handed it to him.

"I'll need a drink."

She brought water from the kitchen while he waited next to the sofa.

After swallowing the pill, Mike handed her the empty glass. "Thanks." He slouched from the room and clumped up the stairs—in oh so many ways, her third child.

Daniel was in his bedroom doing homework, she hoped. Since the suicide attempt, he kept away from his dad. Frightened in case he said the wrong thing and set his dad off again, he'd withdrawn. She missed him but didn't blame him. No teenager should be burdened with caring for his father. She had explained PTSD, but Daniel still blamed himself for his dad's breakdown.

Christopher had also withdrawn. Right now he was watching cartoons. Sarah had met his teacher and discussed the problem. It had been a tough thing to do, confessing to a stranger that her family was broken and there was no knowing when it might be whole again. The school was sympathetic and supportive, more than she expected. Clearly, Mike wasn't the only emotional casualty of war living in Fayetteville.

Sarah called Rosa first. "Can you come over at seven? Brian is on his way from Raleigh."

The relief in Rosa's voice was palpable. "Oh, Sarah. Thank you. Thank you so much."

"No I—" Too late.

"You're a good friend, Sarah."

What the hell. Why spoil Rosa's mood? Sarah didn't know why Brian was coming, although from his tone, she didn't think it was what Rosa hoped for. Still, no point in worrying her unnecessarily. "See you at seven. I'll order pizza."

She contacted Yaz. He was excited to meet Brian again. "I haven't seen Nerdman since Iraq. Finally, I'll can thank him in person for dragging me out of that trailer. Mind you, the last phone conversation we had cost me thirty thousand dollars. I hope he isn't looking for more."

Sarah hoped so, too.

<><><>

When Brian arrived at quarter of seven, Sarah showed him to the kitchen table and sat opposite. "Yaz, Rosa, and Butch are on their way. But before they arrive… Look, Brian, things have been difficult around here."

"Difficult?"

She swallowed, stared at her fingers. How did you explain this stuff to a civilian? "Mike and Butch are suffering after-effects from the last deployment."

Brian tilted his head, waited.

"Flashbacks, depression, that sort of thing. I'm worried that… What I mean…" She took a breath. Sharing this was proving harder than she'd imagined. "If you have bad news about the LightCube project, I don't know how they'll handle it."

"Oh."

She took a deep breath. *Break it down for him. One step at a time.* "Okay. First. Butch has lost his job."

"How?"

"That's not for me to say. I only learned of this today, but that's why I was going to call. Is there any way Rosa can pull their twenty thousand out? Right now, they have no income and plenty of bills."

Brian's mouth opened then closed again. His cheeks flushed. "You know the money was spent with the fabricator."

"Yes, but. Heck, I don't know. Rosa and Butch are fragile, so I got volunteered to ask."

Brian shook his head. "Yesterday I'd have said I'd ask around. I mean, George, or one of his connections, would jump at the chance to buy more shares. And they'd pay a premium because we're so close to integrating the prototype with the game."

"So, what changed since yesterday?"

"That's why I'm here." He slipped his leather jacket off and hung it on his chair back, then fished out a few sheets of paper and handed one to her. "GameSoft received this today."

She scanned the letter, looked up. "What does it mean?"

"It's from the JAGs at Fort Black. They claim I stole code from their VCOM project."

"Did you?"

"No."

"So?"

"So, GameSoft has suspended the LightCube project until I can get this claim rescinded. That's why I came. If I knew who triggered this letter and why, I'll know who to talk to."

Mike cleared his throat as he entered the kitchen. Brian sprang from his seat. "Mike, how are you?" He offered his hand.

Mike glared at Sarah. "How should I be?" His biting tone was filled with suppressed anger, ready to spill over.

Brian threw a confused glance at Sarah. Her stomach turned and twisted like a washrag. What did that letter mean to their investment, to their home. How would Mike react. She dug nails into her palm and steadied her voice. "Brian got here early. Yaz and Butch are on their way."

After Mike and Brian shook hands, Mike pointed to the letter on the table. "What's that?"

Heat flooded Sarah's face. She couldn't catch her breath, couldn't beat Brian to the answer.

Brian picked up the letter. "It's a new development in the LightCube project. If it's okay with you, Sergeant, let's cover this once everyone's here."

Sarah eased out her breath. Brian was a quick study. She sprang to her feet. "Forgive my manners, Brian. How about a cup of coffee?"

"That'd be great, thanks."

She moved to the sink. "Want a one, Mike?"

"Sure."

The doorbell chimed.

"Mike, that'll be Butch and Rosa. Can you let them in?"

Mike headed to the door, and Sarah smiled at Brian and mouthed, "Thank you."

Rosa, Noe, and Butch came in, followed by Yaz, who rolled into the room with a strange mechanical gait forced on him by his prosthetic legs. When he stood still, though, he looked like the Yaz of old. Ironic that the person most damaged in the attack had healed the best. Unlike his battle buddies, Yaz had suffered no emotional fallout. Butch's and Mike's injuries were buried, invisible, and infinitely more difficult to deal with. A sheen of sweat beaded Yaz's forehead, and he was breathing hard.

"You walked?" Sarah asked.

"Just from Butch's place. My physical therapist says it's good for me. Mind you he's a sadist."

Rosa rolled her eyes. "I told him it was too far."

Sarah helped Rosa maneuver Noe's baby carriage into the living room, quietly, so he didn't wake.

"Did you ask about the money?" Rosa whispered.

Sarah nodded. "Just now."

Rosa's voice lifted with anticipation. "And?"

"It's complicated. Let's go into the kitchen and listen to Brian first."

Sarah escaped before Rosa could press further.

Once they sat around the table, a silence fell, and Brian cleared his throat. "Thanks for meeting me at such short notice. There's no easy way to do this, so—" He handed each of them a copy of the letter. "Please read this and then I'll explain." The silence stretched for a couple more minutes while they scanned the cease-and-desist letter.

Rosa put the page down first. "I don't understand."

Her dark eyes fixed on his, forehead creased with worry. Brian's heart sank because he was the one to bring more stress to her. The others looked up and waited.

"GameSoft received this letter today, couriered from the JAG's office at Fort Black. It means someone in Fort Black has heard about the LightCube project, and they are accusing me of stealing their code."

"Did you steal it?" Rosa asked.

"Of course not. But I have to prove that to Adam Barnes, and he's suspended the project until I do."

Mike glanced at Butch and Yaz. "Who the hell at the base would report this to the JAGs?"

Butch slammed a fist onto the table so hard it spilled Brian's coffee. "That bastard."

Brian grabbed what was left of his drink. Sarah jumped up. "Hold still. I'll get a cloth." She scurried across the kitchen and yanked a length of paper towel from the roll. Brian mopped his lap and the table.

Mike hissed, "Swain."

Yaz nodded.

Butch's face had turned scarlet. A violence that rattled Brian to his core glazed the sergeant's eyes. "Who else, but that bastard?"

Rosa touched her husband's arm. "But how did he learn about GameSoft and Brian's LightCube? Did you tell him?"

"Me? I wouldn't tell that prick the time."

"Me either," Mike said. "Yaz?"

"Ha. No chance."

Rosa softened her voice. "So, Butch, honey, maybe it's not him." Butch bunched and flexed his fists. Jawline hard, set, square, the man's looked capable of mass murder.

Brian cleared his throat. "Look guys. The letter's not valid. That's why I'm here. If I knew who triggered this, I could meet them, explain why they're mistaken, and get them to withdraw the complaint. Then we can restart the project."

"How?" Sarah asked.

"I have copies of my original software on file at JAG HQ in Washington. That's the code I used at GameSoft. *I* own the copyright, not the US Army."

"So, you need to show a document or something to the JAGs at Fort Black, right?" Sarah asked.

"It'd be easier if I could speak to the person who raised the complaint. Get them to withdraw. So if General Swain did file the complaint—"

Butch thumped the table again. "He did."

Brian straightened, recoiling from Butch's hostility. "Well if I can meet him, I'm sure he'll be cooperative once he understands the situation."

"That destructive bastard will never be cooperative," Butch said.

Sarah put up a hand. "Hold on, Butch," she said. "What do you need, Brian? I mean how can you resolve this, assuming Butch is correct that Swain is the source of the complaint?"

"It's a timing issue. If I can get him to withdraw the complaint, it'll short circuit the legalities. Otherwise I'll have to write to the JAGs at Fort Black and ask them to speak with Washington to validate my claim of copyright. I was hoping to cut through the red tape. When I started the VCOM project, it took Washington two months of bureaucratic BS to get my code verified."

"Two months!" Rosa's eyes filled with tears. "Butch and I don't have two months."

Butch jerked to his feet. His chair rocked back and clattered to the floor. "Fuck it, Brian!"

The big man's fierce glare sent icy needles prickling down Brian's spine. The muscles on Butch's arms bulged. His pecs twitched under his T-shirt. Brian felt sure the man was ready to take a swing at him. Instead, Butch spun away, and in three strides was out of the kitchen.

"Butch, wait!" Rosa ran after him, chased him out the front door and along the path, pleading, "Butch! Come back, please. Please, honey. Honey, where are you going?"

Sarah followed her friend into the front yard. Brian and Mike stopped on the doorstep. Butch was sprinting along the street, already a block away. At the garden gate, Rosa stood, gripping the pickets, staring after her husband's receding form. From behind, Sarah wrapped an arm around her friend and whispered in Rosa's ear until she turned and the two women hugged. Rosa's shoulders jerked up and down, and the soft sounds of sobbing scorched Brian's heart. This was his doing. Of course he wanted to fix it for Mike and Sarah and Butch, but the sound of Rosa's pain was more than he could bear. Mike stood beside him: eyes dull, shoulders slumped.

What had happened to these warriors?

Behind Brian, Yaz stood in the kitchen doorway, shaking his head. Brian widened his eyes, asking the question.

Yaz shrugged. "Fuckin' Iraq, man." Then he shouted, "Heh, Mike, got any beer?"

Mike turned and squeezed Brian's shoulder. "Come on, Nerdman. Might as well have a drink while we wait for Butch to cool his jets."

Brian had been transported to Bizarro World. The soldiers he'd worked with in Iraq moved toward challenges. But Sarah and Rosa were the ones concerned about the letter, concerned about Butch. Brian shook his head. "I'm good. Got to drive home. You guys carry on." He stepped into the front yard. When he reached Sarah, he tapped her on the back. "How can I help?"

She turned to him with tear-filled eyes. "Get the project back on track, Brian. None of this is your fault, but the LightCube is the only good thing happening in our lives right now."

"I'll work on the Washington angle first thing tomorrow. I'll stay in touch."

Rosa said, "Thank you, Brian." And never had he heard his name spoken with such sadness.

TWENTY-ONE

General Swain swirled peaty malt whisky around the walls of an oversized snifter. He breathed in the aroma and took a sip before raising the glass to his golfing buddy. "Revenge is sweet, Philip."

Dr. Wainwright, sitting opposite his friend in their customary place in front of the clubhouse fire, smiled. "Enjoy it while you can, you lucky SOB."

"Sore loser, eh?"

"Whatever." Wainwright downed his drink and grunted as he got to his feet. "Damn, I'm getting old. Look, I hate to drink and run, James, but Betty has friends coming for cocktails tonight. I have to play the genial host."

"I understand." The general tapped a manicured nail against his glass. "I'll hang on for a while. Don't want to rush the spoils of victory. Same time next Wednesday?"

"Vengeance will be mine." The doctor offered a slack salute and headed for the exit.

Swain placed his drink on the side table, selected a thick log from the pile on the hearth, and tossed it onto the fire. The bark creased, and smoke whistled from the center of the wood. A tongue of flame sprouted from the red ash below the new fuel, small at first, then expanding until it licked the log, wrapping it in yellow heat. As he finished the whisky, the steward appeared, a starched white napkin aligned over his right arm. He collected the empty glass. "Another, sir?"

Eyes locked on the fire, Swain said, "I think I will."

The officer's lounge served generous hand-poured measures. By the time he'd finished his third scotch, the log had crumbled to gray ash, and Swain felt warm inside and out.

He signed his tab and strolled across the thick-pile carpet to the coat check where he collected his overcoat; the spring nights were still chilly. He waited under the awning covering the club's main entrance while a valet brought his Mercedes C300 from the lot.

As he wound along the curved driveway, the whisky's effect starred the edges of the street lamps. He blinked and rubbed his eyes. *Better go easy on the way home. Don't want another DWI.* He'd recently endured twelve months driving with a breathalyzer contraption fitted to his vehicle. A second offense would cost him his license.

Swain swung out of the golf club's wrought-iron gates and navigated through the small suburb that fringed the course. A left on Main Street took him toward town. He maintained posted speed through Fayetteville, even stopping at a yellow light out of extra caution. When he turned onto the back road that led through open farmland to his five-acre country home, Swain gassed the car, enjoying the surge of the six-cylinder engine. In the driver's mirror, he was surprised to see a vehicle closing on him. He glanced at the dashboard; he was running sixty in a forty-five zone. *Shit!* He eased off the accelerator and slowed his car using the parking brake to avoid triggering the rear stoplights. When he hit forty-five, he set cruise control and checked behind again.

The following car was an older model—not a cop. The driver tailgated him with high beams blazing. *Asshole.* That kind of driving caused accidents and, of more concern to Swain, attracted the cops. He signaled right and slowed. Let the prick pass if he was in such a hurry.

When Butch jumped up from Sarah's kitchen table, a volcanic fury scorched his mind, stoked and fed by white-hot flames of hatred for Brigadier General James Swain. Ten years Butch had served his country. Ten years asking, "How high?" every time some college-educated officer without a fucking clue told him to jump. And now he needed something in return there was no, "Thank you for your service, Sergeant." No, "How can we help to repair the damage incurred while doing your duty." Just a, "Get the fuck out, *Oliver.* Put away your begging bowl. Don't you dare ask for more." Wainwright had tried to get Butch a medical discharge with full benefits, but that wasn't fast enough for Swain. The general's career path was littered with the broken families of discarded soldiers. Butch's dishonorable discharge was just another scrap of collateral damage, an unfortunate byproduct of Swain's ambition.

But stealing everything Butch had earned wasn't enough. Not for Swain. That pompous, unfeeling bastard had also stolen the LightCube. The one remaining chance Butch had of giving Rosa and Noe a decent life outside of the military.

Since stopping his medication, Butch had seen things more clearly, seen them for what they were. Sure, he wasn't sleeping. But he had trained for that. He was an American warrior. An American warrior was always ready. That was why Wainwright kept injured soldiers full of drugs. To keep them quiet, keep them dumb.

Now he was clean, the situation was clear as glass. He and Rosa and Noe were pieces of fluff clogging the army's gears. Flush them out. Bring in fresh meat. Restructure and re-equip for the new, smaller, more-nimble army. Well, Brigadier General James Swain was about to learn how nimble this soldier could be when he was protecting his family. This was Wednesday. Butch knew where the general snuck off to every Wednesday.

He sprinted from Sarah's without a backward glance, ran four blocks in record time, opened his garden gate, and tore up the front path. Jogging in place, he dug out his key. Once inside, he flew up the stairs into his and Rosa's bedroom. After tossing his phone, wallet, and a copy of the cease-and-desist letter on the bed, he stripped. In the wardrobe, he located his hunting gear. He dressed for the field: white cotton leggings and long sleeve T-shirt topped with ScentBlocker pants and hooded jacket; thick socks and hiking boots finished the ensemble. He'd be prepared for any eventuality.

Butch opened the gun cabinet and caressed the barrel of his Savage III rifle. He'd bagged his first six-pointer with that gun, and he'd promised himself an upgrade with the profit from Brian's LightCube. "Fat chance of that happening now thanks to General fucking Swain."

He bypassed the rifle, pulled his Glock 9mm from its shaped-foam holder, and released the magazine. After tipping a box of fifty shells on the bed, he loaded fifteen into the mag and slipped it into his left breast pocket. The gun he tucked into his pants. Finally, he snugged Brian's JAG letter into his inside pocket. After locking the gun cabinet, he headed downstairs. Their ten-year-old Camry sat in the drive; he climbed in. The car was a piece of shit, but she started first time—another item he'd dreamed of replacing with the

LightCube windfall.

Before pulling out of the driveway, Butch glanced along the road in case his wife had followed. Clear. Good.

Rosa had the radio tuned to a country station, so he swiveled the dial until he heard AC/DC's "Problem Child." A smile creased his lips—perfect. Butch cranked the volume until the speakers fuzzed. In warrior-mode now, senses acute, reflexes sharp, he felt alive and in control of his own destiny for the first time since returning from the Sandbox. He drove through town, radio blasting, until he reached the golf course.

He parked in the visitor's lot and stashed the Glock and magazine in the glove box. This late in the evening, only a handful of vehicles remained. He made his way to the clubhouse, entering on the lower level through the pro shop. He shrugged off the stare he received from the soldier staffing the counter—Butch wasn't dressed for golf. Mostly officers played the course, but enlisted men were occasionally invited, or they could fill in a tee time when the reserved party failed to show. Another example of grunts forced to feed off officers' scraps.

Skirting past shelves of golf apparel and equipment, he slipped out the shop's rear door into the club. A long carpeted hallway led him to the officers' lounge. He stopped at the double doors and peered through the glass paneling. Only officers were permitted to enter.

But he didn't need to go in.

Swain was there. Sitting in a leather recliner in front of a crackling log fire. And sitting next to him, drinking liquor, was Doctor Wainwright.

Like a bullet racking into its chamber, everything clicked into place.

Wainwright.

The doctor had convinced Butch to spill his guts. Therapy he called it. Whatever they discussed was private and confidential—off the record, never to leave the surgery. But it had left. And it had walked into this room. That's how Swain heard of GameSoft and Brian's LightCube—over drinks with his golfing buddy.

Butch locked his jaw and ground his back teeth. His mission shone star-bright in his mind. Butch was to blame. He had shown weakness. He had trusted the doctor, trusted the military. Paul Cassidy's error of judgment had jeopardized his friends' and his family's last, best hope of financial independence from the US Army. The responsibility to put matters right rested on his shoulders.

From the corner of his eye, he saw a steward approaching. Butch nodded at the man and spun away. He'd seen enough. Retracing his steps to the car, he drove out of the club's main gate and parked in a side road with line-of-sight to the vehicular entrance. If the general headed home, he'd pass twenty yards from where Butch sat. If he had other plans, Butch could follow.

To preserve gas, he killed the engine. A half tank left and no money to buy more—no money for pills, no money for food, no money for an anniversary present. In July, he and Rosa would have been married three years. He'd placed a ring on layaway at the jewelers. White gold with a big, beautiful, princess-cut diamond to replace Rosa's tiny one-eighth carat—all they could afford when they got married. After Brian's project multiplied their money, the mother of his child would wear the ring her finger deserved.

Swain had taken that from him.

Butch was going to take it back.

Hunkered low, so the vehicle appeared empty, he waited.

At nine fifteen, Swain's Mercedes turned left out of the club. A streetlight illuminated the general's pinched face and bony nose as he passed. Butch's pulse quickened. Mission-buzz prickled his skin.

Showtime.

He started his engine but took a deep breath and slow-counted to five before shifting gear—he didn't want to show his hand. Not here. Not yet. He followed, half a click back, keeping Swain in sight but allowing other vehicles to occupy the space between. Three miles out of Fayetteville, the general slowed for his final turn onto a quiet country road, five miles from his home. When Butch rounded the corner, he was five hundred yards behind the Mercedes, so he floored the accelerator.

Swain had sped up, and Butch was doing eighty before the general's taillights grew larger and the gap between the two vehicles narrowed. *He's slowing.*

Camped on the black car's rear, when the right turn signal flashed and the Mercedes moved over to let Butch by, he yanked his wheel left and punched the gas, clipping the Mercedes's left rear bumper. The general's vehicle veered right toward the nearside grass verge. Swain over-corrected, and the car whipsawed left, slewed across the white line, and nose-dived into a ditch on the far side of the road.

Butch slammed on his brakes and skidded to a stop behind the crashed vehicle, illuminating it with his headlights. After a quick check behind at the empty road, Butch grabbed his weapon, slipped in the magazine, and climbed out.

Angled in a six-foot-deep levy, its nose buried in the soft bank, the Mercedes's rear wheels had left the road and continued to spin. Steam hissed in a cloud from under the hood.

The stalled engine ticked.

Butch slid the bolt on the Glock, loading the chamber. He clambered into the ditch and yanked open the front passenger door. Inside, surrounded by deflating airbags, Swain slumped over the steering wheel. Blood trickled from his forehead. With the gun tucked into the back of his pants, Butch leaned across the passenger seat. He dragged the unconscious general by his shirt collar over the center column and out of the vehicle.

The man reeked of liquor.

Fuckin' hypocrite!

Slipping and struggling for traction, Butch dug in his heels and backed the body up the ditch's steep grassy bank. Once he reached the road, he dumped the limp form onto the pavement like a sack of sand. Swain groaned. The sound triggered an animal response in Butch. He slammed the toe of his boot into the general's ribs and screamed, "Shut the fuck up!"

After pocketing the general's cell phone and wallet, Butch returned to the Toyota, unclipped Noe's car seat and stowed it in the front passenger side. Grabbing Swain's armpits, he backed into the Toyota, dragging the body into the rear until the general sprawled across the seat. Swain's nose twisted to the side, probably broken. Butch leaned over the man and clenched his fist. How he wanted to pummel that face, to turn it into mush. But this wasn't about him and what he wanted. This was about Rosa and Noe, about their future, about repairing the damage he'd done to his family and friends. With teeth gritted, he marshaled his self-control—no more mistakes. He had to stay on mission.

Butch closed the car doors and pulled away.

TWENTY-TWO

Brian left Sarah and Rosa staring along the road, hoping Butch would return. By the time they returned to the kitchen, Yaz and Mike were on their third beer. Sarah glanced at the crushed beer cans lying on the table, and her lips tensed into a tight, thin line. The men lowered their beers and stopped talking. Sarah glared at Mike who returned the look with interest. A tired cry came from the living room—Noe was awake. Rosa went to her son.

"Someone has to take Rosa home and check on Butch. It's turned cold out. She can't walk with the baby," Sarah said.

Mike pushed his chair back.

"No!" Sarah snapped the word out with venom, and Mike balled his fists. She softened her voice and said, "You're not used to the new pills yet. And you've been drinking." The glowering look Mike gave his wife churned Brian's stomach.

He wanted to escape before that battle escalated. "I can drop her. Yaz, you need a ride to the base."

"Yup, not cleared to drive yet—won't be long though; I've had hand controls fitted to my old Jeep."

Rosa returned, jiggling Noe over her shoulder.

Brian addressed Rosa, but spoke loud enough for all to hear, "No promises, but I'll speak to George, tell him you and Butch need cash and see if he knows anyone at Militec who might buy you out, okay?"

On the street, Brian cuddled Noe while Rosa folded the baby carriage and placed it in the trunk. The streetlights reflected in the boy's saucer eyes, dark brown like his momma's. Rosa slid into the rear, and Brian passed Noe to her. Yaz reversed his ass into the passenger seat and lifted in his prosthetic legs. "Gotta relearn everything."

Brian started the car. "You're doing great." He glanced at Rosa in the driver's mirror. She was smiling—the first time tonight. It transformed her face; in the dim light, with her baby in the crook of her arm, she reminded Brian of a Da Vinci painting of the Madonna and Child.

Although it was only four blocks, he drove with extreme caution because Noe wasn't secured in a safety seat. When they stopped outside Rosa's home, she pressed her face to the side window. "God damn it! The car's gone."

Brian popped the trunk. "I'll give you a hand."

Rosa carried Noe, and Brian wheeled the baby carriage while Yaz waited in the vehicle. Rosa opened the front door and stepped inside. "Leave Noe's things in the hall. I'll see to them later." She faced Brian and fixed him with a brave smile that failed to soften the strain in her eyes. "Thank you for helping. You're a good person."

Like a schoolboy with a crush, heat rushed to his cheeks. He fished a business card from his wallet. "Here. Call if I can help, okay?"

As she accepted the card, her eyes misted, and her chin trembled. He spun away and stepped out of the house to save her embarrassment. When she closed the door behind him, the temperature seemed to drop. Brian hugged himself and hurried to the car. Yaz had the heater blazing, and Brian blew into his hands before putting on his seat belt. "Damn freezing all of a sudden."

He checked the road—all clear—and drove off.

Yaz grabbed Brian's arm. "Wait! Rosa's forgotten something."

Brian pulled over and reversed. Rosa was running down the garden path, waving her arms. Yaz lowered the passenger window. "What's up?"

Rosa's voice was pitched high. "It's Butch," she said. "Something's wrong. He's... I don't know."

Brian climbed out. She grabbed his arm and pulled him toward the house. "Can you come?"

"Sure."

Behind, Yaz opened the passenger door and shouted, "Give me a hand, here." His legs were out of the vehicle; Brian backtracked and yanked him upright. Rosa ran up the path toward the house. Brian longed to chase after her but held back out of respect for Yaz's feelings.

Rosa waited halfway up the stairs. The baby carriage stood in the hallway where Brian had left it. Noe was standing up, screaming, and rocking back and forth, dangerously near the edge.

Yaz said, "You go up, Brian. I'll take care of this little tyke." He picked the boy up as though he were made of air and blew a raspberry on his cheek.

Rosa sprinted upstairs and Brian followed. He felt awkward being in Rosa's bedroom. It smelled of her perfume, musky but with a hint of citrus.

She pointed to the bed. "Look! What does it mean?" Next to a wallet and cell phone that Brian assumed belonged to Butch lay an open box of shells. Her hand trembled as she indicated the gun cabinet, glass-fronted and mounted on the wall by their dresser. "His Glock is missing."

"Does he usually take his gun when he goes out?"

"No. Never. And why leave his money and phone?"

"I—" More than anything, Brian wanted to help this beautiful, fragile woman, to relieve her fear and grief, ease her pain—to fix things for her. But he didn't know how. "Where would Butch go?"

"Before the DWI, he drank at The Blue Note."

"But why take the gun? And how will he buy a drink with no money?"

"Butch lost his license. He's not supposed to drive."

"Everything okay up there?" Yaz shouted.

Brian put a hand on her shoulder. "Let's go."

She took a step, but instead of passing by, swiveled into him, wrapped her arms around his waist, and grabbed the back of his shirt. As she laid her head against his chest, her body, so delicate and soft, shook with sobs. Brian hesitated, arms held out to the side. He was in another man's bedroom, with that man's wife, but she needed comfort. He wrapped her in his arms, pulled her closer. Anyway, Butch should be with his wife, not running around causing trouble.

When her crying eased and her breathing steadied, she pulled away and looked in his eyes. "Thank you, again." The sadness in her smile, pierced him like a stiletto.

Brian put an arm around her shoulders and moved her toward the stairs. "We'll find him. Yaz might know where to look."

"But you must return to Raleigh, no?"

Noe's shrieking giggles echoed through the house.

"Let me worry about that. Come on before Yaz steals Noe from you."

This time, the smile reached her eyes. "Okay." She led the way downstairs.

When Sarah turned around after closing the front door on her guests, Mike stood inches from her in the hallway.

"Never treat me that way in front of people again." He spat the words from behind clenched teeth. Raising his fist, he jammed it under her jaw and tilted her head back with a mean push.

When she tried to move past him, he blocked her, glaring with black eyes. Exhausted from the cycle of threatened violence, exhausted from tiptoeing around her husband, Sarah backed into the door, closed her eyes, and prayed for it to be over. Five faltering breaths later, his footsteps moved away. The fridge opened, and the top hissed off another beer.

Everything was up to her.

After checking on Daniel, she crept along the landing to her bedroom, turned off the light, and lay on the bed. Eyes closed, she focused on her breathing and tried to switch off, desperate for thirty minutes with no arguments, no violence, no shouting or criticism. Her life had telescoped down to this—a yearning for thirty minutes' peace.

Her phone rang and jolted her awake. She fumbled for the device and checked the screen—Rosa. Sarah noted the time; she had slept for twenty minutes. "Hi—"

Rosa launched into a rapid, panicked description of what she'd found in her bedroom. Sarah sat bolt upright. "Have Brian and Yaz found him?"

"Brian called. No one's seen him at The Blue Note. They're checked a few other bars."

"Butch ever taken the gun out with him before?"

"It's for the home. You know that."

"Maybe you should phone 911."

The line went silent. Rosa sucked in a shaky breath. "I can't call the police on my husband. Can you ask Mike if he knows where Butch is?"

Sarah's gut twisted and bile stung her throat. It had come to this. The thought of speaking to husband made her sick to the stomach. "I'll ask, but—"

"What? But what? What do you know?"

"Nothing." She sighed. "It's just… Mike's downstairs drinking. We had another argument."

"Sarah, please."

She swung her legs off the bed. "I'll speak to him and call right back."

In the bathroom, she washed her face and combed her hair. A worn woman looked back at her from the mirror. Stopping outside each of the boys' bedrooms on her way past, she listened. All quiet for Christopher. Daniel was watching TV. She crept downstairs, jaw clenching at every creak. The kitchen door was open, and she peered in. Mike sat at the table, face buried in his hands, sobbing.

Waves of love and sympathy washed through her. She whispered, "Heh, honey. It's me, don't get a fright, okay?"

He nodded, face still hidden. She moved behind him, wrapped her arms around his shoulders, and kissed his neck. "We'll beat this monster, Mike. Together, we'll beat it." Her words triggered a low, pained growl that rumbled through his back and sent shivers through her breasts.

This was the part of war they didn't tell you about—that your man might return scarred and broken, haunted by what he'd seen and been asked to do. She took a seat opposite him, peeled his hands away from his face, and whispered, "Mike we need to talk. Rosa called. Butch has gone AWOL with a loaded Glock. Any idea where he might be?"

Mike stared back at her with vacant eyes.

Did he even hear her words? She took a deep breath. "Come on. Let's get you to bed. Tomorrow's another day."

Once Mike was settled, Sarah made herself a cup of tea and called Rosa.

Rosa's phone rang. She snatched it up. "Butch?" She held her breath.

Sarah said, "It's me. No news, then?"

On exhale, Rosa sighed out her answer. "No. Nothing. What about Mike?"

"I asked. He hasn't a clue where Butch is, but he says if ammunition was on the bed, Butch wasn't thinking straight. Look,

Rosa, I'm your best friend, but there's no easy way to say this—Butch might be considering doing something stupid, like Mike almost did. I think you'd better call 911."

"I—" A sob caught in Rosa's throat and choked off her words.

Sarah said, "I can't leave the kids. Why not bring Noe over and sit with me."

"No. I need to be here for Butch. In case he comes home."

"Okay. Look, should I call 911 for you?"

"No. I'll do it."

"Promise you'll call me if you hear anything. I'm here for you, Rosa."

"I know." When the call ended, she stared at her phone. What if Butch had gone drinking again? If the police caught him driving with no license, they'd lock him up. How would Butch manage in prison, and without his medication? She pressed *talk* and stared at the phone's screen until it timed out. She should wait. Give him time. Maybe he needed space. But what if he was somewhere with the barrel of a gun in his mouth?

Rosa went upstairs to the nursery. Noe had kicked off his covers and lay sprawled on his back, legs and arms splayed, eyes closed, long dark lashes resting on his chubby cheeks. He had Butch's strong, square chin. She stooped and lifted him. He was a big boy, like his daddy, not yet eighteen months, but bursting out of age-two onesies. Holding him close, swaying side-to-side, she smelled baby powder and chocolate milk.

What if Noe loses his daddy because I didn't call? After easing him back into his crib and tucking in the covers, she crept downstairs and dialed 911.

Sarah settled in front of the TV. She needed a few minutes to unwind, but she left the living room door open in case Mike or the kids needed her. The drugs that got Mike through the day neutered him as a man. Before this last deployment, he would have tracked Butch down, looked out for his battle-buddy, taken charge. Not taken a nap.

When the house phone rang, Sarah jumped a mile, and her heart pumped and raced. She snatched up the handset. "Hello?" She hoped it was Rosa with news about Butch, but it was Brian.

"Did I wake you?"

"No, but Mike's sleeping. Hold on."

She closed the door with a quiet click. "Okay, I'm with you. What's up?"

"I shouldn't have called so late."

"Not a problem. Do you have news?"

"Sort of. On the drive home, I had time to think. After my meeting with Adam at GameSoft, I panicked. I should've engaged brain before charging to Fayetteville and worrying everyone. Anyway, I can't reach him now, but first thing tomorrow I'll contact George at Militec. He dealt with the JAGs in Washington before the VCOM project. I'm certain he can get this mess sorted out, and he's got twenty thousand reasons to act fast. I called to apologize and to let you know I had a plan."

"Thanks."

"Any sign of Butch?"

"No. Poor Rosa's beside herself. She's reported him missing, so now the police are searching for him too."

"Wow! Don't take this the wrong way—I mean regarding Mike, but I can't fathom what's happened with the guys. Well, Yaz seems himself, except the legs." The line went quiet for a few beats. "Gosh, I'm sorry. That was very insensitive of me."

She sighed. "S'all right. I understand what you mean. On the face of it, Yaz came off worst from the rocket attack—but maybe not."

"Meaning?"

"It's hard to explain."

"Look, Sarah. Tell me to butt out if you want, but I worked with Mike for three months, and I hung out with Butch and Yaz most nights in Camp Liberation. I consider them friends. I've seen them on duty and off, and they're conscientious and *really* good at what they do. Tonight, in the kitchen, I hardly recognized them. Well, obviously physically I did, but what I mean is, Butch and Mike aren't the same men I knew in Iraq."

"You've got that right."

"Can I help? Honestly, without the guys, I'd have gone nuts over there. Sorry, I didn't mean—" He sighed. "—I should hang up before I say anything else stupid."

Sarah understood Brian's good intentions, but how could he help with what Mike was suffering through when even his wife was at a loss? "Finish the LightCube and arrange a buyout for Rosa to relieve the financial pressure on her and Butch; that'll help more than you know."

"Like I said, I'm on it first thing in the morning."

A static hiss crackled on the line and amplified an uncomfortable pause. Sarah took a deep breath. Brian was a good man, and his concern was genuine. "You want to know why Butch and Mike seem different?"

"Uh huh."

"Best I can describe the problem is like this: The US military exists for one thing—to break and destroy an enemy. Life is easier for soldiers when they are in a war zone. Training kicks in. They run on adrenaline. Follow orders. Threats are met with instant and overwhelming force. Everyone knows what to do, how to react. They're primed to respond at all times. Does that make sense?"

"Hold on a sec, I'm just pulling into my apartment complex. Wait while I park."

Sarah heard his car's engine die in the background.

"Okay. Yes, I understand," Brian said. "I've seen that happen. Over there, they're either at zero—waiting—or at one hundred, ready to strike."

"Exactly. So when they return home, civilian life seems slow and mundane—no highs and lows, just a steady pace. But their instant-readiness training still operates. A car backfired outside the grocery store last week, and Mike dropped like a rock and took cover, rolled under an SUV and soaked his jeans in a big puddle. Over the years, Rosa and I have learned to cope until our men phase out of deployment mode. But this time is taking longer."

"How so?"

"We think something happened when the rocket exploded. Butch's doctor says he suffered a concussion. Mike was in the trailer too."

"I've heard of NFL players concussed after a big hit, but they always make next week's lineup. So how do they fix it?"

Sarah spat her words. "They don't!" She took a few breaths to calm herself. Brian was asking logical questions. Questions she'd asked herself, but coming from him, from his point of naivety, the questions flared her anger.

"But I thought Butch and Mike were taking medication," Brian said.

"Yeah, they get meds. But drugs don't cure, they just mask the symptoms."

"What will you do?"

She sighed again, exhausted by the conversation, by the circular futility of her life since Mike returned. "I wait, and I hope. The US Army's training programs are the best in the world. They take a man and turn him into a soldier, teach him to pull the trigger, to kill and move to the next target. But when that soldier comes home, the army has no boot camp to un-train him, to change him back into a civilian. Butch, for example. He was kicked out of the military because he's not deemed a *good piece of gear* anymore. The unit commander wants a full complement of battle-ready assets to fulfill his mission. Butch didn't match his commander's requirements, so he threw him away. That fixes the army's problem. Meanwhile, Rosa has to pick up the pieces."

The line went silent for a few beats until Brian said, "I'm ashamed to say my first response tonight after he rushed out of your house was to blame Butch for hurting Rosa. But this isn't Butch's fault, and yet he's the one who has to pay."

Sarah said, "Thanks for caring, Brian, but this isn't your problem."

"Well, in a way I feel it is. Look, I'll phone you tomorrow with good news I hope. And, Sarah, I'll do everything possible to get the project restarted."

"Thanks."

"If you hear from Butch, call me. No matter the time, okay?"

"I will."

Pete Barber

TWENTY-THREE

Butch drove the Toyota along the dark country road toward Swain's home. Through the open driver's window, he smelled rosemary and fresh-plowed earth. On his left, a lone bullfrog croaked. Heart rate elevated, senses heightened, battle thrill soaring, a smile crept across his lips. He'd missed this. Missed being alive. After four miles, he turned onto the asphalt drive leading to the general's McMansion. After parking at the front entrance, he climbed a set of six marble steps. Before ringing the doorbell, Butch slipped the Glock into his inside pocket, out of sight.

The hall light came on, filling the door's stained glass panels with color. "Who is it?" a woman asked. Her sharp, overloud voice masked a nervous undertone.

"Staff Sergeant Paul Cassidy, ma'am. I have the general with me. He's been in an automobile accident."

The locks turned, and she cracked the door, leaving the safety chain in place while she peered out. Butch saluted her. "General Swain is in the car, ma'am. He's injured." Butch skipped down the steps to the Toyota and opened the rear door. Behind him, the light increased as she opened the front door. He stepped away from the car, so she could see into the back seat.

Her hand jerked to her mouth. "Oh!" She opened the door, ran to the car, and stared at her husband's prostrate form. "What happened?"

"On my way home from a hunting trip, I spotted the general's car in a ditch a few miles along the road."

"Did you call the police?"

Butch cleared his throat. "The general has been drinking. I didn't think he'd want the police involved."

"Thank you, Sergeant. I understand. Let's get him inside? I'm sorry, your name again?"

"Sergeant Cassidy, ma'am." Butch grabbed Swain under his armpits and slid him from the back seat. "Can you take his feet?"

Dressed in a silky multicolored top and pale cream pants that did her ample figure no favors, her eyes narrowed and her mouth twisted as though disgusted by the thought. After a momentary hesitation, she grabbed the general's ankles, straining to keep the shoes away from her clothes.

Butch scanned her body and saw no evidence of a phone; the pants were too tight, the blouse too sheer. He reversed up the steps into a large, tiled lobby; she followed, supporting Swain's feet. Butch could have managed the bag of bones without assistance, but he wanted to keep her from calling 911.

"Is there anyone else here who can help?" he asked.

"No. It's just James and me." She gasped the words, breathing hard from the exertion of climbing six steps. Once she cleared the door, Butch dropped the general, cracking his head against the tiled floor. Still supporting her husband's legs, Mrs. Swain's mouth gaped as Butch whisked past her, closed, and secured the front door. When he pulled the Glock from his inside pocket, her eyes widened.

Butch motioned with the gun barrel. "What's your name?"

"What's the meaning of this?"

"No name. Okay."

"Are you crazy? Don't you know my husband's a general in the US Army?"

Butch grinned. "Oh, I *know* who he is and what he is." He scanned the lobby. White Italian tiles covered the floor. A long, sweeping staircase curved up one wall. "Nice place."

He read her eyes, saw her intention. She dropped the general's feet but had hardly moved before Butch was behind her—right arm around her chest pinning her arms, left hand pressing the gun under her chin. She squealed.

"Look. I don't give a damn about you, or your husband. So if you want to live, you'll listen and follow orders. Surely a general's wife knows how to follow orders." He screwed the barrel into her neck, hard enough to make her gasp. "Do we understand each other?"

She nodded.

"Good. Now, I'm sure this lovely home has a downstairs bathroom."

She nodded again.

"Where?"

"Farther along the hall."

"Okay. I'm going to let go, so you can grab his feet again. Try anything else and I'll hurt you."

"What do you want?" she croaked. "I have money upstairs. It's not much, but it's yours. Just leave us alone."

"Oh, I need money all right. Your husband made sure of that."

When he let her go, she spun and faced him, her voice filled with hope. "Let me get it for you. I have two hundred dollars in my purse." She took one step toward the stairs.

Butch pointed the gun and barked, "I won't say it again. Pick up his feet."

She did as she was told. "My name is Patricia," she whispered.

Butch grabbed the general's armpits, reversed across the lobby, and down the hallway. He passed the open bathroom door. "After you, Patricia."

She backed into the doorway, and Butch used the general to push her into the bathroom. Once inside, he dropped the general again.

"Stop doing that; he's hurt enough, you brute!"

Butch laughed. "You can't imagine what I'd *like* to do to him. But I need him alive. For now."

"Tell me. What? What do you want from him? I can get it for you."

"No, you can't."

In three seconds, he had surveyed his surroundings. The bathroom door had an ornate, brass knob with a traditional keyed lock below. "Where's the door key?"

"In the wall cabinet."

"Get it." When she opened the cabinet door, he glanced at the contents: aspirin, Band-Aids, no weapon. She handed him a large key.

"Now, Patricia. I'm going to leave you here. You have water to drink, a pot to piss in, and," Butch indicated the medical supplies in the cabinet, "if you give a shit, you can patch him up. Stay here. Stay quiet, and this will be over soon. But when he wakes, let him know Paul Cassidy has nothing to lose."

Tears filled her eyes. Her voice shook. "But what do you want?"

"That'll wait till morning."

169

Butch closed the bathroom door and turned the key. After closing window blinds and locking external doors, he opened the fridge. Ignoring a six-pack of beer, he grabbed a can of Coke and took it into the living room. With the TV on low, he settled on the sofa. Sergeant Cassidy was on a mission; it would be a long night.

At ten thirty p.m., Officer Justin Yule and his partner Officer Mason Parkes pulled to the side of County Road 197, twenty yards past the scene of a motor vehicle accident. They were responding to a call made by a passing motorist. The black car lay nose down in a ditch. The passenger door was ajar, and the headlights illuminated the thick grass of the verge. Officer Yule climbed into the ditch and played his flashlight inside the vehicle. The Mercedes was empty. He leaned into the cab and sniffed. The car stunk of liquor. Blood splatters had dried on the dashboard and on the deflated airbags.

He shouted to his partner, waiting by the police cruiser, "Car's empty. Smells like a honky-tonk. Someone's hurt though. Call in the registration. I'll check the road in case the driver got disoriented and wandered off."

A search of the ditches one hundred yards either side of the accident drew a blank. When Officer Yule returned to the squad car, his partner had the ownership details on his computer screen. "Registered to Brigadier General James Swain. He lives four miles north of here."

"Think he could have walked home?"

"Who knows. No one's reported him missing though. Let's pay a visit."

The police officers drove to Swains' house and rolled up his driveway, stopping behind a rusty Toyota with a bent rear fender and a cracked taillight. The old vehicle looked out of place parked in front of a three-quarter-million-dollar home. Officer Parkes punched the vehicle's registration into his computer and picked up a missing person's report for Sergeant Paul Cassidy. "His wife called the station thirty minutes ago—Iraq veteran. He's armed, and he's been off his meds for a few days. She's worried about his mental stability, potentially suicidal."

"Maybe he was a Good Samaritan, saw the accident, and gave

the general a ride home," Officer Yule said.

"Hmph. If he did, he's driving on a revoked license—DWI three months ago."

"Let's see who's in." Both officers climbed from the vehicle. Parkes remained next to the squad car. Gun drawn, legs braced, he focused on the front door, covering his partner. Yule went up the steps and rang the bell. Westminster chimes sounded from the hallway.

When the doorbell chimed, Butch sprang to his feet and checked the time—eleven twenty p.m. The bell sounded again. At the front window, he eased back the curtain enough to snatch a glimpse of a squad car in the driveway, parked behind his Toyota.

Damn it—should have moved the car.

"Help! We're being held against our will. Help!" Patricia Swain's voice, high-pitched and demanding, made the hairs on Butch's arms prickle to attention. Standing in the living room doorway, Glock hanging by his side, he listened, head withdrawn in case the cop peeked through the stained-glass vanity panels either side of the front door. The bathroom door muffled her voice. But would it carry outside?

"Help! Help!"

If he shouted for her to shut up, the cop would hear him. And he'd be seen if he crossed the hallway.

Mrs. Swain continued to yell, but the bell didn't ring again. A couple minutes passed. Butch heard a radio exchange outside, too distant to make out content. He edged back the curtain and peeked out again. One cop was shining a flashlight into the Toyota.

The other, sitting in the squad car with a mic pressed to his lips, locked eyes with Butch. He jerked away from the window.

Shit!

The house phone rang—a shrill and ominous sound that echoed through the empty hallway.

"Help us! Help!" Swain's wife elevated her screams.

Butch ground his teeth, willing her to shut up. No matter. The authorities would work out what was happening soon enough anyway.

With the police officers busy in the driveway, Butch dashed

across the hallway and pounded up the stairs. In the first bedroom, he peeled back the comforter and yanked the top sheet from the bed. A glance out the window showed both cops still occupied. He ran downstairs and into the kitchen, carrying the bunched sheet under his arm. In a drawer, he found a roll of duct tape and a box of pushpins. *Those'll do nicely.*

TWENTY-FOUR

At five after midnight, Rosa's doorbell rang. She sprang to her feet.

Thank God!

She ran from the living room, along the hallway, and yanked open the front door. Two police officers, a man and a woman, stood on the doorstep. "Mrs. Cassidy?" A gust of wind swirled into the hall and raised goosebumps on Rosa's bare arms.

"Yes. I'm Mrs. Cassidy. Have you found my husband?"

"Has he contacted you since you reported him missing?"

His brusque tone sent a shiver of dread through her. She looked from one officer to the other, seeking a clue in their eyes. Why ask that question? Their flat, noncommittal faces turned her fear to anger. "I called *you*, remember? I told the desk sergeant I didn't know where he was. If I'd heard from him, I'd have phoned the station. This isn't a game. I'm worried sick!"

The policeman held up his palm. "Calm down, please, Mrs. Cassidy. I'm just checking."

She reached out, grabbed his sleeve, and shook his arm. "Why are you here? Why not phone to ask whether I'd seen him?"

He turned to the policewoman, raised his eyebrows. A look passed between them. "We've found his car," she said.

Rosa tightened her grip. Something was going on. Something they weren't telling her. "Is he hurt?"

"May we come in?"

Rosa released the officer's arm and backed into the hall. "Keep quiet; the baby's sleeping." She led them into the living room. The policewoman's eyes scanned the home as though taking an inventory. Was she looking for Butch? Didn't they believe he was missing?

"Take a seat." She pointed to the couch.

The officers sat together on the sofa while Rosa perched on the edge of a recliner, opposite them.

"Mrs. Cassidy—"

"Rosa."

He smiled. "Rosa, do you have any idea where Mr. Cassidy might have gone?"

His condescending tone irked her, but she checked her temper—for Butch's sake. "No. My friends checked The Blue Note and a few bars along Main Street, but Butch hasn't had a drink since... since his DWI."

"When did you last see him?" the woman asked.

"Seven thirty-ish. We were at a friend's house when he lost his temper and stormed out. I didn't follow, figured I'd let him cool off. When I got home, the car was missing. So was Butch."

"Why was he angry?"

Rosa looked from one to the other. She didn't want to tell them her business, but what else could she do. They'd find out eventually. "He was fired yesterday."

The policewoman glanced at her partner. "We thought he was a sergeant in the army."

"He was. Because of the DWI, they Chapter Fourteened him."

"Chapter Fourteen?"

"Dishonorable discharge."

"Because of a first-offense DWI?" The policewoman shook her head. "That can't be all."

Tears welled in Rosa's eyes. After a couple deep breaths, she said, "That's all it takes for them to throw a good soldier away."

The policeman shook his head. "I'm sorry," he said, and sounded it. "Rosa, why might Butch visit—" He pulled a small notepad from his inside pocket and flipped a couple pages. "— Brigadier General James Swain?"

Rosa jerked back in her seat as though the man had connected with an uppercut. "He's with Swain?"

"Well, that's what we're trying to discover. His car is parked in the general's driveway. Butch may be inside the house. But no one is answering the door or the phone. What do *you* think is happening?"

Finally, the tears won, and they spilled down her cheeks. Rosa wiped them with her sleeve. What had her man done? She sucked in a faltering breath and on the exhale said, "Swain signed Butch's discharge papers."

The police officer sprang to his feet and nodded toward his partner. "Marion will stay with you. In case your husband shows up."

"Where are you going?"

Marion looked at her partner and gave a small shake of her head. The policeman cleared his throat and said, "I'll update you when we have more information."

Rosa stood. "You're going after him, aren't you?"

He stopped at the door and said, "Mrs. Cassidy, you need to stay here and leave us to handle this."

"The hell I will."

He froze. The policewoman got to her feet, stepped forward, and laid a hand on Rosa's arm. "It's for the best," she said in a soft voice. "Look, we don't know whether your husband is at the general's home, just that his car is parked in the driveway. While my partner finds out what's going on, I'll keep you company."

Rosa yanked her arm from the policewoman and leaned in, so their faces were inches apart. "Am I under arrest?" She spat the words.

"No, of course not."

"Well then, you need to leave my home. Now!"

Rosa hustled them out, ignoring their protests. When they left, she stood for a few seconds, her back against the front door, trying to focus. Butch was at Swain's house; she knew it and so did the cops, but surely he wouldn't shoot anyone. Foggy confusion swirled around her head.

Think. Plan.

First, get Noe situated. Then, go to Butch. But he had the Toyota. She needed a car.

She called Sarah and told her about the police visit. "I have to take Noe to my mom's. Then I'm going to Swain's home. I don't know what Butch is planning, but I'm afraid for him. He believes he's lost everything. The LightCube was his lifeline. He told me so before we came over this evening. Then Brian brought the letter, and now Butch feels he's painted into a corner. I've been too hard on him. It's my fault, and I have to make it right. I have to let him know we're going to be okay. I know it's a big ask, but I need to borrow your car."

Sarah's response was instantaneous. "No chance. But I will drive you."

"What about Mike."

"He's got a belly full of Ambien—out for the count. I'll leave a note for Daniel. He'll take care of Christopher if he should wake. Poor kid is getting used to being the man in our house. We'll drop Noe off at your mom's on the way."

"This isn't your problem, Sarah."

"Look, Rosa. Next week or next month or next year, Mike might bring home a Chapter Fourteen, and I'll sure as hell want you by my side when that happens."

Rosa choked back the lump in her throat and whispered, "Thank you." She hung up and called her mother, woke her. "I have to bring Noe over. I'll be there in twenty minutes. No, I'm fine, Mom. Yes, so is Noe, but Butch has gone missing." She rocked from foot to foot, desperate to get moving, to take action, but her mom kept firing questions. Rosa ended the call with her mother in mid-sentence and charged up the stairs to get her son. He woke, but barely. By the time she got him ready and downstairs, the headlights of Sarah's car lit her hallway.

Sarah leaned across and opened the rear passenger door. "Christopher's child seat is too big. Sit in back and hold him."

Rosa slid in and closed the door, cradling her son.

"Thanks, Sarah," she whispered.

"Let's save the discussion till we've dropped him off. Okay?"

"Okay."

Rosa's mom lived on the other side of Fayetteville, a ten-minute drive. Sarah stayed in the car while Rosa carried Noe up the front path. Her mother opened the door dressed in a fluffy pink housecoat, hair in curlers. Rosa handed over her son as though he were a hot potato. Her mom was still asking questions when Rosa climbed into the passenger seat.

"Ready?" Sarah asked, glancing at Rosa's mom, standing on the doorstep, eyes wide and mouth open, Noe in her arms.

"Go."

"Where to?"

"General Swain's home, but I don't know where it is."

Sarah drove around the corner, out of sight of Rosa's mom, before pulling to the side of the road. She searched Swain's name on her smart phone, his address popped up, and she punched it into the GPS.

"Okay, we're on our way, twenty minutes. Now talk. What's happening?"

"They found Butch's car parked at Swain's home."

"Oh?"

"The police think he's inside, but he won't answer the door or the phone. When I told them Swain had signed the Chapter Fourteen, they panicked."

"Could Butch hurt Swain, d'ya think?"

"Maybe. Since he stopped taking his meds last week, he's been on edge. The slightest noise triggers him. Two nights ago, I woke at three in the morning, and he was standing flat against the bedroom wall in his jockeys, peering out the window with a baseball bat in his hand. I didn't speak in case I set him off. He stood there for an hour before coming back to bed. I don't think he's slept much since."

Sarah nodded, but didn't ask what Rosa planned to do about Butch's behavior. No point. There was nothing *to* do. This was their new normal. Mike suffered the same night terrors. Drugs dulled the effects, but the soldiers were programmed to respond to a perceived threat. All it took was a bump or a creak, and they *knew* the bad guys were waiting around the corner. "What will you do when we get to Swain's place?"

Rosa shook her head. When she spoke, her voice cracked. "I don't know. Butch despises Swain. I'm worried he's planning something very bad. If I can speak to him, maybe I can persuade him to give it up before it's too late."

A few miles from their destination, Sarah slowed. Ahead, two police cruisers blocked her lane. Between them was a black sedan stuck in a ditch. One officer waved a flashlight and pulled them over. He checked Sarah's license and registration and sent her on her way.

"Wonder whether anyone was hurt," Rosa said.

They drove on. Rosa called out mailbox numbers until the GPS told them the house was coming up on the right. She turned in to the driveway and jammed on her brakes. A police cruiser parked diagonally across the road blocked their path. A uniformed officer climbed out and approached. Sarah lowered the window.

"May I help you?" he asked.

Sarah looked across at Rosa who bent low to see the man's face. She shouted, "I'm Rosa Cassidy, Sergeant Paul Cassidy's wife. The Fayetteville police told me he was here."

The officer played his flashlight inside the vehicle. He asked for identification, and they surrendered their driver's licenses. "Wait here." He strode back to his car.

Silence settled. Sarah glanced at Rosa—sunken cheeks, pale skin. The fingers of her left hand, balancing on the center console, trembled. Sarah reached out, grabbed Rosa's hand, and squeezed. "It'll be okay, you'll see."

Rosa nodded to the windshield. The police officer was returning.

"Looks like we're about to find out."

TWENTY-FIVE

At one thirty a.m., Butch peeked out the living room window. Four squad cars blocked the driveway, positioned in an arc around his Toyota. In the center of the lawn, a white van with a satellite dish mounted on the roof sat broadside to the house. Two sets of spotlights, raised on poles and powered by a generator, lit the front of the home. Dozens of police officers huddled in groups, keeping their vehicles between them and the house. These assets were in addition to two black vans that had parked in the backyard.

Butch had secured the bed sheet to the front door frame with pushpins, draping the glass panels so he could move unobserved across the hallway. The police had arrived faster than he expected, but it didn't matter. Only the mission mattered.

The house phone rang again; they'd been calling every ten minutes. At least Patricia Swain had quit screaming for help every time the ringer sounded. Butch checked the kitchen one last time. The rear door was triple locked, including a sturdy deadbolt. He'd lodged a chair beneath the knob for additional safety. On a solo mission, the rear was his blind spot. The authorities had made a show of strength out front, but if it came to forced entry, they'd probably come through the kitchen.

Butch picked up the phone.

A man spoke in an easy Southern drawl, his voice even, his words clearly articulated. Butch smiled, recalling the hostage-training program he'd completed before his second deployment. Ironically, during the role-play, his team chose him as lead negotiator because of his Southern accent. He'd loved that course, planned to apply to the police force once he retired from the army—ha! The leader's primary objective was—don't spook the hostage taker. "I'm Captain Manny Marshall of the Fayetteville police department. Am I speaking with Sergeant Paul Cassidy?"

Butch let the words hang for a few seconds and listened to the captain's breathing. No nerves showed, but he'd be ticking like a time bomb—the first couple minutes were critical. Butch had never felt calmer. He was negotiating for his family and his friends. The poor choices he'd made since returning from Iraq had negatively affected everyone he loved. It was time to man up and make a positive contribution.

"This is Paul Cassidy," he said.

"Sergeant Cassidy, I'm here to listen to you and make sure everybody stays safe."

"Not Sergeant anymore, Captain. Thanks to General Swain, as of today, I'm back on the block, just a nasty civilian. Call me Butch?"

"Thank you for clarifying that, Butch. I'm Manny. First off, we saw blood in your car. Are the general and his wife okay? Does anyone need medical attention?"

Nice touch. Getting a headcount confirmation under the guise of concern.

"The general had a fender bender. I pulled him from the car. He's banged up—nothing serious. Mrs. Swain is looking after him."

"Good to know. And you, Butch. Are you okay?"

"Everyone's fine."

"So no one's hurt, and you may have saved the general from lying in a ditch half the night. That's admirable work."

Butch smiled. Manny was complimenting him, gaining his trust, minimizing the seriousness of the situation—hostage negotiating 101. Time to up the ante. "Manny, can we cut to the chase, now?"

The line went quiet. He waited a five count for the captain to speak. Butch wanted to retain control of the conversation.

"I'm listening," Manny said.

"I want one thing from you. As soon as I get it, Patricia Swain can take her shit-bag husband to the hospital and have his broken nose straightened."

"Butch, you said he was okay. If his nose is broken, we should get him to a doctor." Manny articulated concern, but his even, controlled cadence never wavered.

Butch snapped, "Call back when you've got a better answer," and hung up the phone.

<><><>

When the police officer reached Sarah's car, he bent his knees until his face was level with her open driver's window. He handed back the licenses. "Ladies, I will pull to the verge. You can move on through. Another officer will meet you farther along the drive."

Rosa leaned across Sarah, rested one hand on the steering wheel, one on Sarah's thigh. "Is my Butch here?"

He screwed up his face as though the response would be painful. "I'm not at liberty to say. Please drive on and speak with the other officer." He stood, double-tapped the car's roof, then climbed in his vehicle and pulled over.

"What the hell's going on?" Rosa asked.

"Guess we'll find out soon enough." Sarah shifted into drive and rolled by the police car.

Rosa stared at the police officer as they passed his car. "Why wouldn't he tell me about Butch?"

They rounded the curve in the driveway and saw dozens of police cars parked on the lawn and surrounding Butch's Toyota. Rosa let out a squeak. Her hand shot to her mouth.

Sarah said, "I don't think they'd have invited us to the party if Butch wasn't here. Do you?"

Rosa began to sob. Sarah put one hand on her friend's shoulder as she guided the car toward a tall man waving them down with a flashlight. He wore an orange Day-Glo vest with SWAT emblazoned on his chest. Sarah leaned out the driver's window.

"Ms. Cassidy?" he asked.

She pointed to Rosa. "This is Mrs. Cassidy."

"And you are?"

"A friend. Where's her husband?"

"Please pull to the side of the driveway, exit the vehicle, and follow me."

Sarah snapped, "Look, my friend's upset. Where's her husband?"

His face fixed into a mask. He braced his legs and spoke in a firm voice, a voice used to giving commands. "No need to get angry, ma'am. Do as I asked, and I'll take you to someone who can answer that question." He tilted his head. "Please."

Sarah tapped Rosa's arm. "Come on." After parking on the lawn twenty yards behind the line of police cars, they climbed out. Rosa, hunched over, shuffled around the car hood. Sarah moved to her, looped an arm over her friend's shoulders, and pulled her close.

They followed the SWAT guy. Rosa, staring at the ground, saw nothing, but Sarah took it all in. The Swain's front lawn resembled a movie set crammed with extras dressed in police uniforms. But what sent Sarah's pulse racing was a man in black coveralls flat on his belly on top of a jeep, peering through the telescopic lens of a sniper's rifle balanced on a tripod and trained on the house's front window. Sarah moved her hand up Rosa's neck, making sure she kept her head low.

SWAT guy stopped at a white panel van, opened the rear door, and made a "go in" gesture. Sarah slid her fingers down her friend's back and took her hand, maintaining contact. She leaned close and whispered, "Stay calm, Rosa. I've got your six. Let's go find Butch."

The van swayed as they climbed four steps. Banks of electronics crowded the far end of the vehicle, but the first twelve feet was open space. A folding table set against the left sidewall had a large, old-fashioned speakerphone in the center. Three picnic chairs facing each other sat centrally. A broad-shouldered, white-haired man stepped forward and offered his hand. Sarah checked Rosa: cheeks pale and drawn, eyes vacant—in shock. She gave her friend's fingers a squeeze and with her free hand executed a clumsy handshake with White-hair.

"Captain Manny Marshall," he said, and dipped his head. "Fayetteville police."

Rosa reminded Sarah of a child who'd lost her mother, displaced, confused, terrified. Sarah empathized. Rosa was a good friend and as strong as the next army spouse, but this whole performance meant bad news for her husband. Sarah would have been scared witless if Mike were barricaded in a house surrounded by this three-ring circus. These people couldn't understand what Butch was going through. How come the authorities didn't leverage this much support to *help* their veterans? Why were these resources only expended against them? Sarah stepped forward, maintaining her grip on Rosa's hand, not easing up.

"I'm Sarah Braeman, Rosa's best friend. We're in this together. Where's Butch?"

Manny nodded, gave her a knowing smile. "May I call you Sarah?"

The calculated control in his voice chafed like gravels in her sock. She straightened. He had twelve inches on her, but right then and there, she'd have taken him on and not stopped till it was over. "You can call me Mrs. Braeman. Now answer my question, or my friend and I are out of here in three seconds." She glared at him, at his face filled with condescension, and boiled inside but didn't blink.

He remained silent.

"Three... Two... One." She took a step toward the door.

Manny raised his hand. His expression changed, became serious. "Mrs. Braeman. I get that you're angry, but I'm just doing my job."

"Yeah, well, Rosa and me are army wives and we're doing ours. Where's her husband?" Still focused laser-like on the big policeman, she waited three beats of her pounding heart before pulling Rosa's hand again, turning her this time. "Come on, Rosa. We're wasting our time here."

"He's in the house."

Sarah stopped, looked back.

For the first time since they'd entered the van, Rosa lifted her head. She pulled Sarah's hand, continuing for the door. "I need to go to him."

Manny stared at Sarah, widened his eyes. "That's not possible, Mrs. Cassidy."

She whipped around and faced him. "He's my husband. He needs me."

"What's he done wrong?" Sarah asked.

"Nothing much, I hope. But I'm not sure."

Rosa dragged Sarah to the exit, but the guy in the SWAT jacket blocked the way.

"Ladies, please," Manny said. "I can't allow you in the home. It's a crime scene."

Sarah snapped back, "You said Butch hadn't done anything wrong. What crime?"

Manny sighed. "Look, if you want to help Butch, and I think you can, please sit." He tapped the backs of two chairs. "Please."

Rosa glanced at Sarah who nodded and said, "If it'll help Butch."

"I think it will," Manny said.

They sat, facing the police officer.

"Thank you," he said. "Here's what we know: Butch is holding General Swain and his wife hostage in the house."

Rosa sprang to her feet. "I have to go to him."

"Mrs. Cassidy. Hear me out. Please." He pointed to the chair and waited until Rosa sat before continuing, "According to *your* police report, Mrs. Cassidy, Butch is armed. And we just learned he was discharged from the army yesterday, and that General Swain, as company commander, was instrumental in that act."

Rosa said, "Just learned. From?"

"From Butch. I spoke to him by phone moments before you arrived."

"Is he okay?" Rosa asked.

"He told me everyone is okay, although the general's car was involved in an accident earlier this evening."

"That was his Mercedes in the ditch." Sarah said.

"Yes. And we found blood in the rear seat of Butch's Toyota. Butch pulled him from the wreck and brought him here."

"Then he's a hero. Not a criminal," Sarah said.

"We don't have enough information to make that deduction."

Sarah fixed him with a hard stare. Captain Manny Marshall was easy to dislike. "So how will you get *more* information?"

Manny shook his head. "Mrs. Braeman. I'm not the enemy here. All I want is Mr. Cassidy and his hostages safely out of that house."

"And how will you achieve that?"

"I was about to call Butch when I heard you'd arrived."

Rosa's head popped up. "Let me speak with him?"

Manny held up his palm for silence. "Butch told me there's something he wants before he'll release the Swains. What is it? What does he want?"

Rosa's mouth gaped. She looked at Sarah, then back at Manny. "How would I know?"

"You may not. I'm just trying to learn as much as possible before I speak with Butch again. Understand this, once an HT makes demands, his situation changes."

"HT. What's an HT?" Sarah asked.

"Hostage taker."

Sarah pursed her lips. Damn these men and their clever acronyms and stupid ego games. "So what happens if Butch makes a demand?"

"Well, he's guilty of extortion for one, and maybe worse,

depending on what he asks for. If I knew ahead of time, I could help him more. That's all I want to do."

Open-mouthed, face blank, Rosa stared at Sarah.

"Mrs. Cassidy," Manny said. "Are you sure you don't know what Butch wants? Help me to help him."

Rosa shook her head; tears spilled down her cheeks. "No" caught in her throat.

Manny stared hard at her for a few seconds. As Sarah was about to say something to support her friend, the captain said, "Okay, I'll call Butch now, but I need your word. Both of you." He glared at Sarah. "That you'll remain silent unless I ask you to speak. Mrs. Cassidy, I know you want to help your husband. So do I. Let's do it together, okay?"

Rosa wiped her eyes with the back of her hand, and whispered, "Okay."

"I'll put Butch on speaker. As soon as you understand what he wants, signal me. Then we'll work together to get him out of this mess. But allow me to do my job. I'm a specialist hostage negotiator. I know what I'm doing." He softened his voice and leaned in. "Look, I served eight years as a marine. I did two tours of duty in Iraq. I'm on Butch's side. Let me take the lead, understood?"

Manny slid his chair across to the table, put on a headset, and flicked a switch. The women watched him from the middle of the van. A dial tone came from a set of speakers embedded somewhere above Sarah's head. When Butch answered, Manny said, "I'm sorry for the delay, Butch; we've had a few technical issues. Is everyone in the home still okay?"

"Yes."

At the sound of Butch's voice, Rosa cracked. With her face buried in her hands, faltering sobs shook her body. Sarah rubbed her friend's back and stretched her jaw, clearing her ears, straining for any clue to help Butch.

"Butch, you wanted to tell me something."

"It involves a business venture myself and my friends are invested in."

"Go on."

"We've received a cease-and-desist letter from the JAGs at Fort Black."

"Okay. I'm with you so far."

Sarah's hand shot up like a schoolgirl with the right answer.

"I—"

"Butch, hold that thought. I hate to do this, but I need a couple more minutes to fix a glitch in my audio. Wait by the phone. I'll call right back." He hung up, pulled off the headset, and locked eyes with Sarah. "Explain," he said. "Fast."

Sarah explained the demand Brian had received from the JAGs.

"But you say this letter was sent in error."

"Yes, Brian Matthews, our business partner, owns the software code, and an original version is in escrow with the JAGs in Washington."

"How is General Swain involved?"

"Butch thinks Swain triggered the letter."

"And what do you think?"

"I think he's right."

"Okay." Manny waved to the man guarding the door. "Charlton, get contact information for Brian Matthews from Mrs. Braeman. Get him on the phone. Find out who we need in Washington. Wake them up. Let's get this demand met before Butch makes it."

Manny pulled on his headset and called Butch again. This time he left the speaker off.

TWENTY-SIX

Butch slammed his fist against the living room wall. A framed picture of James and Patricia Swain and their two grown children rattled but held. Why would Manny treat him this way—push his buttons, test his resolve? The tactic went against every tenet of hostage negotiation. Why was the man stalling? Were they planning a forced entry? A last resort, according to Butch's training. Perhaps procedures had been updated. But that made no sense. First priority—keep the hostages safe. He strode through the hallway, stopped at the kitchen door, and peered around the corner. The SWAT vehicles hadn't moved. The drivers remained at the wheels. In the rear of each van, he knew, an assault team waited, primed and ready.

The phone rang. He rushed back to the living room and snatched up the handset.

"What the hell are you playing at?"

"Stay calm, Butch. I'm doing my job, trying to get you out of this situation with minimum collateral damage. Your wife and her friend, Sarah, just arrived."

Butch's knees buckled. He leaned against the wall for support.

"Butch? You still with me?"

"I'm here."

"Good. Now listen carefully. Before you make any demands, before you take that step and make things worse, let me update you. As we speak, my number-two is on the phone to Washington. He will track down whom ever he needs in the Justice Attorney General's office and make sure they contact the JAGs in Fort Black tonight and get the cease-and-desist letter rescinded."

"How—"

"Doesn't matter. I'm going to hang up and give you two minutes to think things through. But Butch, consider this. Where we're at right now is the best your situation can get. So far as I'm

187

concerned, you rescued General Swain after his car was in a fender bender and brought him home. If the letter is your only issue, it's being handled. Any further demands or threats you make will stack the odds against you. Think carefully. The choice is yours. I'll call in two minutes."

The line went dead.

Butch replaced the phone. A smile crept across his face and he shook his head. Maybe if he'd stopped the damned meds sooner, his life wouldn't be in the shitter. No doubting it, everything had improved since he regained his warrior edge. Manny's response was unexpected, but change was the only guarantee in a conflict. All he had to do was roll with it.

Two minutes later, the house phone rang.

"Butch," Manny said. "Talk to me."

"Is Rosa there?"

"Yes. She's here."

"May I speak with her?"

"That can be arranged. But Butch, we're working our butts off for you. How can I be sure you aren't wasting our time?"

Quid pro quo. "Stand by." Butch hung up the phone and headed to the bathroom. He turned the key in the lock and jerked the door open. Patricia Swain perched on the edge of the bath. She had propped her husband against the side of the tub. Bloody washrags soaked in the sink. The general didn't move, but his wife sprang to her feet and in two strides she was on him. Before he could react, she slapped his face. "You bastard. Let us out of here. James needs a doctor. He's lost a lot of blood, and you've broken his nose."

As she swung a second time, he grabbed her hand, stopped the blow, and used her momentum to pull her out of the bathroom. From behind, with one arm around her waist, he lifted her like a child—a kicking, screaming child. He booted the door shut and turned the key in the lock.

"Let. Me. Go," she hissed.

Butch released the body-hold and stood her up. Maintaining his grip on her wrist, he whipped her around, so she faced him. "Listen. Listen good."

She bared her teeth, preparing to scream, but whatever she saw in his eyes changed her mind. Fear displaced anger. When he lifted his hand for silence, she winced, expecting a blow. But she shut her mouth.

"You ready to listen?"

She nodded.

"Good. God knows he deserves it, but I'm not going to harm your husband. I'm going to open that." He pointed to the front door. "And you'll walk out." She opened her mouth to speak. He touched his finger to his lips, and she fell silent.

"Keep your hands high in the air so they don't shoot you. Understand?"

Her eyes widened. She nodded.

He pulled the copy of Brian's letter from his inside pocket and handed it to her. "Ask for Manny. Give him this. Tell him what happened here, no embellishments because he'll check the details with me. Got it?"

She grabbed his arm. "What about James?"

"Manny is getting something for me from Washington. When he has it, I'll leave your home, and the doctors can take care of James. Are we clear?"

"Why should I trust you after what you've done to us?"

Butch pried her fingers from his forearm. "Lady, you have no idea what I'd like to do to your husband. But I won't. Don't worry about me. Worry about getting that letter from Washington. Come on." He led her along the hall, threw the locks, and slipped the safety chain. Butch stood behind the door, shielded, with Patricia Swain to his side, so she'd be visible as the door opened.

As he turned the latch, she put her hand against the door and stopped him. Looking deep into his eyes, her voice cracked when she said, "Don't hurt my husband."

"Ma'am, until yesterday I was a US Army Sergeant. I'm proud of my country and of my service. I could never knowingly harm a fellow American."

Butch eased the door back. "Hands up."

She reached high and stepped outside. He slammed the door behind her and threw the locks.

Sitting beside Rosa, Sarah stared past Manny's shoulder at the TV monitors next to the phone. The policeman straightened and spoke into his headset. "The front door's opening. Pearson, take no action unless instructed by me!"

189

"Roger that."

The clipped response echoed in the van. Manny flicked a switch to turn off the speaker. Sarah wondered whether Pearson was the sharpshooter she'd seen when they arrived. The image of that man's rifle trained on the front of the home raked icy fingers down her back; she shivered. Rosa leaned closer to the screen, blinking tears from her eyes. She whispered, "Is it Butch?"

Someone stepped onto the front doorstep and the door slammed behind her.

"It's a woman," Sarah said.

Manny spoke into his mic. "Hold your positions." Then he flicked a switch, and his voice issued from speakers mounted outside the van. "Ma'am. If you're able, please walk toward the white van."

The woman, arms raised high, made her way down the steps. When she reached the driveway, she broke into a run. A uniformed officer emerged from behind the row of squad cars and met her at the front lawn. He wrapped her shoulders with a gray blanket and put his arm around her so they blended into one large shape. In a couple strides, they slipped out of camera shot.

Manny pushed his chair back, stood, and smoothed his shirt. The van door opened and the policeman Sarah had seen on the monitor guided the woman up the steps.

"Mrs. Patricia Swain," the officer said.

Rosa sprang up and elbowed past Manny. "Butch is my husband. Is he all right?"

Sarah stood behind Rosa and gripped her friend's shoulders aware that this woman wouldn't give a damn for Butch's wellbeing. Patricia Swain glared at Rosa and screamed, "That man's a lunatic. He's beaten my husband, broken his nose. He locked us in the bathroom without a thought for James's injuries." She rotated her head, assessing the van's occupants, and locked eyes with Manny. "Are you in charge here?"

"Yes, ma'am." He offered his hand. "Captain Manny Marshall. Fayetteville police."

Patricia Swain ignored the captain's proffered hand. A short snort of derision escaped her nose, which she angled up as though Manny smelled unpleasant. "Well, Captain, what the hell are you waiting for? Go and rescue my husband."

Manny made calming signals with his hands. "Yes, Mrs. Swain, we will, but first I need to understand what we're dealing with."

"You're dealing with a lunatic is what. A madman. A savage."

Rosa squirmed from Sarah's grip and invaded Patricia Swain's personal space. When their faces were inches apart, Rosa shouted, "If Butch is a savage, your no-good husband made him that way. After ten years' unblemished service, he tossed my man away like a piece of lint on his dress-blues, and—" Rosa's voice broke. She grabbed a fistful of Patricia Swain's blouse in her right hand and pressed her case, shaking the woman with each word: "Tell me. Tell me now! Is... he... hurt?"

Sarah grabbed her friend's arm and pulled. "C'mon, Rosa. Let Manny handle this. It'll go faster."

Rosa pushed off as she released her grip, hard enough to force the woman to take a step back. "This *cabrona* better watch her mouth when she's talkin' about my Butch."

Manny nodded a thank-you to Sarah and shepherded Mrs. Swain to a chair. "Take a seat, ma'am, please."

She straightened her blouse, accepted the offered chair, and sat, keeping a wary eye on Rosa.

In a low and steady voice, Manny said, "Now, Mrs. Swain, explain what happened."

With mission-buzz roiling his belly, Butch slid the security chain back on the front door and repositioned the bed sheet. He jogged to the kitchen. A glance told him the rearguard were still in place, and unmoved.

So far, so good.

Every plan had its weaknesses, and he was approaching his point of least certainty. Since he'd gotten into the house, he'd been in control; now the unknown came into play. He turned the key in the bathroom lock and yanked the door open. The general remained slumped against the bathtub: no challenge. Butch crouched before the man. When he lifted an eyelid with his thumb, it elicited a groan. General Swain didn't look so intimidating sat on the floor with his legs splayed like an infant. His wife had done a half-assed job cleaning the blood from his face. *Probably afraid she'd break a nail.*

Grabbing Swain's shirt collar, he dragged the officer like a wet towel across the tiled floor and through the shiny, hardwood-floored hallway. In the living room, he had to grab under the man's arms to traverse the thick-pile carpet. When he dropped the general at the center of the room, the man grunted and moved a hand to his face.

Butch positioned a straight-backed chair in the far corner of the room, aligning it to face the window. As he pulled the general upright and tossed him over his shoulder, air whooshed from Swain's lungs, and he muttered a few indecipherable words—*soon be awake*. He flipped the man into the chair and strapped him with duct tape: arms at his sides attached to the backrest, thighs strapped to the seat, and calves bound to the front legs.

With his hostage immobilized, Butch went back to the bathroom and emptied the bullets from his Glock's magazine into the bathtub, leaving one in the chamber. Then he returned to the living room, sat near the window, and waited. He was good at waiting; he'd gotten plenty of practice in Iraq.

Staring at the man whose callous desire for advancement had ruined Butch's life, he felt no anger. General Swain was following orders, doing his job. The US Army didn't care if he was self-centered, arrogant, and power-hungry. The military was a machine. Any cog that fit and turned the right way was a valuable part of the mechanism. Butch had just been unlucky—wrong place, wrong time. A few years earlier, at the height of the Iraq invasion, a unit commander, desperate for human assets, would have laughed off the DWI. The mission had changed. That much he understood and accepted. But he couldn't allow his friends, his wife and his son—Oh God! His son. He couldn't allow the army to punish them for his mistakes.

The phone rang. He picked up.

"Butch, it's Manny."

"Uh huh."

"Just listen. First, thank you for releasing Mrs. Swain unharmed."

Butch let the line's silence do his talking.

Manny cleared his throat. "I have a copy of the letter, and Mrs. Swain told me everything that happened since you brought her husband home. I explained her options to her with your wife and her friend listening. She understands that you *helped* the general. Heck, if you hadn't pulled him from the car, he might have lain there all night, maybe gotten exposure, right? She's pledged not to press charges if you bring the general out unharmed, or if you let us in. Surrender your gun, and we can resolve this in the best way for you and your family. What do you say, Butch?"

"I released Mrs. Swain. Now let me speak to Rosa."

Another mission-critical weakness in Butch's plan, not the worst he foresaw, but still, he'd surrendered control to Manny by asking a question to which he didn't know the answer. Manny made him sweat for a ten-count before Butch heard, "Fair enough, here she is."

"Butch!"

Rosa's voice landed like a punch to the gut. His chest emptied of air, and he forgot how to fill it again.

"Butch? Are you there?"

Tears stung his eyes. "Y——." His voice betrayed him. He swallowed. "I'm here."

"Thank the gods. Honey, everything Manny said is true. Sarah's here with me. I heard the *cabrona* promise no charges. Manny is on our side. He's a former marine. You can trust him. Butch, it's time, sweetie. Come back to me. Let's work through this together as a family. Please, my husband. I need you. We need you." The fear in Rosa's voice tore a guilty hole in his heart. Then she whispered, "I love you," and started to sob.

Butch opened his mouth to speak, but no words came. He took a few deep breaths. He had to stay on mission—action fulfilled objectives, not emotion. "What about Brian's letter?" he asked.

Rosa's sobs had deepened; she stuttered, but couldn't collect herself. Hands scuffled with the phone, and then Sarah came on the line. "Hi, Butch."

"Hi, Sarah. Thanks for helping Rosa."

"No problem. You're on speaker, so I heard everything. Manny's people have hustled the JAGs in Washington, roused them from their beds. They're in contact with Fort Black. If Brian's telling the truth, and the code is in escrow, I'm sure they'll get the letter rescinded."

Butch nodded—one weight lifted. "If Brian's lying, there's nothing I can do. Sarah, do you think he is?"

"No."

"Me neither."

"Butch. Rosa wants you again."

Before he could respond, his wife's voice, soft with sorrow, whispered in his ear. "Butch, I need to tell you something. Hold on." Butch heard her ask someone to turn off the speaker. "Okay," she whispered, "it's just us now, baby. You have to let this go. Come out before this thing goes bad."

This was the pivotal moment—man-up and fix his self-generated problems, or live his life drugged up, feeling sorry for himself, punishing his wife and kids for what *he* had lost in Iraq. He straightened to attention, chest out, legs locked, teeth clamped so tight his jawbone pushed at his cheeks. Butch stared at Swain: strapped to the chair, saliva dribbling from the side of his mouth and pooling on his shoulder. "I can't, Rosa. There's something I need to do for us, for our family."

"*Booch*," she breathed his name. Her soft Spanish lilt speared his chest and blanked his mind, sucking away at his resolve. "Baby, it's not just you and me and Noe anymore. *Booch*, I'm pregnant."

Butch's legs gave, and he staggered backward into the table.

The hum of the police generator filled the silent room. A cold reality chilled him, lifted the hairs on the arm that held the phone that connecting him with his wife. Rosa's vision for her family's future was beautiful. But thanks to General Swain, for this damaged grunt—unattainable. Her dreams of a wonderful life for his son and his unborn child could be realized only one way—his way. Still, he asked, "Are you sure?"

"*Si*. I tested twice. Come out, honey. I know you hate Swain, but he's not half the man you are. He's not fit to buff your boots. Hurt him and you'll hurt us too." Sobs stole her voice. He waited, wanting to hear her voice again. After a few ragged breaths she managed, "I need you, Butch. I need my warrior. The babies need you. They need their daddy."

In the chair, Swain coughed, and winced. He straightened a crick in his neck. When he tried to move his hand, his eyes sprang open, and he looked to see why his arms didn't work. Then he lifted his head and locked his gaze on Butch who was rocking back and forth on the balls of his feet, straining his ear against the phone, his last connection to his wife. But she didn't speak, just sobbed.

Butch said, "Rosa, put Sarah on, please."

He heard the handover.

"Hi, Butch," Sarah said.

"Sarah. I need you to promise me something?"

"Of course, anything."

"Look after—" This was the point of no return, of total commitment. Ironically, the news of his wife's pregnancy had made a difficult decision easier. Despite Manny's promises, if he walked from this house, he would sink into a mire of laws and fees and loss. He'd become a lead weight chained to his family's ankle. To save them from drowning, he must sever the link that bound them. Butch coughed, clenched his gut, sucked in a breath, and spoke on exhale, his voice strengthened by an inner certainty that he was right. "Sarah, you're a good friend. Promise me you'll take care of Rosa as though she were one of your own."

"Of course. I'm here for all of you."

"Thanks. You can put Manny on the line now and tell him to turn on the speaker so everyone can hear."

Manny spoke with a calm voice of command. "Okay, Butch, speaker's on. Now I need you to come out with hands high. Leave the gun in the house. Don't make any sudden—"

Butch pulled back the curtains.

"What's going on, Butch?" Uncertainty crept into the policeman's tone. "Where's General Swain?"

Butch dragged the table away from the window and stood with his back against the large central pane, in full view. He pointed across the room with his Glock. "The bastard's over there. Strapped to a chair."

Two of the police observers standing behind the line of vehicles shifted position.

"Can you see him?" Butch asked.

Manny paused, then: "Yes, we see him. Butch, I need you to put down the gun and show me your empty hands."

Butch pointed the gun at the ceiling.

And pulled the trigger.

The shot boomed out of the van's speakers. Rosa's eyes sprang wide. She jumped from her chair, grabbed Sarah. "What's happening?"

A clamp strangled Sarah's throat. She couldn't speak, just shook her head and put an arm around Rosa and stared at the monitors.

A man's voice, pitched high, screamed from the speakers, "Shot fired! Shot fired!"

A second voice—steady, calm, chilling—said, "I have a clear shot."

"Pearson, stand by!" Manny said.

"Who's that speaking?" Rosa asked.

Sarah's hand went to her mouth. Now she was certain who Pearson was. *Come on, Butch.* She held her breath, strained her ears, hunting any sound, any notion that he was ready to surrender. Things were moving too fast.

Another male voice said, "HT is sighting the gun on the hostage."

Manny leaned forward, neck muscles bulging, knuckles white against the tabletop. "Butch! I need you to drop the gun. Now!"

On the monitor, Sarah watched Butch lower his arm until the Glock pointed at the general. Swain's mouth was open. He was saying something. Butch, his back to the window, held the phone in his free hand, at arm's length. Swain's high-pitched voice sounded over the van's speakers. "Don't do it, Cassidy. I'm begging you. Don't do it." The general sobbed. "Please—"

From behind Sarah, Patricia Swain screamed, "Shoot him! Shoot him before he kills my husband!"

Manny's voice cut through the general's pleading, and his wife's anger.

"Pearson, take the shot!"

A sharp crack rang out beyond the walls of the van. The home's front window glass shattered. A plume of red sprayed from Butch's scalp as he jerked away from the window and dropped out of camera shot. Rosa muscled past Sarah and leapt on Manny's back. The impact toppled him from the chair. On the floor, Rosa pummeled him. Her balled fists slammed, again, and again, into his neck and head.

"Get her off me!"

The guard moved from the door and grabbed Rosa's shirt, lifting her with one hand. She writhed and twisted until she regained her feet, whirled around, and threw an uppercut that connected with the guard's chin and forced him back.

Sarah, frozen to the spot, mouth gaping, throat filled with sawdust, stared at the TV. Through the bloodstained and shattered window, she saw Swain, still strapped to the chair. A second monitor displayed four men in coveralls using a battering ram against the front entrance. The door gave way followed by a loud bang and a bright flash of light.

She dragged her gaze from the monitors and looked for her friend. Rosa was curled in a ball, crumpled against the van's sidewall like a discarded trash bag, violent shudders racked her body every couple of seconds.

A series of voices came from the speakers:

"Alpha Clear."

"Bravo Clear."

"Delta Clear."

"HT is down. Repeat, HT is down."

When Patricia Swain stepped out of the shadows at the rear of the van, Sarah gave a start. She'd forgotten the woman was there. Mrs. Swain tapped Manny's shoulder. He had regained his seat, hunched over the monitors with a bloody handkerchief pressed to his nose. In a shaky voice, she whispered, "My husband, is he—?"

Manny put up his hand and spoke into the mic, "What's the status of the hostage."

"Stand by. Stand by. Hostage is unharmed."

Patricia Swain swayed, then folded to the floor like a rag.

Manny barked at the guard, back in position by the door, "God damn it! Get her out of here." He glared at Sarah and pointed to Rosa. "And keep her away from me."

TWENTY-SEVEN

At five a.m., Sarah pulled up outside her house. Rosa hadn't spoken since they left the Swain's home. She had begged, and screamed, and threatened, and fought the captain, desperate to enter the house, to see her husband. But Manny had the place on lockdown until his people completed their work. All the way back, Rosa, hunched over in the passenger seat, had let out tiny sobs. Each whimper scratched a new scar across Sarah's heart. "Come on, Rosa, let's get you inside."

Rosa looked up, realized where she was. "I need to collect Noe. I need to go home." When she broke down again, Sarah understood. The thought of home without Butch must seem inconceivable. How would *she* cope if Mike had been the one in Swain's house? Nausea churned her stomach.

How? She had no answer. Would it come to that?

She didn't know.

"It's been a long night. Come in. Get a shower and a bite to eat, then I'll drive you to your mom's." Rosa's Toyota was still at the crime scene. Manny said they couldn't pick it up until tomorrow.

Sarah walked around the hood and helped Rosa out of the passenger seat. "Come on, now."

She guided her friend up the path, opened the front door, and stopped on the doorstep. Broken pieces of drywall were strewn across the hall carpet. Three fist-sized holes had been punched in the wall.

Christopher, Daniel!

She needed to go to her children, but first she had to shepherd her wounded friend through the hallway and into the living room. With Rosa parked on the sofa, Sarah ran from the room, speaking over her shoulder. "I'll be back in a minute. I have to check something."

Rosa stared at the TV, although it wasn't on, and nodded. She

199

had stumbled through the wreckage in the hall without commenting.

Sarah ran to Christopher's bedroom. His sheets were rumpled, but the bed was empty. Heart pounding, her mind blanked, overloaded, overwrought, and she stood rooted to the carpet.

Daniel whispered from behind her, "Mom."

She spun around and her heart rattled her ribs. "Where's Christopher? What happened? Where's your dad?"

Daniel put a finger to his lips, made a *come on* hand signal, and led her into his bedroom. Christopher lay asleep in Daniel's bed.

"Thank God." She held Daniel at arm's length and gave him a quick appraisal, saw no damage. "Are you all right?"

"Dad went nutso again." Fear vibrated through his voice. His cheeks were gray, sunken, old before his time. She opened her arms, and he came to her. Tall and lean, he gripped her around the shoulders and squeezed. His breathing came in stutter-steps, and she waited until the spasm passed—no teenage boy wanted his mom to see tears.

How much damage was this chaos doing to her young man? It had to stop.

Once Daniel regained control, she pulled away and looked in his reddened eyes. "Where's your father now?"

"In the bedroom."

"Daniel, lock the door after me. Stay here."

"Mom—"

Sarah raised a hand. "I'll be fine. Stay with Christopher. He needs you here if he wakes." She cupped his cheek, then reached up and ruffled his hair. Forcing a lightness she didn't feel, she said, "You're a fine big brother, Daniel. You did good. But I've got this. Don't worry." She hoped these were the right words. She hoped exhaustion from the night she'd spent, and her anger toward the world, didn't leak into her voice. Daniel's smile was as false as her voice. Her brave boy was pretending to be okay for her sake. She waited on the landing until the lock clicked behind her.

Good boy.

The sound of Rosa's sobs drifted up the stairs. Sarah gritted her teeth and took five reluctant steps toward her bedroom. She turned the knob and cracked the door enough to peek inside. The curtains were open. A drab pre-dawn light draped the room. Mike was curled under the covers. Sarah knew better than to be close when he woke, so she stood in the doorway and whispered, "Mike."

He grunted and rolled on his back.

"Mike?"

He jerked upright and roared, "Where the hell have you been? Is this what you did while I was in the Sandbox—whored around all night?"

Tears filled her eyes. This was more than she could handle. Where was her warrior? Where was the strong, protective soldier who had swept her off her feet and promised to lasso the moon?

"Well?" he barked. Fierce eyes locked onto hers, Mike sprang from the bed and faced her, six feet away, wearing only his jockeys, legs braced, shoulders tensed, biceps and forearms tight and ready. He pointed at her.

No.

He pointed past her. "What the fuck's she doing here? Oh, I get it; she's your whoring buddy."

When Rosa touched her on the back, Sarah jumped. Her friend hooked an arm over Sarah's shoulders, so the two women filled the doorway.

Rosa spoke in a robotic, emotionless voice. "Butch is dead."

Mike's jaw went slack. His eyes moved back and forth between them. He opened his mouth. A tiny grunt came out.

Rosa said, "They killed him. And they'll kill you too because they don't need you anymore. You and Butch are *bad gear*."

A car drove by outside. The house creaked and settled. Sarah broke the silence. "That's where we've been. Trying to help *your* friend. Mike, what happened here? Christopher's sleeping in Daniel's room. Daniel's terrified. The hallway's a mess. What did you do?"

"I—" He dipped his head like a scolded child. His shoulders drooped, and a wave of contempt washed through Sarah. This wasn't her husband. Her husband had died in Iraq. And they'd sent home an imposter.

"Get dressed," she snapped. "We'll wait downstairs. But, Mike. Look at me."

"What?" he said to the carpet.

"Look at me."

He lifted his head. His face, lined and worn before his time, no longer moved her to pity. Sarah was all used up. "Unless you plan on being part of the solution, go back to bed and don't bother coming down."

At noon, Sarah returned from driving Rosa to her mom's house. She shut the front door, leaned against it, and took a few deep breaths. Mike had cleaned up the mess on the floor although three jagged witnesses to his rage still gaped in the wall.

Dressed in fresh cammies, he stepped from the kitchen. "I've made coffee." At least he had dressed. Nowadays he mostly slouched around the house in sweatpants.

"Where are the kids?"

"Daniel's at school. I took Christopher to your mom's. He's staying the night over there."

"Thank you." Sarah slid down the door until she sat on the floor.

Mike came to her, crouched, then sat beside her and draped an arm over her shoulders. He kissed the top of her head. "I'm sorry."

Sarah cleared her throat—no point in pretending anymore. "Mike. We can't help Butch, but you have to help us. I can't go on—"

"Shush, now." He stroked her hair, so softly, so tenderly, that it tore a rent in her emotional dam and last night's terrors broke through and she sobbed and wailed until her chest ached.

Even after she was all cried out, he remained still, his arm around her, strong, silent.

When he spoke, his voice was filled with a gentleness she'd missed. "Come on. I've got a P&J sandwich with your name on it. Then you'll shower and rest. While you're sleeping, I'll be at the base. If this monster can be beaten, I'll beat it. But, Sarah, look at me."

She did as he asked and saw the sincerity in his eyes.

"If I'm permanently broken, I won't hold you back, and I won't blame you for moving on. This is my challenge to overcome. I have to accept responsibility. Otherwise, Butch—" The name caught in his throat. "Otherwise, Butch died for nothing."

"I don't want to lose you, Mike."

"I don't know why you'd say that. I don't deserve it. But I'm sure glad to hear the words." He stood, and Sarah took his hand and let him pull her upright. She glanced at the holes in the wall.

They could be fixed.
But could Mike?

<><><>

Three days later, Sarah answered a knock at the front door. Rosa stood there, alone, looking older, thinner—no jacket on, shivering.

"Where's Noe?"

"We're staying at Mom's. I had to swing by the house to pick up a few things, thought I'd drop by."

"I've left messages," Sarah said.

Rosa nodded. Sarah stepped back to let her enter.

"Is Mike home?" Rosa asked.

"He's at the base medical center. This new doctor is helping. Younger and better informed than—"

A cloud passed across Rosa's face.

"Sorry," Sarah said. "I'm sure you don't want to hear that Doctor Wainwright wasn't very helpful."

Rosa shrugged.

"Coffee?" Sarah asked.

"Sure."

They moved to the kitchen. "We'll find out on for sure Monday, but it looks as though they've found Mike a place in a new mental health program at Walter Reed Hospital. The doctor says they've been reporting good results. Mike'll be away for three months, but they're keeping him on active duty. He's dreading the group therapy, but I'm proud of him for going."

"That's good."

Once they settled at the kitchen table, Sarah asked, "How are you?"

"Okay, I guess."

"Noe?"

Rosa took a faltering breath. "Oh. He keeps asking for his daddy. I change the subject—don't know what to say." She fished a Kleenex from her bag and dabbed her eyes. "The funeral's next Monday."

"Mike told me. We'll be there." Sarah leaned across and took Rosa's hand. "If there's anything we can do."

Rosa nodded and gave a half smile. "I know. Thanks. Manny

phoned me yesterday."

Sarah eased back in her chair. "Really?"

"Butch's gun was empty. They found the bullets in the bathtub."

"What does that mean?"

Rosa swallowed, and swallowed again, struggling for words. "Suicide by police officer Manny called it."

"Excuse me?"

"I received a letter from the insurance company. They got the police report. Butch's Whole-Life policy will pay out because the police shot an unarmed man."

Sarah reached across and squeezed her friend's hand. "You think Butch knew?"

Rosa nodded. "*Sí.* He fixed it all—forced the JAGs to rescind the letter, then arranged for me and Noe and the baby to get the money from his life insurance. My Butch thought of everything. Except he didn't think we'd rather have had him back."

TWENTY-EIGHT

Eight months later - Cape Fear Valley Maternity Hospital, Fayetteville, NC

To be on the safe side, Sarah kept her arms underneath Christopher's as he held Rosa's two-day-old baby for the first time. "He's got a pointy head," Christopher said.

Rosa, sitting up in bed, laughed, and stroked Christopher's cheek. "It'll round off in a few days, *chiquito.*"

He nodded. "Okay. I'm done now, Mom."

Sarah took baby Paul and handed him back to his mom. "There are Legos on the table in the corner."

Christopher didn't need a second invitation.

"How are you feeling, Rosa?"

"Oh. Good, I suppose. I mean, Paul is healthy and feeding well. He's a good baby, slept most of the night last night. I should be out of here tomorrow. But—" She sighed, and Sarah understood what a bittersweet moment this must be for her.

"How's Mike?" Rosa asked.

Mike had returned home four months earlier from the Walter Reed rehab center. "He's good. He was planning to come, but changed his mind at the last minute—said he'd seen enough of hospitals for a while. Men are such wusses." As soon as the words left her mouth, Sarah wanted them back. Butch's death was a constant elephant in the room nowadays. How could she complain about life with Mike when Rosa had lost her man? Sarah suspected the real reason her husband hadn't come was because he couldn't handle seeing Butch's son.

"Things are ticking along," Sarah said. In fact, life in the Braeman home had settled into a familiar pattern. Not the same as before. It never would be. A part of Mike had died in Iraq never to return. Although the rages had stopped, night tremors still woke him. Coping techniques learned during rehab helped, but he still couldn't ride shotgun without bobbing and weaving from imaginary IEDs, and sudden loud noises often sent him ducking for cover. He'd learned to joke about the episodes, and the humor helped. The prescribed drugs still seemed a heavy load to Sarah, but Mike's body had adjusted. And at least he would never be deployed again. "Mike's working as a trainer, now, and enjoying the challenge."

"That's good. And how is Bravo?"

On his return from rehab, Sarah had surprised Mike with a Labrador puppy. A dog was supposed to be a steadying influence, and that's how it had proven for her husband. Dogs don't judge. And Bravo was always on alert, which took some of the perceived responsibility for watching for the bad guys off Mike's shoulders.

"They're inseparable. I often wonder who Mike would save first in a fire, me or the dog. Listen, on the drive over, Brian called. He's on his way to Fayetteville. I told him to meet us here. I hope that's okay."

Rosa's eyes widened. "I look a mess."

"Really? You've just given birth and you still look as though you came from the spa."

"Pass me a comb and mirror."

Sarah fished them out of the bedside table, but couldn't hide her grin.

"What?" Rosa said.

"I think you like him."

"Pah." She swatted away the comment and tidied her hair. "Why is he coming back so soon? We're not due to meet until next month, right?"

Butch's death had devastated Brian. His visit to Sarah's home with the cease-and-desist letter was only the trigger; Butch's pathology stemmed from Iraq, not from the LightCube. But that didn't stop him blaming himself. After the shooting, Brian visited Fayetteville every other week. Rosa, Yaz, and Sarah gathered at her kitchen table, where the project had started, while Brian gave an update. Once Mike returned from rehab, he joined them. So this visit two days after their previous meeting was a surprise.

"Apparently, he has papers for us to sign."

Brian arrived thirty minutes later. His face went beet red as soon as he laid eyes on Rosa, who had freshened her lipstick and sprayed on perfume. He shook her hand. "How are you?"

"I'm good."

"You look great. I mean considering. That is—" He cleared his throat, and his face turned crimson. "How's Paul?"

"Thriving."

"Oh, I brought this." Brian fished a teddy bear stuffy from his briefcase and handed it to Rosa.

"Do you want to hold him?" Rosa asked.

Brian glanced at the baby. "No. I mean. I'm not sure how."

"Here." Smiling, Rosa held out her son. "You can't break him. I promise."

Brian nestled the baby in his arms. He swallowed, hard, and his voice cracked as he said, "He has your eyes." Brian's gaze never left the child's face.

"So, what brings you back again so soon," Sarah asked.

"Oh. Hi, Sarah. Sorry. Excuse my manners. Yes." He returned Paul to his mother and sat beside the bed, opposite Sarah. "The first LightCube game ships in less than twelve months."

Sarah waited.

"Well." Brian took a folder from his briefcase, "Adam Barnes pulled me into his office this morning and gave me this." He handed each of them a single sheet of paper.

Without glancing at the document, Rosa said, "Tell us, Brian. What does it say?"

Once again, color rose in Brian's cheeks. Rosa flustered him. Sarah thought it was cute. She suspected that was another reason he visited so often—an excuse to see Rosa.

Brian grinned. "Actually, it's great news. This—" He held the paper high and waved it back and forth. "—is an offer from GameSoft. They want exclusive distribution rights to the LightCube. And to protect their investment, they want to buy a controlling stake in our company."

Sarah looked up from reading the document, eyes wide. "They've offered ten dollars a share."

Brian, still grinning, nodded. "Yup."

When Rosa cried out, Sarah and Brian froze. The noise she made contained no joy; it was the chilling, primal sound of raw animal grief. Paul's eyes popped open, and he screamed.

Rosa's offer document fluttered to the floor.

Sarah jumped up. "Here, let me." She took the baby from her friend.

Rosa gulped in deep breaths and gathered herself. She pointed at the box of Kleenex and Brian passed them to her. "I'm sorry. That is great news, Brian."

Sarah's paced, and shooshed the baby.

"It's just—" Rosa took a faltering breath. "Why didn't he wait?"

Sarah just shook her head. She had no answer.

Brian reached forward and took Rosa's hand. He pulled another tissue from the box and dabbed her eyes. "Butch was the bravest man I've ever known. He did what he did because he loved you and Noe. And because of him you have Paul. This—" Brian pointed to the paper. "—was what he wanted to happen. Nothing can bring Butch back, Rosa, but whatever I can do to help you and Noe and Paul, just name it. I'm here for you."

Sarah took Rosa's other hand. "Me too."

THE END

A NOTE FROM THE AUTHOR

Dear Reader:

Thank you for taking the time to read *When A Warrior Comes Home*. If you enjoyed the tale, please consider telling your friends or posting a short review on Amazon. Word of mouth is an author's best friend and much appreciated.

In researching this story, I read hundreds of first-hand accounts written by caregivers, soldiers, and veterans. Sarah, Rosa, Mike, Yaz, and Butch are not real. Any similarities to actual events experienced by real persons are coincidental. However, I know from my research that for thousands of men and women much of the pain and suffering illustrated in this story is a close reflection of their daily lives. I set the story in 2008-09. Since then, the US Army has made significant improvements in the diagnosis and treatment of PTSD and TBI.

But much is left undone.

Pete.

Special thanks to my beta readers:
        Susan, Sheryl, Cherrie, and Big Al.
Editing – Laurie Boris and Carolyn Steele.
Cover – Debbie at TheCoverCollection.com.

ABOUT THE AUTHOR

Born into a blue-collar family in Liverpool, England, Pete Barber immigrated to the US in the early 90s and settled in North Carolina.

After surviving near-death experiences at ages six and eighteen, he led a haphazard life, putting bread on the table as a plumber, computer programmer, salesperson, marketing executive, hotel operator, real-estate developer, and llama breeder.

Pete loves chickens and dogs, and writes fast-paced fiction that makes people think--what if?